WHEN THE WHISTLING STOPPED

A Novel

* * *

DAVID J MATHER

A PEACE CORPS WRITERS BOOK

Mrs Carl Bonifacious
2569 Kay Conley Rd
Rock Spring GA 30739

When the Whistling Stopped

A Peace Corps Writers Book

An imprint of Peace Corps Worldwide

Copyright © 2014 by David J Mather
All rights reserved.

Printed in the United States of America by Peace Corps Writers of Oakland, California.
No part of this book may be used or reproduced in any manner whatsoever without written permission except in the case of brief quotations contained in critical articles or reviews.

For more information, contact peacecorpsworldwide@gmail.com. Peace Corps Writers and the Peace Corps Writers colophon are trademarks of PeaceCorpsWorldwide.org.

ISBN: 1-935-92545-8
ISBN-13: 978-1-935925-45-3

Library of Congress Control Number 2014941666
First Peace Corps Writers Edition, May 2014

FOR LINDY,
ALWAYS

Author's Note

Although it has a much different story line, *When the Whistling Stopped* is a sequel to my first novel, *One For the Road*. Both take place primarily in southern Chile. This time around, I have included a translation of the Spanish words and idioms in a **Glossary** at the end of the book.

Acknowledgments

I would like to thank the following people. First, my usual crew of readers: Judy Barker, Allie Farrar, Kate Hewitt, Joyce Killebrew, Don Metz, Nini Meyer, and Alex Sawyer, who read, and sometimes re-read the novel, in its early, painful stages. I took note of all their suggestions, acting on many.

A huge thank you to nurse extraordinaire Andrea Wyle for all the information on paraplegia. I would also like to especially thank Janet Post who magically appeared when the book needed to be copy edited. Her proficiency in both English and Spanish was invaluable.

Thank you to artist and friend Jennifer Brown who created the cover artwork.

As with my first novel, I would like to thank the Coronado family for their warmth and hospitality. It was during our stay with them in Valdivia, Chile, that the idea for the novel was born, and much of the physical research accomplished.

Finally, a tremendous thank you to my wife, Lindy, without whose support and computer expertise, this book would have remained page-less.

When the Whistling Stopped

Prologue

The truck turned onto the Pan American Highway and started down the steep hill to Valdivia. María Elena laughed at one of Hernán's jokes while the two workers who had helped load the truck were sitting on top of the tightly stacked firewood, each with a hand on the headboard and the other on his hat. They squinted into the wind. Hernán downshifted and began to ride the brakes of the heavy truck. The brakes were soon smoking. Smiling, María Elena was saying something to Hernán when suddenly the brakes let go and the truck began flying down the hill. There was a terrible grinding as Hernán frantically tried to jam the transmission into a lower gear. Sheer panic painted María Elena's face.

The truck went faster and faster. Catching up to a much slower moving bus, Hernán had to pull out on a curve to pass. He couldn't prevent the wheels from hitting the soft narrow shoulder, causing the truck to tip. The two workers screamed. Hernán tried to keep the truck on the road, but the shift in weight was too much. The truck rolled over, crushing the two workers. Firewood scattered in all directions as the truck rolled again with María Elena being thrown from the cab. The truck continued to roll until it struck a huge bolder.

Chapter One

Tom slowly climbed down the ladder from the loft, and walked over to the pitcher pump. After splashing water on his face, he went out to the porch to split stove wood. A beautiful New England summer morning. Within minutes he had the spruce kindling and small pieces of poplar crackling like ladyfingers in the Glenwood; just a quick fire for coffee because the cabin would warm up soon enough. He removed the cast iron rings of the stove so he could put the kettle of water directly over the flames. Wrapping stiff, callused hands around the kettle, absorbing its warmth, he looked around the cabin.

His reading glasses and an open letter lay on the little table next to the easy chair in front of the stone fireplace. How late had he stayed up reading it over and over? With cup of steaming coffee in hand, he took the letter and glasses out to the rocker on the porch. Down in the valley to the east was a snake of fog twisting its way above the Connecticut River with New Hampshire's White Mountains on the horizon. If those mountains were snow-capped volcanoes, he thought, the view would be just like Cufeo. How long had it been? Must be close to thirty years. He did the math. My God, it had been thirty years!

His banty rooster stopped strutting around long enough to crow. Tom smiled. Everything just like Cufeo: chickens wandering around, a couple sheep, a pig, cabin built out of rough lumber, rusty roof, no electricity, year-round outhouse, wood for heat and much of the cooking. He even had a *faja* to wrap around his lower back for support. About the only difference was he didn't have to fetch water from a spring—that plus it could get twenty-five below.

He hadn't wanted to leave, but after María Elena's death he couldn't stay—everything there reminded him of her. He had left Chile, traveling a year around South America. When he reached Panama, he found a U.S. soldier in the Canal Zone who sold him a motorcycle that he rode through Central America. He had hoped that being constantly on the move and seeing new things would help him forget. But it didn't.

When he arrived in the States, he visited an old friend in Vermont. While the friend was at work, he took long walks. Nearby was an abandoned dirt road, and at the end of it he discovered an old cellar hole next to a clump of overgrown lilacs. There had been a farm here in its own little valley. Old stone walls mapped what had been fields, but now the fields were covered by young forest. He knew that with some hard work it could be made into a beautiful little homestead. He tracked down the owner and bought the property. As he worked the land, he fell in love with it. He learned how to use a chainsaw and cleared the overgrown fields. He scrounged and recycled materials for the cabin. He poured himself into the project, scattering seeds of permanence that quickly took root. He soon did not have the desire to travel again. He did not have the time; there was just too much to do.

Months passed, and then years. He never got over María Elena. He continually wished her at his side so they could work together and share the joys and hardships of rural life. He talked to her often in his mind. People thought him a hermit, crazy to live without most modern day conveniences. He did not bother to explain.

He put the cup of coffee down, and picked up the letter and glasses. Taking a deep breath, he began to read.

Dear Tomás my brother,

We were all so surprised when your friends arrived at the farm. We were also very happy to know that you are alive and healthy. But most of all we are happy to be able to write to you to tell you how much we miss you and that we pray that you will return one day. You are and always will be an important member of our family. There is so much news to tell you that I do not know where to begin. As you can tell I am not writing this letter. It would take me two long winters to put my words down on paper and then you would not be able to read them anyway. Flor is writing this.

Well we are all much older now and thank God most of us have been lucky to still have our health. My leg bothers me a little more each year but I am too stubborn to let it slow me down much but I did stop playing soccer years ago. Your little trees have done very well and are not so little anymore. But the face of Cufeo is changing. Several families could not pay off their forestry loans and have sold their land to some big lumber companies which is very sad because the big companies paid very little for the land and are taking advantage of all their hard work. Others of our friends have died and their children wanted to live in Valdivia. The big companies bought their land too. The companies are planting trees everywhere. Many of the farms have been torn down. Sometimes when you look around you don't even know where you are. One good thing is they have improved all the roads and trucks can go up to Lote Once even during the winter rains. But now there is the noise of these big trucks taking the logs to the mills. I think we have gained some things but lost others.

Jaime Martinez asks about you whenever I see him. I am happy that I can tell him where you are now and what you are doing. Jaime still lives on the farm in Los Guindos and is married. He has several children but they have moved to Valdivia. His youngest sister Lilia lives with him. She has never married and we think that is because of the rape so many years ago.

About a year after you left Flor and I were married in your 'ramada' in the 'copihue' clearing. We were pleased to finally use it for such a happy occasion and it has become a family tradition to marry there. Flor and I have three children. My eldest son is named Tomás for you and my second—Guillermo—for my father. They too were married at the 'ramada.' My youngest is a girl who we named Amanda for Flor's mother. She is very intelligent and I am more than a little proud to say she received a scholarship from the university in Valdivia that pays for everything. You will see in the pictures that she looks very much like María Elena and she is now the same age as María Elena was when she died. Tomás I do not know what you feel these days but I hope you have healed. I still miss and will always miss my sister. Some nights I am very sad but there is nothing I can do about it and life has to go on. Flor has been a wonderful 'señora' and mother and we have food on the table every day and we are healthy. One should be thankful for that.

Many years ago Sr. Kurt came up and asked to see the land you protected in my sister's memory. He looked very good—like a rich and important man. One of his sons—Carlos—came up with him. He was a very nice boy and Amanda showed him around the farm while we talked. It was summer so Sr. Kurt could drive almost all the way in his big pickup truck. I rode with him in front and all the children in the back. It was quite an outing. He could not believe the size of the old trees and said trees like those were very rare and valuable now and that I should keep an eye out for any timber thieves. I go up as often as I can and there are others in the area watching. Everyone knows the story behind the land and it is treated with much respect. We walked down to the clearing and Sr. Kurt saw your wedding 'ramada.' It made him sad. I told him the story of when you were building it and how the condor came to you then at the exact time María Elena died—that you thought her spirit was in that bird. Sr. Kurt said he believed anything was possible when it came to things like that and maybe especially so because of the special bond you had with my sister.

Well Tomás my brother there is much more to say and after your friends leave with this letter I will think of even more. But I will end it now. Maybe we will never see you again but deep in my heart I think we will. Remember, my home is always your home. Everyone sends their love. Please return to Chile some day soon before we all get too old.

With the biggest 'abrazo' possible
Juan

Tom went into the cabin to get the envelope of pictures. The pine trees were so tall! He knew they grew fast down there—that was the point after all—but that big in only thirty years? Other than the trees, everything looked the same: the schoolhouse, the Rodríguez farm, the Montoya farm. Then there was Juan with his impish grin. He had grey flecks in a still full head of hair, and he had his arm around a stout Flor Gonzales. Ha! Even now he remembered Juan looking at her that last day before they left the farm. Those HAD been looks of interest! Standing on either side of them were two young men. One had an arm around Juan's shoulders, and the other had an arm around Flor's waist. Kneeling in front were three young women. Tom stared long and hard at the one in the middle. She took his breath away. She had a beautiful smile and a long thick dark braid. She was the spitting image of María Elena. He could not put the picture down.

But, he had a barn roof to do. He carefully put the pictures away, and, after a quick breakfast, headed to the barn. Over the years he had done about everything there was to do with wood. He had planted trees in Chile, but here he cut them down to clear the land, and for firewood. Occasionally, he cut a few saw logs which helped to pay the taxes. He had worked thinning young woodlots for large landowners, helped foresters cruise timber, marked trees for selective harvests, had even been a sawyer in a sawmill. He had also built houses and the furniture in them. There wasn't much about wood he didn't understand.

He tied a nail apron around his waist and put the shingling hammer into its holster. Picking up a bundle of cedar shingles, he climbed up to the scaffolding. The sun was out with not a cloud in the sky, perfect roofing weather. He arranged the shingles along the guideboard, splitting some to make them fit right. With his mind full, he began to methodically nail.

Early on, back in the States, he had spent some of the traditional holidays with his father and mother in Massachusetts. He was their only child. Per usual, his father did not understand what he was doing with his life; but later, for some reason, his father began to relate to the simplicity of it all. His mother never got it. His father would come up more and more often. He loved to sit out on the porch in the autumn, watching the golden leaves flutter and fall to the ground. They would talk of Chile and María Elena then. He told his father about her beauty, her strength, all the things she could do, and all the things she did. His father repeatedly apologized for the callous letter he had sent, insulting their engagement. He had thought his son was out of his mind to marry a peasant girl. Instead of coming to their wedding, he and Tom's mother had gone on a cruise in the Greek Islands. They said that he hadn't notified them early enough. His father had sent a large check instead. Guilt money, Tom had called it.

She had died only days before they were to be married. Tom used his father's money to buy the land where he had built a *ramada*—a three-sided structure made out of saplings—where they would have said their vows. It was a special place with a beautiful clearing covered in red *copihue* and a grotto of huge *alerce* trees. The clearing looked out onto a nearby volcano and a tall waterfall. When Tom told his father how the money had been spent, his father said that it was probably the best thing his money had ever bought. He wanted to go there to see it with Tom. Tom thought hard about that. Maybe enough time had passed, over ten years. Finally, Tom agreed and they made some tentative plans; but they never went because his father died of a stroke. Tom had no idea what to do with the pile of money he inherited. His old friend recommended a financial adviser.

By noon Tom was famished. He lay down his apron and hammer while gauging his progress. It was slow going, and he figured it would take him until early fall to finish. He walked up to the house to make lunch. As much as he tried, he couldn't get the letter out of his mind.

Like always, the New England summer passed too quickly. Fall arrived and the foliage wasn't particularly good. There had been a lot of cloudy and rainy days, and the reds and oranges were dull. Tom finished the roof, and began to stack cordwood for the winter. He had never forgotten that first winter when he slept every night with long-johns, wool socks, and a hat, coming down each morning to get a hissing fire going so he could thaw out the pot of water left on the stove. When the water warmed, he used it to thaw the plunger of the pitcher pump. Only then could he start to make the coffee. Ever since, he had his wood under cover before the first snowflake fell.

He endured another New England winter. Nights were long, and Tom thought more and more about the three years he had lived in Chile. He realized that he still deeply missed Cufeo, and began to consider returning. Life in Vermont was fine, but the void created by María Elena's death had never been filled. None of the women he had gone out with came close to measuring up. He knew that it was not fair to compare them to her; yet he couldn't help it. He also knew that if María Elena had lived, their life together would not have been perfect: they would have quarreled and had hard times like everybody else. It was unrealistic to think otherwise. But his memories of her were perfect, and that was all he had. And that was all he would ever have. His father had been a duck hunter and he had some old pen and ink wildlife prints. Growing up, Tom always had a favorite. When he saw the print after María Elena's death, it took on new significance. Titled "Alone," it was done by an artist named Bishop. It showed a single goose flying way up in the clouds. Tom had read that geese mated for life. He was that goose.

But what about the decades of hard work here? he asked himself. Yes, decades! The homestead he had carved out, the cabin and barn he had built, the road he had brought back? The friends he had? Could he leave all that, start over? But it was in Chile where he had first learned to appreciate simple rural living. And it was so beautiful in those hills looking out at the snow-capped volcanoes with the Andes shimmering way off. He had felt a warmth of family life there he never had in the States. He couldn't totally explain the draw, even to himself, but it was deep. The tug of war lasted the winter, but he finally decided to return.

He hoped the decision was the right one because he was leaving no tracks. He was very fortunate that his financial advisor had picked stocks and mutual funds well. His significant inheritance had grown into something quite significant indeed—he would never have to worry about money. When the spring mud dried out and it was possible to drive in, he put his property on the market. He thought he would feel sad about leaving the land; but, strangely, did not. Rather, he felt lighter without the responsibility. He also felt proud that he had been a good steward for so many years. He sold his pickup and most of his tools and other possessions. He also gave a lot of stuff away. Some personal items he stored in his old Peace Corps trunk which he left in the loft of a friend's barn: he would send it when Tom was settled. As the day of departure drew near, Tom was a little nervous, but he was also ready.

Chapter Two

No doubt about it, something was poisoning the river. She looked up from the microscope, rubbing her eyes. She was exhausted. For hours she had been examining slices of swans' livers and samples of the *luchecillo* and other aquatic growth. Many small vials of river water were arranged neatly in the center of the large lab work area. The swans had died of malnutrition, their livers full of iron and other heavy metals. The plants she'd found should have been green and luscious, but they were brown and crusty from the iron. The water had varying amounts of chlorine dioxide. She'd bet anything it was from that new pulp mill upriver. It had to be.

She was alone in the university lab on an early Friday evening. The other students were out enjoying the fine late spring weather, getting a head start on the weekend. She looked at her watch and sighed. How did it get to be so late? She cleaned the counters and put everything away. Pulling her lightweight sweater from the back of the stool, she looked around making sure everything was in its place. Finally, after turning out the lights, she carefully locked the door behind her.

She was a very beautiful girl with a stunning figure. Her raven hair was in a long thick braid, and she was wearing a brightly colored T-shirt and jeans. Even though it was very warm, she put the sweater on as she left the building. If she walked up to the bus-stop without covering the T-shirt, the young men on the street would whistle and click at her. She approached a small group of students kicking a soccer ball around between two university buildings. One of them passed the ball to her, saying, "Hey, Amanda! Come join in."

She bounced the ball off one foot then the other a few times without letting it hit the ground. "Thanks," she replied, "but I have to go home to get ready for an *asado* out in the country. Lucky for you guys, though, because I'd just show you up." She flipped the ball up high and, with her braid swinging in an arc, headed it back to them. The young men laughed as they continued their game. All eyes were on her as she walked away.

She approached the bus stop where she would take the #5 *micro* round about Valdivia, out to the suburb of Las Animas. She lived there with her great uncle and aunt, Pablo and Miriam, who had plenty of room in their house because their two sons had married and left home. Amanda's parents had wanted her to go to school in Valdivia rather than in the one-room schoolhouse in Cufeo, so she had moved in with Pablo and Miriam to begin the third grade. She was a senior now at the university, one of the very few students ever awarded a full four-year scholarship.

The studies at the university came easy to her; it was the social life that was difficult. Most of the students were from upper middle class families—sons and daughters of merchants, ranchers, high-up civil servants, lawyers, doctors, successful businessmen. She was the daughter of *campesinos*—small farmers who eked out a living selling firewood and charcoal, and growing pine trees. Waiting for the bus she thought about her parents. They had worked so hard, going without comforts their whole lives. Most of her fellow students had no idea what that was like. In their world they had electricity and indoor plumbing, washing machines, servants. Their parents had a car to take them to visit their grandparents on the weekend—they didn't have to slog on foot for miles on slippery muddy roads and trails. They had bicycles when they were kids, and new fancy clothes whenever they wanted. They thought nothing about buying candy and going to a movie.

Living off campus didn't help her social life. She had no close friends, although the coeds were polite enough to her face. She would pass a group of girls in the hall where they might nod when she walked by, but no smiles. Some would pointedly look at her cheap, worn clothes before turning away. She suspected that they talked about her behind her back. The boys were different, of course, no surprise there. They were always nice, flirting shamelessly; but she knew that was because she was pretty and had a great body. And she knew the girls were jealous of that.

The little red and white *micro* pulled up. Full of workers from the Kuntsman Brewery and the university, she squeezed in to where she could hold on to the back of a seat. The bus left the Isla Teja and crossed the Valdivia River. After a couple of turns it stopped for shoppers at the central plaza. The bus was soon so jam-packed that the driver didn't even slow down as he passed the usual stops on Calle Arauco. When the passengers thinned out, Amanda sat down. After the bus crossed the Calle Calle River, she got off at the first stop. She walked the rest of the way on backstreets to Pablo and Miriam's.

Amanda was studying science at the university with hopes of becoming a veterinarian. She had always loved animals. During the summers and holidays when she was a little girl, she made sure it was her job to feed the chickens and pigs, let the sheep out in the morning and bring them back in the evening. When the apple trees had a good year, she would sneak some of the fruit for the horses, and she loved watching the oxen chomp on the hay she gave them after their hard day's work. She helped her father treat the animals' various maladies, and would watch the ewes give birth whenever she could. Many a cold and rainy night she and her father would sit up to pull out a baby lamb that had gotten turned around. The summer when she was ten, she watched the cat give birth to six kittens. She excitedly went to tell her father. He put on his hat and strode purposefully out to the shed. She had followed, watching in horror as he scooped up the kittens to drown them in the wooden barrel under the eaves. There was no extra money to feed pets, he explained. Every animal had their job to do, and they only needed a couple of cats that they already had. Amanda never watched their dog or cat give birth after that.

Her great uncle Pablo used to make his living buying and selling animals. He didn't make much money, but he was good at it. He would travel the province looking for young oxen that matched up in size and color, bringing them back to train in the two fenced-in hectares he rented behind the house. Amanda would sit on the fence for hours to watch. He would lead the young team around with a *garrocha*—a long skinny pole that rested on the middle of the yoke—and teach them to back up by lightly tapping their noses. If he wanted them to stay where they were, he would leave the pole leaning against the yoke. As long as the *garrocha* was in place, the oxen wouldn't budge. Pablo let Amanda help with the animals. When she was a teenager, she began to accompany him on his buying trips. He began to ask her opinion and, not long ago, he had told her father that she knew as much about animals as he did.

Amanda still missed her family. She was as close to her brothers as she could be, considering they lived apart nine months out of the year. After teaching her how to play soccer, her brothers made the other boys let her play with them in front of the nearby school. It didn't take long before she was good enough so that no one objected again to her playing. But in Valdivia she was a loner. When she was young, Miriam had to force her to mix in with the neighborhood children. Amanda much preferred to take her schoolbooks down to the bank of the Cruces River to study. It was there she had fallen in love with the swans.

The Cruces was one of the three rivers that joined in Valdivia before heading out to the Pacific. It was where most of the swans congregated—thousands of them. She would watch the swans for hours. She enjoyed seeing them interact, softly whistling at each other during the molting season. She laughed when they tipped themselves upside down while dabbling for food. She made sure she kept her distance during the breeding season when the parents closely guarded the nests and toted the fluffy baby swans on their backs.

When she entered the university, her trips to the river became much less frequent. To keep her scholarship, she had to pour herself into her studies. It was only a few months ago when she began to notice the number of swans had dropped off drastically. The plumage of those that remained looked drab and unkempt. She had found several swans inexplicably dead on the riverbank. She suspected that somehow they were being poisoned. She approached her department head at the university to voice her concerns. She wanted to do an independent study to see what was wrong. Because she was a high honors student very much respected by her professors, her request was quickly granted. The department head said that if she could substantiate her suspicions, he would try to get the university to spearhead an investigation.

Amanda opened the little gate in front of Pablo and Miriam's house. It was like all the other houses on the street—small, wood sheathed, corrugated metal roof with a single stovepipe sticking out. She walked along the side of the house, stopping at the kitchen door. She heard a radio playing a *cueca:* Pablo must be out back, working on the new saddle. She entered the kitchen where she found Miriam filling the large kettle with water.

"Here, *abuelita,* let me do that," Amanda said, taking the kettle out of her hands. Although Miriam was her great aunt, Amanda called her 'little grandmother.' "You go sit down. I'll prepare the *onces.*"

"Ah well, that would be good. Thank you, child."

Miriam was much shorter than Amanda, and much stouter. All the years of eating white bread three times a day, every day, had finally caught up with Miriam, Amanda thought. But as round as she might be, Miriam was still strong. How could she not be? She had lugged so many pails of water, washed clothes by hand, handled heavy pots and kettles, and kneaded bread dough all her life. She was also a fireball. It was she who kept the family, including her grandchildren, on an even keel.

Amanda opened the refrigerator to pull out butter and homemade blackberry preserves, some meat spread, and cheese. Miriam had already put the sugar, honey, and silverware out. Amanda sliced the morning's thick round loaf of bread before placing the steaming kettle on a little piece of wood in the center of the table.

"You better go get Pablo, dear, or he will work until dark. I swear that man will never eat anymore unless he is led to food."

Amanda went out to call Pablo. In a short while he entered the kitchen. As he was about to sit at the table, Miriam asked, "What do you think you're doing, old man? Don't you have sense enough to take off your hat and wash your hands before you eat, eh?"

Pablo wore a white short-sleeve shirt and thin woolen pants held up by suspenders. His straw hat was flat with a wide brim, much like his fancy felt *huaso* hats. He wore his fancy hats only in parades, when he occasionally went to buy animals, and on important social occasions. For sure, Amanda thought, he would wear one tomorrow at the *asado*.

"Aii, woman! Don't you ever get tired of nagging me!" He gave her a sharp look, but hung his hat on the rack behind the door before washing his hands. Miriam shook her head as she stirred her tea. They always bickered, but Amanda knew they were devoted to each other.

Pablo filled his *maté* cup with the coarse tea.

"Old man," she repeated, "why don't you drink some tea or Nescafé? *Maté* is bad for your heart!"

Pablo put in two teaspoons of sugar before he filled the cup with hot water.

"Now I can't have my *maté*? What else do you want me to give up, eh? Maybe I should just go down to the bar and spend our money on wine with the drunks there, eh woman? At least there, no one will nag me."

He angrily sucked through the hot metal straw, burning his mouth. He jerked back. Miriam chuckled, but didn't say anything. Amanda made herself a cup of tea.

Miriam said, "Just like María Elena, dear. She always put honey in her tea. But you know that, don't you?" Miriam passed her the bread.

"Yes, *abuelita*, you have told me many times."

"Here, take some bread. You're so skinny! I swear you eat like a bird."

"No, thank you." Amanda reached for a small slice of cheese instead. "I will be eating plenty tomorrow."

"Now she is nagging you, too. Leave her alone, woman! If she's hungry, she'll eat. And she's not skinny, she looks good. Haven't you seen all the boys watch her when she walks by?"

Amanda blushed.

"And she's right. Tomorrow we will all stuff ourselves at the *asado*. What time is Javier picking us up, old woman?"

Javier, their eldest son, ran a small garage halfway across town near the cemetery. He was the wealthiest member of the family, and had a small pickup. They would all pile in it tomorrow.

"Mid-day. He can't get away until then. And he still has to pick up his family first."

Pablo frowned.

"We'll be the last there then. He can't find somebody to fill in at the garage?"

Miriam shook her head.

"You can go out earlier if you want, Pablo. You can take that old crowded bus. And you can walk all the way up carrying maybe the wine jug and some other things. But not me or Amanda; we'll wait for Javier. Right, dear?" Amanda nodded, but didn't look at Pablo.

After a final sip of *maté*, Pablo leaned back in his chair. Smiling, he said, "It will be good to see Tomás again. I wonder how much he has changed…or how much he will think we have changed, eh? And I wonder what he will think when he sees Amanda here, looking so much like María Elena? Her death destroyed him, you know," he said to Amanda, "and that's why he left. Even though none of us wanted him to leave, it was the right decision. His sadness was like a wolf in his stomach—it was eating him up inside."

Amanda nodded. Everyone in Cufeo had told her about Tomás. Maybe it was because she looked so much like her aunt that people had to tell her about Tomás and María Elena. She heard about their love and how they worked so hard together for the community. And how he had lived amidst their poverty, and was responsible for bringing so many trees to be planted; over a million, her father had said. She wondered what Tomás would think now that most of the farms he worked so hard for had been bought up by big rich companies. And that much of the pine was being delivered to the new pulp mill which was poisoning the river.

Miriam yawned as she rubbed the fingers of her arthritic right hand.

"Come on old man, it is time to go to bed. Will you be an angel, Amanda, and clean up? I feel very tired tonight. I must be getting old."

Amanda smiled and began to clear the dishes.

"Of course. You two go on."

Pablo and Miriam went upstairs while she washed the dishes. When she was finished, she made another cup of tea. She was excited about the lamb roast tomorrow, curious and eager to meet Tomás, plus she hadn't been home in well over a month. She was very much looking forward to seeing her parents and brothers. It was always when she was about to return to Cufeo when she realized how much she missed it. A good thing she was so busy here, she thought while finishing her tea.

Upstairs she pulled the little brown leather suitcase that had belonged to María Elena out of her closet. She ran her hands over the supple leather. Papá had made it out of a cowhide he had scraped and tanned. He was so clever; he could make just about anything. Yet, they were poor. When she finished packing, she went back downstairs to take a shower in the only bathroom. She had to light the gas hot water heater in the hall because the household was run on such a tight budget that the pilot was never left on. A plastic curtain hung precariously around the small tub, a leaky hand-held sprayer lay balanced on the faucets.

It felt good to get out of her sticky clothes, and running the hot spray all over her body was heaven. She reached for the soap and lathered up. As she washed, she wondered if she would ever have a real boyfriend—someone she could talk intelligently with, someone who was not just interested in her body. And, of course, someone who would make passionate love to her some day. But enough of that; she still had to dry her hair before bed. And she needed a good night's sleep; tomorrow would be a long day.

Chapter Three

The guide, oars poised, was in the stern of the raft when Carlos pushed off. Like the others, Carlos wore a life vest and bright red helmet. He also had his waterproof Nikon around his neck. It was going to be another scorcher, he thought, so unusual for around here. Two other guides, one in a kayak and the other in a small, single-man catamaran raft, followed them to the center of the river.

For the first kilometer, Carlos was able to take as many pictures as he wanted of the Futaleufú Valley with its beautiful mix of mountains, fields, and lush green forests bisected by the turquoise river of the same name. But things changed in a hurry when they came to a basalt gorge. Spuming mountains of white danced above them as they began to bounce and dive. The raft was thrown sideways with the helmsman fighting to turn them around. Their kayak escort disappeared upside down in a hole, but quickly reappeared after a combat roll. Shaking the water out of his ears, the kayaker professionally negotiated more holes and rapids. Carlos watched him go into a gigantic standing wave where somehow he completed a roll in mid-air. The kayaker waved his paddle at them, obviously part of the show. Carlos had to get a picture of this guy doing the impossible: his readers would love it. But reaching for his camera was a big mistake. At the moment he had the kayaker framed, the raft went down into a huge hole. Carlos lost his paddle as he was bounced out. Clutching the camera close to his chest, he ricocheted off boulders like a pinball. He dropped into another hole where he was sucked down underwater. Shit, this is it, he thought; but no, he was re-circulated to the top where he gasped for breath. Under he went again, but was soon spit out downriver. The current shot him around a tremendous boulder, and he dropped several feet into an absolutely monstrous hole. He couldn't see the raft or escorts anywhere, just walls of white in all directions. He was sucked under, totally powerless. Down he went, much deeper than before, tumbling around like he was in a gigantic washing machine. When he finally surfaced, he just caught a breath before he was pulled under again. He went way down. He was running out of air when suddenly all the turbulence was gone. It was as if he was floating in a dream. He wondered if he had drowned. People who had been revived from drowning said the end was very peaceful; but he knew he was alive when he saw the bottom rushing by. Suddenly, up he popped, twenty meters downstream of the hole. He sputtered and gasped, weak as a child, his life vest keeping him afloat. The guide in the catamaran maneuvered over to him. Carlos felt himself be lifted by the back of his life jacket until he could clutch the rear of the nylon deck with what strength he had left. They made it into shore where Carlos crawled onto the bank.

"Are you all right?"

Carlos, still trying to catch his breath, looked up at the guide.

"*Sí*, but if not for you, I would have drowned."

The river guide shook his head.

"You were under the water for a long time."

"I was holding my breath for the rest of my life," Carlos muttered.

The river guide looked at him closely.

"Do you want to rejoin the raft? They will be waiting in the eddy around the next bend ... Or maybe you should stay here and climb up to the road to bus back with us when we return?"

Miraculously, Carlos still had his camera around his neck. The river guide noticed.

"This is also a good spot to see the other rafters come down. You can take pictures..."

The photo incentive was unnecessary.

"I'll stay."

The guide nodded and pushed off. Carlos wavered as he stood, never more grateful to be on terra firma. He tested his legs before slowly climbing up to a good vantage point. Looking out to the monster hole, he considered himself fortunate to be alive. If he wanted to make thirty, maybe it was about time to tone down his little adventures. But, really, who could ask for a better job? A roving reporter, someone who could travel from one end of the country to the other, writing feature articles for the Sunday edition of a big Santiago paper. And the job hadn't come from luck—he had talked his editor into it. He had carte blanche to write on anything: local politics, human interest, travel, the environment, whatever. And being an excellent photographer had helped swing the deal. That was over two years ago. Since then over sixty of his pieces had been published, and he had even been considered for the National Journalism Award for his exposé of the dangers facing miners in Copiapo.

But he was also a realist. He knew that much of his success was because he had been privileged. His family was very wealthy, sending him to the best schools. He had followed in his father's footsteps, graduating from college in the United States. His father had gone to R.P.I., whereas he attended the prestigious school of journalism at Columbia University. When he returned to Chile, he applied for a job as a fledgling reporter. It was the degree from Columbia plus his father's contacts in Santiago that had opened the door. But he had earned the rest. He was smart, sensitive, and a very hard worker. He came to the office early and left late. He didn't stand around the water cooler bullshitting with the others. Even when he was not working he always carried his camera, just in case, and once or twice that had paid off big time. He attracted attention—he was up and coming.

He had decided to write an in-depth travel article on some of Chile's most beautiful areas on the northern edge of Patagonia. He would go first by boat to the Glacier San Rafael, then north by car on the Carretera Austral to the thermal springs of Puyuhuapi, and then here, the kayaking and rafting center of Futaleufú close to the Argentine border. Next on the list was Parque Pumalín, and finally the Valley of Cochamó near Puerto Montt where hard-core rock climbers from all over the world came to scale what they called Little Yosemite. From there he would wind up his southern trip with a brief visit to his family in Valdivia before returning to Santiago.

He saw some rafts approach the monster hole. Pulling the camera from around his neck, he zoomed in on the passengers, their faces a mix of fear and excitement as they dropped down into the hole. Perfect, he thought, as the motor drive shot frame after frame.

He wanted to write about the Futaleufú River not only because of its incredible beauty, but also to tell of the threat by ENDESA, the energy corporation that wanted to dam it. Many rafters and kayakers considered the Rio Futaleufú with its huge waves and madly turbulent 'rodeo holes' as the most challenging whitewater in the world. One section, known as the Gates of Hell, had over forty Class IV and V rapids with names like *purgatorio* and *terminador*. Not only would the whitewater activities be wiped out, but the environment would be seriously impacted in countless ways. He hoped his pictures would effectively show the beauty that would be lost if the dam went through. His next stop, Parque Pumalín, was the other extreme: a prime example of how man could protect the pristine.

Parque Pumalín was news, not because it was huge—over three hundred and twenty thousand hectares—or because it was unbelievably picturesque. Rather, it was because it was so controversial. Privately owned by a North American named Douglas Tompkins, the park extended from Argentina to the Chilean coast, effectively cutting the country in half. Tompkins had had agents secretly buy up the land for him. Being a millionaire *gringo*, the prices would have gone through the roof if he hadn't. But when the people of Chile found out, they didn't trust him. What was he up to? Was it another CIA plot? Was he setting up a new Jewish State? Was it going to be a nuclear waste dumping ground? What were his real motives?

Tompkins went on national TV to defend himself, saying that all he wanted to do was to protect a piece of this earth forever from man's wanton destruction. But the press, playing on people's fears, sensationalized the way he had purchased the land. Carlos believed Tompkins was sincere, that much of the criticism was fomented by far-right politicians because they didn't want such a huge chunk of real estate removed from the possibility of exploitation. Carlos wanted to write an honest, informative article, and he wanted to dramatically show what Tompkins was trying to protect through his pictures.

He made the easy day's drive from Futaleufú, passing through the little town of Chaitén at the park's eastern edge. After settling in the cabin he had rented for two days, he began to explore the park. On the second day, he took a three-hour hike up the Sendero Cascada through thick temperate rain forest. After crossing a broad stream so clear that it was like looking through glass, he came to a bamboo ladder. A thick rope lay draped over the boulder above it. He climbed up and tested the rope, and pulled himself the rest of the way up. He had been listening to a waterfall for some time now, but still hadn't seen it. He followed the footpath, outlined by small cairns, around a rock wall. And there it was. Magnificent! And the light was just right, he thought while reaching for his Nikon. The waterfall was so tall that even holding the camera vertically he couldn't fit it all in. He opted for shooting the lower section, a glistening torrent of water cascading past emerald-green ferns into the jade-colored pool.

Taking off his hiking boots and socks, he stuck a foot into the water. By God, it was cold! The morning, though, was already warm, and he knew it was going to be record hot again. The temperature yesterday had been thirty-three degrees, unheard of for Patagonia. The shower of water hitting the pool beckoned. He turned around; no one was coming. What the hell, he thought, and began to strip. He was very tall for a Chilean and well built. He also was a *rubio*—fair skinned and blond from his German heritage. He walked naked over to a large flat rock about a meter above the water. The water was clear and deep. It took his breath away when he dove in; his *bolas* felt like they had shrunk to the size of pebbles and were looking for a way to re-enter his body cavity. He treaded water until he caught his breath, willing himself to swim over to the curtain of water; he just had to feel it falling on his head. He reached the falls, but didn't linger. He swam quickly back and pulled himself out of the pool. Toweling off as best he could, he lay down on warm sculpted stone where, in a few minutes, he dozed off.

He woke some time later to giggling behind him. Startled, he turned. Three young Chilean girls were above him on the trail. He knew they were Chilean because of their well-kempt dark hair, their perfectly neat hiking outfits, and the way they giggled at his predicament of lying with his rear end exposed. He quickly reached for his pants.

The tallest girl said, "Better cover up, Señor. You are getting sunburned." They giggled again. Carlos sat up and, ouch, they were right—his butt was indeed a bit sensitive. Keeping his back to them, he wiggled into his clothes. He wondered how long they had been there.

"Excuse me, girls, I seem to have fallen asleep. I hope I have not offended you."

The girls looked surprised when they heard his Spanish. Probably thought he was an American or German—it happened all the time. The tall one spoke up again.

"Oh no, Señor. You looked very comfortable, and we would not have disturbed you if you were not so pink. I think maybe you will have a problem sitting down tonight." They started giggling again.

Shouldering his camera, Carlos walked up to the girls.

"A beautiful spot, eh?" They nodded. "How about a picture of you down by the pool? I work for a Santiago paper and am doing an article on the park. Who knows? Your picture might make my paper."

The girls looked at each other excitedly. Carlos took out his camera and framed them at the water's edge. He didn't have to tell them what to do. They posed, smiling their best smiles. He'd bet family members and schoolmates had taken their pictures a thousand times. He smiled at them.

"Thank you—all set. Enjoy yourselves, girls. And I highly recommend a dip. It's a bit cold, but very refreshing." They waved as he walked away.

Carlos returned to the trailhead. His last stop in the park would be the Sendero Alerces where he wanted to take pictures of the enormous trees, then on to his final destination of the Valley of Cochamó. His only regret with the park visit was that Tompkins had declined an interview. Carlos had spoken to him by radio from the park's information center. The North American had been polite, but guarded. He said he had been burned too many times by journalists who had taken statements out of context.

The *alerces* were gigantic, almost four meters through, and thousands of years old. They matched his memories of the giant sequoias he had seen in California. The trunks tapered as they rose to the sky, and although there were no branches down low, up above they were so thickly covered with moss and lichens that they looked hairy. Carlos stepped up to one of the behemoths to place a palm against the flaky reddish-grey bark. It had a spongy feel to it. He suddenly remembered that he had touched an *alerce* before, and how ironic was that! It had been when his father had wanted to see the piece of land outside Valdivia which for years he had paid the taxes on for a friend from the States. Now that friend had recently returned to Chile, and there was to be a celebratory *asado*. His father wanted him to go; maybe he would see those trees again.

He had been seventeen when, on the way to see the American's land, his father had stopped at a little farm where the *campesinos* greeted him like an old friend. The farmer and a pile of kids had jumped into the truck, and they rode up to the land where, besides the trees, there was a beautiful clearing that looked out on a waterfall. Carlos also remembered that the farmer had a very pretty young daughter who was quite smart. Sitting in the back of the pickup, she had told him all the names of the trees they passed, and what the wood of each was used for. He wondered if she still lived there. What was her name? He couldn't remember. He guessed she had been maybe five or six years younger than him, which would make her about twenty or so now. She was probably married, he mused, with several kids in tow—most likely stout like all the other *campo* women, and worn from hard work.

It didn't take long to walk the *alerce* trail. He returned to the largest tree for a couple more pictures. When he was done, he patted the trunk and bowed his thanks. After loading his pack and camera bags, he boarded the car ferry only a couple of stone throws away from his cabin. The ferry would take him across to Hornoprien where he would continue on to Cochamó and Little Yosemite. Gazing out towards the volcanoes to the east, he thought about his trip. Other than almost drowning, it had been wonderful; he was proud to live in such a beautiful country. With all the photos and notes, he was also eager to begin writing. He would start at his parents' farm in Valdivia. It was going to be pretty boring there after all his adventures, and it would give him something to do until he returned to Santiago.

Chapter Four

"Did you marry me or your sister, eh Jaime!" she asked while rocking her granddaughter on her knee.

"Quiet woman, she will hear you!"

"I don't care!" But she lowered her voice. "What if she does? It would do her good to know what I think." The baby spit up some of the milk she had for breakfast. Jaime's *señora* brusquely wiped her mouth. The baby made a face and shook her head.

"Lilia does more than her share of work around here," Jaime said. "She does all the gardening and most of the laundry. You should be thankful for that."

"She does work hard," she admitted grudgingly, but added, "when she is not having one of her 'spells.'"

"Quiet, I say!"

But Jaime's *señora* was just getting warmed up.

"And I do nothing? Who cooks the meals and mends your clothes? And feeds the animals? And what about this baby, eh? Did I ask our daughter to bring her here for us to raise?"

Lilia heard them through the wall of her bedroom. She knew what Jaime's *señora* thought, and agreed with her that a household should have only one woman. But what could she do? She had no other place to go. She was stuck here. Jaime did his best to maintain the peace; he had even built her this room off the side of the house so she could have some privacy. But two women were still one too many.

She looked around the room. She had made it as cheery as she could. She had painted the walls and ceiling an off-white which Jaime's *señora* had thought a terrible extravagance. It was the only painted room in the house. The single window, with potted flowers on the sill, was framed by green muslin curtains. There were a few jars with cut flowers scattered about, and the quilt she had made was colorful. There were several of her bird carvings sitting on a long shelf above the small writing desk she had built out of some old planks. She was proud of the desk. She had scraped the boards smooth with shards of glass, oiling them until they were a lustrous deep dark brown. She loved to read there at night with the soft glow of the kerosene lamp bringing out the richness of the wood.

Lilia got out of bed, purposely making noise so Jaime and his wife would stop arguing in the kitchen. Once dressed, she took the chamber pot outside through her private door, and walked over to a wide wooden shelf with a tin basin on top, and a bucket of spring water underneath. She washed her face, and returned to her room. Finally, she entered the kitchen.

Jaime looked up from his *maté*.

"Good morning, sister."

Jaime's *señora* ignored her while shifting the baby on her lap. Lilia bent over the baby who smiled up at her. She caressed the little head before walking over to prepare a cup of *maté*.

"How was your trip to town, Jaime?" she asked after taking a sip of the strong tea. "I hope your little truck didn't give you problems this time." Last night she had gone to bed late, but he still hadn't returned from Valdivia. She had suspected the worst. His little pickup was more trouble than it was worth, always breaking down. He would be better off tending to chores and cutting firewood rather than spending so much time tinkering underneath that old truck.

"Everything went fine. And I got the spools of thread and that library book like you wanted. They are on the shelf by the door." Lilia looked eagerly over. "And guess what! I saw Juan Montoya in town. He told me Don Tomás has returned from the United States. He is in Camán! Can you believe it!" Lilia's mouth opened in surprise. "Juan was buying some supplies for an *asado* to celebrate his return. We are invited."

"Don Tomás! Really!" Her brother nodded. "That is wonderful!"

She took a thoughtful sip of *maté*.

"I wonder what he looks like now?" Tomás was ten years her senior which would make him fifty-one. She thought back to those months he had lived with them—so clueless when he arrived, hardly speaking a word of Spanish. The whole family had struggled to understand him which had made things very awkward. But she and Tomás had soon bonded. While he helped her bring in the sheep in the late afternoons, she pointed out all the flora and fauna. Soon she was the only one who could understand his horrible Spanish. At night after clearing his dishes from the big table, they would talk about what they had done during the day. She remembered crying when he decided to move out of their house to a more central location for his work.

Jaime put his cup in the sink basin. When he returned to the table, he was surprised to see Lilia's eyes lit up and a big grin on her face.

"Sister, I have not seen a smile like that since you were a little girl!" Jaime's *señora* looked over at Lilia. She was surprised too. Jaime continued, "Lilia, you are showing your teeth like an old horse with its chin tickled. What makes you so happy?"

"Do you remember that night at the big table after I had taken Don Tomás to see the colony of burrowing owls?"

Jaime began laughing.

"Of course! I couldn't count all the times I teased him about that."

He and Lilia laughed until they had tears in their eyes. Jaime's *señora* looked from one of them to the other.

"Do you two mind if you let me in on the joke? Or is it something private?" she asked peevishly.

Lilia wiped her eyes with a corner of her skirt.

"Oh, it is not private at all. Most everybody in Cufeo heard about it at some point."

She started laughing again. The *señora* frowned.

"I am sorry, I don't mean to be impolite. What happened was *chuchos*—the little owls—was a new word for Don Tomás. He always carried a little notebook around to write down the words I taught him. But he misspelled it, and that night when I came out to sit at the table with him, he told me how much he had enjoyed the day. He said the best part was seeing all the little *chuchas*. He said they looked so soft and cuddly that he wished he had one right there at the table to pet."

Jaime's *señora* looked at her husband in disbelief. Jaime smiled back at her.

"I was shocked and hoped that Mamá and Papá hadn't heard him. I told him he had used the wrong word, and what he said was that he wanted to pet the soft cuddly part between a woman's legs." Lilia started laughing again. She could barely continue. "And you should have seen the look of horror on his face. He was so embarrassed! And he was scared to death Papá had heard and would come out and kill him for saying that to his ten-year-old daughter." Lilia wiped her eyes again. "Anyway, Jaime and his soccer friends must have teased poor Don Tomás about that a thousand times."

Suddenly Lilia remembered another *chucho* story, and it was not a happy one— far from it. Her smile vanished. It was as if a dark cloud passed over her face. She stood up abruptly to walk over to the stove where she reached out toward the kettle of water, but left her hand dangling. She had gone somewhere else. Her brother and his *señora* knew exactly what was going through her mind. They didn't say a word. Jaime stood up to bring her back to her chair, while the *señora* began to clear the dishes.

After breakfast Lilia collected all the soiled clothes in the house. She carried them outside to the pasture where she dumped them in a heap next to a large smoke-blackened cauldron that she filled with buckets of stream water. She let the clothes soak before starting a fire underneath. As she waited for the water to heat up, she sat on a stump and began to shape a piece of wood with a small knife. She loved to carve birds and animals. She had always loved watching wildlife, which was one reason why she was a good carver. She could see them alive and perky in her mind, but it was her sheer talent that made them so lifelike.

She became so engrossed with the carving that she let the fire go out. She dipped her fingers in the water; luckily it was still plenty warm. Now the real work began. She began to rhythmically rub the clothes up and down against a beat-up old washboard. Jaime's *señora* complained that they needed a washing machine more than Jaime's old truck. Lilia couldn't agree more, except for one thing—no, two: they didn't have electricity or running water. Lilia straightened up to stretch. Her back was not what it was twenty years ago. How many years had she been doing this? She bent over again—she didn't even want to know.

Her older sisters had done the wash when she was real young. Her job then was to take care of the animals and help in the kitchen. She had especially loved bringing in the sheep. Sometimes she would walk all over looking for them. It was hard now to remember how happy she had been back then, but that was before… No! She couldn't let herself think about that! But the memory took over. It always took over.

She stopped wringing out one of Jaime's shirts, becoming motionless like in the kitchen earlier. She closed her eyes as tight as she could, willing the picture to go away; but it wouldn't. She knew it would haunt her for the rest of her life. Her childhood had ended that day.

It was the last time she had gone out looking for the sheep. She had been twelve years old and an early bloomer. Her threadbare clothes, clinging to her nubile body, were much too small for her. Her mother didn't even have the money to buy her a bra. Lilia had never noticed Jaime's friend, Jorge, paying any attention to her; but he had watched her for a long time, and he was a brute, a big, dumb, hairy brute…

When she came to, she noticed that Jaime's shirt was on the ground. She picked it up and brushed it off before hanging it on a bush to dry. She had to take a walk. That's what the old doctor from Osorno told her to do when it got bad. She had loved that old man. He had been so patient with her. She had moved out of Cufeo after the rape because everything at home reminded her of that day. She lived with her grandparents in Osorno for many years, and it was her grandmother who had found the special doctor. He knew how poor they were so he never charged them. Lilia saw him for years. But he was old, and one day he died.

When they looked for a new special doctor, they were all too expensive. Except for one; but he said he wanted to meet Lilia first. Her grandmother brought her to meet him, and he agreed to treat her for free. She was eighteen years old. At first he asked many of the same questions as the old doctor, but after awhile the questions were different. Had she had a man since? Didn't she think that might be the best thing? If she could have good sex with a man, then maybe the dreams and memories would go away.

She noticed immediately when he began touching her. She didn't like any man doing that. At first she assumed it was casual, but it happened more and more often. It had started with a hand on a shoulder or a pat on the hand. It progressed. One day he led her into his office with his hand on the small of her back. The next session he was listening to her intently when he leaned forward to put a hand on her thigh. She stiffened and began to shake uncontrollably. He yanked his hand away, flustered. She left his office, never to return.

After her grandparents died, she moved back to Cufeo. But her parents soon became ill, and eventually moved into Valdivia to be closer to the doctors. Jaime was stuck with her. She knew Jaime loved her, but she was a disruption. Jaime had found her that day, and he had immediately gone after Jorge, nearly killing him. Jorge had lost an eye, and his brain was addled from so many blows to the head. But Jaime had been severely beaten too. Every time she looked at him, she saw the scars from that fight. It was impossible to forget. The whole thing was a disaster. Her life was a mess, and she was making a mess out of other people's lives. But she shouldn't think that way. She should just go on her walk. Like the old doctor said, it was the best thing she could do.

Chapter Five

Tom asked the driver if this were the local bus to Paillaco. The driver looked up from his newspaper and nodded. Tom walked towards the rear. As he sat down, he noticed the driver staring at him in the mirror. Tom thought, I'm a *gringo* again, better get used to it. The driver put the paper down and got off the bus. He walked over to the pile of luggage and sacks that would be loaded on to the roof. Included in the mix was Tom's old frayed backpack. Reaching down, the driver turned it from side to side. When he hefted it, he smiled. Standing nearby was his young assistant. The driver asked him something, and the assistant nodded. When the driver returned to the bus, he walked directly to Tom's seat.

"Pardon me, but is your name Tomás?"

"Yes," Tom answered, surprised.

Slapping his thigh the driver laughed.

"I thought so!" He extended his hand. "Tomás, you may not remember me, but I am Juan—'Juanito'—the bus driver's assistant when you used to ride the bus."

Tom remembered the little assistant well, but it was hard to find him in this portly middle-aged driver. He shook his hand.

"Forgive me, Juan. It has been so many years."

"Yes, it has been a very long time. We all have changed much, I think," the driver said, patting his belly. "I was not sure it was you until I saw your backpack. I would not forget that one, eh?" He chuckled while shaking his head. "It was always so heavy. Are you going to the Camán Road?" Tom nodded. "Then I will let you off there. It is good to see you again."

"For me too, Juan."

The bus was filling up fast with the small farmers and their families who lived outside of Valdivia. They looked much like they did thirty years ago. When the bus was full, Juanito started the engine. After letting it warm up, he pulled slowly out to Avenida Picarte, heading east. Several kilometers out of town, they passed the boulder where María Elena had died. Someone had put fresh flowers in front of the boulder. Tom bet that it had been Miriam, probably for him. He looked towards the front of the bus. Juanito was watching him in the mirror. He knew, Tom thought; he remembered. Maybe he had been working on the bus that day when the truck had tried to pass.

Juanito let him off at the top of the hill. Tom thanked him, and his assistant who climbed like a monkey to the top of the bus to retrieve the pack. Tom began the long walk up to Camán. The road looked good. There was a rusty old grader parked off to the side which had been used recently; the ditching was freshly beveled and not a pothole anywhere. He was excited. Ever since he had landed in Santiago he had felt a pleasant sensation growing in his belly. It was really happening! He really was back in Chile walking the Camán road again! A few plastic bags were caught in the branches of bushes in the pasture, left there by the wind. They reminded him of the Rodríguez sisters who had hung the laundry to dry on bushes like these around their house. Here and there he saw pieces of retread. That was a new look. Few trucks used the road back then so that about the only litter was the occasional blown-out shoe sole. He began to sweat heavily. He was in good shape, but he was not in his early twenties anymore, and his pack was loaded with presents—among other things, Buck hunting knives for the men, and small decorative cans of maple syrup for the women. He heard a truck rumbling up from behind. An old *cacharro*, a firewood truck similar to the one María Elena had ridden in that day, slowly approached. It pulled up along side where it stopped, idling loudly. One of the two workers standing in the back, holding on to the headboard, asked if he wanted a ride. Tom thanked him, but when he said that he wanted to walk, they looked at him as if he were crazy. The driver put the truck in gear and pulled away.

When he came to the steep part of the road where it was slow going, his shoulders began to scream. At the top, he put his pack down and leaned against it. For the first time, he could see the snow-capped volcanoes in the distance. Just the same, he thought. After a few minutes, he rolled his shoulders a couple of times before hoisting his pack and hooking his thumbs into the shoulder straps to ease the pressure. At least this was the level section, only a mile or so to go. It wasn't long before he heard a horse coming from up the road. It was coming hard and fast. Suddenly, a rider came around the bend who must have seen Tom about the same time because he started to yip like a drunken soccer player returning from a tournament. Tom could see that he had one leg extended almost straight out. Juan! Tom began to wave like a madman. Juan was waving his hat, yipping loudly with a big grin on his face. The trucker must have told him that there was a crazy *gringo* walking up the road, carrying a backpack, who didn't want a ride: Juan knew it had to be Tom. Tom jumped up and down, waving both hands, not easy when you had a forty-pound pack on your back. Juan began yelling, "Tomás! Tomás!" Tom's eyes blurred, and he realized he was crying. Tears of joy? For María Elena? For years lost? He didn't know and didn't care. What he did know was that now, after all these years, he, Tomás, had finally come home.

* * *

The first day after settling in, Tomás borrowed a horse from Juan who helped him with the saddle.

"I see you have not forgotten how to cinch a horse, eh, Tomás? When was the last time you rode?"

"When we went up to the *copihue* clearing the day I left."

"You're joking!"

"No, it is the truth. I imagine I'll be a little sore by this afternoon, but I want to look at the land that you have watched over all these years."

Tomás rode out through the gate, and Juan watched as he slowly traveled up the La Paloma road. He knew Tomás had another reason for making the long ride.

Tomás rode all morning. He couldn't believe the change. Everywhere he looked was Monterey pine; gone were the scattered farms and open pasture, there were no views out to the volcanoes, new well-graveled spur roads occasionally spun off to the right and left. All the roads were in excellent condition, maintained by the big companies that had bought up the farms. Although muffled by pine trees, he could hear a distant skidder and chainsaws. He reined in his horse, listening closely. That high-pitched whine sounded familiar; he'd bet the skidder was one of those old red Timberjacks. And the chainsaws sounded familiar, too. He guessed they were Stihls. But they seemed out of place; they were Vermont noises. There had been no chainsaws before, just those heavy long-handled axes.

It was all uphill to his land. As he passed a gravel road to his right, two snow-capped volcanoes were visible on the horizon. Tomás recognized the view. This had been the trail that led down to the farm of the *gerente*—manager—of the co-op he had worked with for three years. But there should have been a house and a one-room school on the corner. And where was the cross marking the grave of the little girl who had been killed by a mountain lion? There were only pine trees in every direction.

    He knew right away when he came to his land because the pine was replaced by old growth hardwoods. It was a welcome change. He began to identify the different species, gratified that he could still remember many: *radal, avellano, roble, tineo, ulmo, rauli.* The diversification of species, he knew, made for a healthy forest; bugs or disease had a tough time spreading if trees that weren't in their diet blocked the way. Not so with a monoculture like the pine plantations where a blight could easily run rampant. He thought of the huge stands of spruce wiped out by the budworm in Maine, or the hemlock devastated by the wooly adelgid in North Carolina. Of course, plantations could always be sprayed with some noxious chemicals with unknown long-term consequences.

    Tomás found the trailhead without a problem, even though the old lightning-struck tree that had marked it was no longer standing. He carefully rode down the narrow, steep trail to the *alerce* grotto. One of the trees had died. After hobbling his horse, he inspected the fallen giant. He was relieved to see no signs of foul play: it looked like it had died of natural causes, but it created quite a hole in the canopy. The rest of the *alerce*, his old friends, looked just the same. How would he notice a change in them anyway? What were thirty years to trees that had been around for several thousand?

    He started down the path towards the *copihue* clearing. The path was much more obvious now; from all the wedding traffic, he thought. The trail zigzagged, and he crossed the stream twice before he could see light ahead through the trees. When he heard the waterfall, 'butterflies' began to flutter around his stomach. He left the woods, stepping out on to the broad shelf. It had changed, but not much. To the left was the white ribbon of water that plunged a hundred and fifty feet. Directly ahead loomed Volcán Puntiagudo. Unlike the view down the *gerente's* road, the volcano was right there in his face. It was ruggedly immense, and the snow at the peak sparkled in the sunlight. Below him were the *copihue* vines, but they weren't in bloom. Thirty years ago when he left, it had been a red sea. He looked at where the condor had landed, the vines sagging under its weight. He walked over to the wedding *ramada*. It looked like it had been worked on recently: must have been Juan. Juan would have known he would ride up here first thing. He sat in the *ramada*, looking out. It was so peaceful.

"Well, *mi querida*," he said softly, "I'm back. I never thought I'd return, never thought I could. But I'm glad to be here. You wouldn't believe how much I've missed you all these years."

He lay down, putting his hands behind his head. It was here they had first made love. He remembered it so clearly. He had napped afterwards. When he awoke, María Elena was standing naked, gazing out at the volcano. She was humming softly and brushing out her hair. He had never seen her hair loose before; she had always worn it in a long thick braid.

"María Elena!" he had exclaimed.

She turned, smiling at him. Her beauty awed him.

"Did I not tell you that the first man to see my hair free would be my husband? Well, *mi amor*," she said as she dropped the brush onto a corner of the *manta*, "you are my husband: we are married now."

She had straddled him and they made love for a second time. Tomás smiled at the memory before easing into a peaceful sleep. When he awoke he couldn't remember feeling so rested. He felt embraced by her spirit as he made his way back up the path.

Once he had decided to return to Cufeo, he had thought a lot about building a cabin somewhere on these two hundred and fifty hectares. Not down in the clearing, though, that was María Elena's spot. He walked around looking for possible sites. He took bearings with a compass, calculating where the sun would rise and set at different times of the year. He hoped to harness both the sun and wind for electricity: there was as much, maybe more, alternative energy technology available now in Chile as in the States. He also wanted easy access to the main road; he had had his fill of maintaining a mile-long driveway back in Vermont.

There was a wide plateau only a stone's throw from the road with a southwestern exposure, and, when he climbed one of the hardwood trees, he saw that there was a terrific view of the waterfall and volcano. He walked up a nearby hill that was still on his land. It faced north, providing some protection for the plateau during the winter. He found a couple of seeping wet spots. He'd bet anything they were springs. It would be easy to run a waterline from one of them down to a cabin. He returned to the plateau. He would have to clear some of the trees, but he was convinced it was the perfect spot to build.

Chapter Six

Juan tried to hand the lasso to Tomás.

"I know it's an honor, Juan, but do I really have to? I mean, you could do it; no one's around."

"It is a tradition, Tomás, you know that. Come on. It won't bite you."

Tomás hefted it. The last time he had a leather lasso in his hands was a lifetime ago. It had a good solid feel.

"I better practice."

"Suit yourself. I'll have some *maté*, and then we'll come out." Juan walked over to the house.

Tom stepped back from the corral, uncoiling some of the rope. He made a big loop which, along with several small coils, he held in his throwing hand. He started to swing the rope above his head, taking aim at a fence post. The toss slapped the post. Too short. He made a bigger coil and tried again. Got it—barely. He practiced several more times. He was the guest of honor, supposed to lasso the lamb that would be roasted. The last time he had tried to rope a lamb had been back in the late '60's.

Juan, Flor, young Tomás and Guillermo, along with their *señoras* and children, came out to the corral. Soon they all stood leaning against the corral waiting for Tomás. Tomás slid a couple of the gate bars back, and entered. The sheep were all bunched up at the far end.

"Which one, Juan?"

"The one with the long black tail."
Tomás looked over at the flock, then back at Juan.
"There are two with black tails."
Juan laughed.
"The male, of course! The one furthest to the right."
Tomás approached the flock swinging the lasso. They began running around the corral, but were too tightly packed for him to throw. When he walked straight at them, they parted. The black male lamb hesitated. When it started to run, Tomás had a clear shot. He remembered he never led enough. This time he threw twice as far ahead of the animal and, I'll be a son-of-a-gun, he thought, got him! Tomás drew the rope across the small of his back, leaning backwards to brace against the lamb's tugging.

"Well done, Tomás!" Guillermo said as he walked up to the struggling animal. Young Tomás came over to help his brother take the rope off. They dragged the lamb away.

Young Tomás said, "Papá, you told me Tomás was terrible with a lasso."

"Did I say that?" Juan asked with his impish grin. "You must have me confused with someone else." When Tomás gave him a look, Juan and his sons laughed. "One thing I do know," Juan added, "is that Tomás won't slit the lamb's throat."

"You got that right!" Tomás said.

Young Tomás threw a short rope over the thick branch of a shade tree. He tied an end around one of the lamb's rear hooves before hoisting it with Guillermo's help, and tying it off. Juan was wearing his new Buck hunting knife which he pulled from its sheath. After fingering the blade, he smiled at Tomás.

"I won't need a stone for this one, eh? I could shave with it. And the blade is perfect for skinning."

Juan put on an old stained leather apron while Flor walked up with a small metal basin. When Juan cut the lamb's throat, Flor captured the blood to make *niache*, the traditional first dish of an *asado*. After mixing in garlic, lemon, and salt, she let the blood coagulate before slicing it up like a dish of brownies. Tomás was the only one who refused a piece. Once the lamb was gutted, skinned, and impaled with a hardwood pike, it was carried to the fire which Juan's sons had been tending since sunup. There was a fine bed of coals between the two y-shaped supports where they placed the skewered lamb. Juan occasionally rotated the lamb while Guillermo and young Tomás took turns basting it. Just like old times, Tomás thought; about the only difference was that now pine trees blocked the view of the volcanoes. The men talked and joked while the lamb slowly cooked. After awhile Tomás stood up.

"I think I'll stretch my legs, and go see if Volcán Osorno is still out there somewhere."

"You'll need to go to the new road down some in the plantation, Tomás. Otherwise the trees will be in the way," Juan said.

They watched Tomás disappear through the little gate in front of the pine.

"He's going to their stump," Juan said sadly to his sons. "That is, if he can find it now, with all the trees."

Amazing, Tomás thought, the trees in the lower pasture were less than two feet tall when he had left. The volcanoes, especially Osorno, were always in view. Not now. He retraced his steps several times before he found the big half-stump with the center burned out ages ago. It hadn't changed much. Must be *lingue*, that wood never rotted. The stump had been their backrest when he and María Elena came down to watch the sunsets. The happiest moment of his life was when he had proposed here and she accepted. It seemed extra big now with just him leaning against it, and he felt hemmed in by the ten-inch-diameter pine trees. It didn't take long before he knew the stump's magic was gone.

He stood up and brushed off the back of his pants. Being the guest of honor, he should get back. When he came to the gate, he saw that Kurt had arrived. At one time he and Kurt had vied for Maria Elena's favors, before becoming fast friends. A young man stood next to Kurt, handing a big jar of what looked like honey to Flor. The resemblance between the two men was strong: had to be Kurt's son. They towered over the Chileans. Tomás rushed up to embrace Kurt.

"What took you so long, Tomás? I thought you'd return way before this."

"You know me, Kurt, I'm not one to rush things." They both laughed. Kurt introduced Carlos who shook hands with Tomás.

"A pleasure, Sr. Young."

"Please, Carlos, call me Tomás."

Tomás turned back to Kurt.

"I owe you, old friend. I don't know how I can thank you enough for paying the taxes on the land for all these years."

"No bother, Tomás. I have a secretary taking care of things like that, and writing one more check took her maybe a minute or two each year."

"Still, I am in your debt. And I have a small present for you. I'll be right back."

Kurt was an outdoorsman who loved to hunt and fish. He gratefully accepted the Buck hunting knife. Carlos admired it with his father while Juan brandished his, telling them how well it skinned the lamb. The men walked over to the fire. Kurt, asking questions about the States, and Tomás talked non-stop while the others listened. A little crew cab pickup riding low came through the main gate. Crammed with passengers and baskets of food, it stopped near the house. Six passengers untangled themselves from the back, four more from the cab. Tomás rushed up to greet them. Among them was Amanda. She shook his hand.

So this is the famous Tomás, she thought. Good looking enough, although weathered like a *campesino*. Even his hand is rough like Papá's.

"I see you have your aunt's leather bag."

She looked at him in surprise.

"Yes. You have a good memory, Don Tomás."

"Please call me Tomás: we are family. And as for that little suitcase, I remember it alright. I carried it many times, including once all the way up here from the highway. But I am forgetting my manners. Let me take you over to introduce my friend Kurt and his son Carlos."

Amanda looked over at the two *rubios*. The older one looked familiar. He was staring at her. Kurt inclined his body slightly as Tomás introduced Amanda. Carlos said, "I believe we met years ago, Señorita, when we went up to see the *alerce* trees."

Now Amanda recalled where she had seen Kurt before.

"That's right! And you must be the boy I rode with in the back of the truck."

Wow, Carlos thought, this girl is beautiful! Juan called over from the fire.

"Hey! What am I? An outcast! Amanda, you can't come give your own father a hug!"

Amanda rushed over. Kurt quickly turned to Tomás.

"She looks exactly like María Elena! You didn't even react. What, do you have ice in your veins!"

Tomás laughed.

"Believe me, Kurt, that's not the case. I was warned. I even saw pictures of Amanda before I left the States. If I hadn't, you'd probably have to pick me up off the ground right now."

Amanda took turns hugging everyone. Different-aged nephews and nieces began to mingle and dart about. Miriam came out to gauge when the lamb would be ready.

Juan asked her where the wine was. She rolled her eyes, saying it would be put out on the porch directly. Young Tomás, with an arm around his sister, said, "The lamb won't be ready for awhile. I think we should get a game of soccer going over by the school. What do you think, eh sister?"

Amanda was all for it.

"We can play half-field with Papá as goalie." She looked at Carlos. "How about you three *rubios* against us three *morenos*?"

"No offense, Amanda," Carlos said, "but three men against two and a girl?"

Young Tomás gave his sister a little squeeze while winking at Guillermo. He looked back at Carlos.

"Don't worry. It will be fair enough. And it's just for fun anyway."

Tomás, Kurt, and Juan immediately started making excuses. We're old they said. Tomás said he'd pull a hamstring. Kurt said he hadn't played in years. And Juan said he was just an old cripple. But they were outvoted. Juan recruited Pablo to finish cooking the lamb, and they headed over to the soccer field. As they crossed the road, a man and woman approached on horseback. Tomás didn't recognize the man until he saw the scars and misshapen nose; a late middle-aged Jaime. Jaime jumped down to give Tomás a fierce *abrazo*. Both began laughing and talking at the same time.

"Jaime, your scars have healed well. You're not as ugly as you were."

"And you, Tomás, are so thin! Don't they feed you in that country of yours, eh?"

The woman remained on her horse.

"And I see you still haven't learned any manners, Jaime. Don't you think you should introduce me to your *señora*?"

"Ahh, I can see you are so old now you need glasses, too. Why should I introduce you to someone you already know? Tell me that, eh?"

The woman dismounted. She was tall and slender, high-waisted with long legs. Tomás guessed she was in her thirties, maybe early forties. She was a handsome woman. She held out her hand.

"Hello, Tomás."

Tomás took her hand but had no idea who she was. Then she smiled.

"Lilia?"

She nodded.

"Lilia!" He threw his arms around her and gave her a big hug. Feeling her stiffen under his embrace, he immediately stepped back; but she was smiling.

"Lilia, you're…you're all grown up, a woman now! Look at you!"

Lilia laughed as Tomás shook his head admiringly from side to side. She said, "It looks like you're on your way to the soccer field, don't let us interrupt."

Tomás tore his eyes away from her.

"Jaime, come on over to the school. The lamb's not ready yet and we're going to have a quick game. But you have to play with us *rubios*."

Jaime walked over to the field while Lilia went up to the house. She sent down one of the older grandchildren to even up the teams. Young Tomás threw the soccer ball out to the center of the field, saying, "Come on, let's start. You *rubios* can have first try."

Tomás lined up with Carlos in the center, while Jaime and Kurt spread out a little towards the wings. Tomás called out to Jaime.

"Remember how we used to do it?"

Jaime nodded. Tomás touched the ball to Carlos and then went around him to his right side. When Amanda approached Carlos, he passed Tomás the ball. Tomás dribbled up the field. When he was challenged, he lofted the ball over to Jaime who had started running down the left sideline. It was a good lead but Jaime wasn't as fast as he used to be, allowing young Tomás to sprint over to the ball first. He passed it to Guillermo who worked it with his brother back up to mid-field.

Tomás teased Jaime.

"I guess all the bread and potatoes have slowed you down some, eh old man?" Jaime didn't reply. He couldn't; he was breathing too hard. Some of the grandchildren came over to watch. The *morenos* lined up with young Tomás in the center, Amanda to his right. Young Tomás passed the ball to Amanda who quickly dribbled around Kurt. She picked up speed and with so few players she decided to head straight towards the goal. Only Carlos was between her and Juan. Carlos smiled confidently as she approached. She put on a burst of speed. Carlos backpedaled in response. Amanda slashed to her left as Carlos challenged her. But as she went left she tapped the ball to the right. It was a simple but effective move. Carlos's momentum was towards Amanda, away from the ball, and he had to compensate. By the time he did, Amanda had run around him, caught up with the ball, and was at the goal in seconds. Juan, instantly on his toes, was set to spring either way.

"Ready, Papá?" Amanda asked, laughing. "Be careful now! Don't get hurt!"

Suddenly Amanda stumbled causing Juan to relax for a split second. But it was only a ploy. As she seemingly started to fall, her left foot shot out, sending a rocket through the upper right hand corner. Juan didn't have a chance: he had been caught flat-footed. He hadn't even tried to stop it.

"Papá, you don't remember that one?" she teased. "It was you who taught it to me!"

Juan shook his head as he limped off to fetch the ball. There were no nets in the goals. Tomás walked back with Carlos to midfield. In English, Tomás said, "Well, you can pick it up now."

At first Carlos didn't understand. Then he smiled.

"Ah yes. An American expression. I haven't heard that one for a long time. You're right. She faked me 'out of my jock.'"

They played for awhile longer. It wasn't even close: the *morenos* were younger, faster, and had the advantage that three out of four of them had played together their whole lives. Their passing made the *rubios* look silly, and they scored at will. The *rubios* didn't score a goal. As they walked back to the farm with grandkids in tow, young Tomás looked over to Carlos.

"Good thing we had a girl on our team so we could keep the score down, eh Carlos?" Carlos didn't bother to reply; Amanda had scored most of the goals.

In the shade of a *ramada*, Pablo carved the lamb up into steaming hunks. The meat was flanked by large bowls of salad, potatoes, and loaves of fresh bread. There were small bowls of spicy pepper sauce, and at the end of the hardwood plank table were several berry pies. In the corner were plastic cups, a demijohn of wine, a big bowl of white wine punch with strawberries, and a pitcher of lemonade.

Carlos, still sunburned, sat down gingerly next to Amanda. Amanda noticed.

"You look like someone who just rode a horse for the first time."

"Nope," he muttered. Amanda waited for him to say something else, but he began eating.

"So I guess you're not going to tell me why your rear end is sore."

He looked up chewing. When his mouth was clear, he said, "Sunburn."

She rolled her eyes.

"Right." She started cutting her meat.

"No, really. I, er, went swimming under a glacial waterfall and it was freezing. When I got out I warmed myself by lying on a big flat stone. And I fell asleep."

Amanda laughed.

"And where was that?"

"Parque Pumalín."

Amanda looked up with interest. She said, "I have wanted to go there since I first heard all the controversy about Tompkins. I know several students who have gone, and they say it's just beautiful."

"It is."

They continued eating. She looked at him. Well dressed and well spoken. From a rich family. Someone with all the advantages.

"So you were there swimming and playing. That must be nice. I wish I could afford to do that."

"Actually, I was on assignment."

"Assignment? For what?"

"An article. I am a reporter and, like you said, with all the controversy, the park is news. I'm writing an article now which, if accepted, should be out in a couple of Sundays. There also should be some good pictures of the park in the article you could look at," he said, trying to impress her.

"I can't afford to buy a Sunday paper," she said curtly. She looked out towards the small flock of sheep grazing on her father's only remaining pasture. A large gray dog guarded them. Carlos felt the rebuff. He changed the subject.

"So you don't live here anymore...you live in Valdivia?" She nodded. "What do you do there?"

"I'm a student at the university."

"Really!"

"That surprises you doesn't it; a *campesina* going to the university?"

"Yes, frankly, it does. You just said that you couldn't afford to buy a paper. Then how on earth can you afford the university?"

"Full scholarship."

She stood up before he could reply.

"I think I'll go get a piece of pie. Excuse me."

Carlos watched her walk away. She didn't return.

After bolting their meals, the grandchildren asked permission to be excused. They rushed over to the *tejo* pits where they took turns throwing leaden discs back and forth, trying to get closest to a string stretched across the middle. The adults moved to the long porch in the front of the house. Juan brought the demijohn of wine over.

"It's really terrible that the big timber companies are the ones benefitting most from the trees we planted," Tomás said. "And you're right, Juan. It's changed so much here that it's hard to know where you are. With most of the farms torn down and all the trees, it just doesn't seem like Cufeo anymore. I find it sad."

"Not to mention that many of the trees end up at the new pulp mill which is poisoning the rivers," Amanda said.

Kurt looked at her evenly.

"What do you mean, Amanda? I've been told the mill has the most up-to-date technology available for treating wastes, and that it is closely monitored. It has never failed to meet all requirements which, I might add, are quite strict. So, what are you talking about?"

A harsh staccato noise interrupted them.

"What is that!" Carlos exclaimed.

"I don't know how you say it in Spanish," Tomás answered, "but in English it is called a 'jake brake.' There's a truck somewhere braking through its engine."

It was so loud that conversation was impossible. Juan stood up with the demijohn of wine. He filled the men's cups before walking to where the driver could see him. As the truck passed, he pointed to the bottle. The driver laughed and shook his head. It was several minutes before the *campo's* sunny stillness returned. Amanda turned to Kurt.

"I am doing a research project for the university in Valdivia, and have been monitoring the water quality of

Las Cruces River. There is the presence of very high levels of iron and other heavy metals which is most likely caused by their bleaching system of chlorine dioxide. There is no industry further up river from the mill, and the waste of the other factories in Valdivia is totally different. As for why the mill's testing comes out negative, I can't explain that. But something bad is going on. The poisons are killing our swans. Valdivia is, or maybe I should say 'was,' one of the largest breeding grounds in South America for the black-necked swan. Not anymore."

Kurt nodded.

"Yes," he said. "I have heard there aren't as many of them now. The merchants who depend on the summer tourists have started to complain; but I have heard nothing about it being because of the mill. It just seems the swans are moving somewhere else."

"That is because their food can't grow in the river anymore. And they're not just migrating; those are the lucky ones. We have found the carcasses of over two hundred. And more are dying each day. They are the ones not strong enough to leave."

Carlos began to smell a story: new mill causing major pollution with huge human interest angle with all the dying swans.

"What is your next step, Amanda?" he asked.

"More water samples. And I have to somehow prove, without a doubt, the effluent is coming from the mill. I'd love to snoop around, but the mill is fenced in and guarded twenty-four hours a day."

"Maybe I can help," Carlos said. "Dad is a significant investor in that mill." He turned to his father. "Maybe I could drop your name and ask the owner for an interview. I could say my paper is interested in doing a story on the mill's state-of the-art technology." He looked back to Amanda. "I don't know what I could find out, but at least I could take a look around."

"Wait a minute son, don't go poking your nose in there and causing trouble. The owner, Ivan Morales, is a powerful man. He has many happy investors from around Valdivia, and important friends in Santiago. He's no one to take lightly; I say this for both your sake and the paper's."

"Dad, I'm a reporter. It's my job to poke around."

Amanda smiled at the exchange. She looked at Kurt.

"Are you one of those 'happy investors,' Kurt?"

"Yes. As long as I don't know that the mill is doing anything wrong, then yes, I am. Morales is paying big dividends, and the value of the stock has soared."

"But you would want to know the truth, wouldn't you, Dad?"

"Of course."

Carlos turned to Amanda.

"What do you say? I'll help you with this if I can have first crack at the story." He glanced at his father. "That is, if there is a story."

Power of the press, she thought. What could be better?

"Agreed."

Kurt sighed resignedly.

"But, son, both of you, be careful…please."

Chapter Seven

A short distance upriver from the town of Valdivia, a black-necked swan left the cover of the reeds. He was a beautiful bird, over four feet tall with a wingspan of seventy inches. His body was white except for his velvet black neck and head, and he had a large red knob at the base of his bill. A thin white line ran past his dark brown eyes. The swan was searching for food. He extended his long neck down into the water, but he was weak, and the effort caused him to tip awkwardly over.

The swan was looking for *luchecillo*, the waterweed that made up over ninety percent of his diet. The plant had mostly disappeared from the river, and what remained had turned brown and crusty with very little nutrition. Several months earlier the swan's mate had starved. A few weeks before that, he had lost his off-spring that he had guarded day and night, and helped to feed. The cygnets had often climbed up onto his back, and he carried them around for hours. They too had died from starvation, and because their livers, like his, were riddled with iron.

He and his mate had lived on the river for close to twenty years, raising many young, protecting the eggs from gulls, and the hatchlings from minks and foxes with their powerful wings. Other than during incubation, they were gregarious, swimming and feeding with others, softly whistling every now and then. But with the loss of the food source, most of the swans had died or left for the wetlands of Paraguay and southern Brazil. The pair had lost the instinct to migrate; this was the only home they knew. They remained until they had become too weak to fly.

After losing his mate, normally a cob would have searched for a new female. But he didn't have the energy to fight another male, nor to perform the mating ritual of rhythmically dipping his head in the water, then stretching his long neck upwards as he swam around the female, calling with chin upraised. There were no females around anyway. He only searched for food and slept, hunger his constant companion.

The swan continued swimming downriver, but didn't find anything more to eat. He paddled in close to shore, approaching a boat launch where a gravel road met the river. On the sides of the road were patches of thick grass which the swan eyed for some time. Finally, he couldn't resist the lure of the grass, although it was unnatural for him to leave the water. The swan hadn't seen the fox that had followed him along the river's edge, and was now hiding in brush at the edge of the grass. The swan climbed out of the river. He was clumsy, extending his long wings to maintain his balance because his bandy pink legs were designed for swimming, not walking. He looked so helpless that the fox could barely restrain itself. When the fox began to creep forward, the swan caught the movement out of the corner of his eye, and quickly faced the fox, whistling and flapping his wings. But the fox held its ground. The swan tried to angle towards the water, but the fox wouldn't let him. He bit the swan, making it squeak in panic. The fox bit him again, this time in the neck, and the swan began to bleed heavily, his wings sagging to the ground. He tried to put up a fight, but the fox ripped another chunk out of the long neck, transforming the squeaks into a gurgle. Losing his balance, the swan toppled over. The fox was on him in an instant.

Chapter Eight

The black Mercedes stopped at the entrance to the pulp mill. The watchman, wearing an eye patch and a pistol on his hip, hurried out of the guardhouse.

"Jorge, I will only be here for an hour or so. Wash and wax the car, and do a good job this time. I want to see my reflection in its shine."

"Yes, Don Ivan. Yes, sir."

The guard, following the car at a trot over to its usual parking spot in front of a three-story building, opened the door for Ivan Morales. Well dressed in a dark suit, and ignoring Jorge, Morales took the elevator up to his office where he placed his briefcase on the large walnut desk. He walked over to the picture window that dominated the room. Hands clasped behind him, he looked out at the labyrinth of steel pipes, pumps, vats, and huge holding tanks that gleamed in the sun. Men wearing bright yellow hardhats scurried below, checking gauges, climbing metal rung ladders, and writing on clipboards. To his left, the Las Cruces River flowed slowly past the mill on its way to Valdivia and the Pacific Ocean beyond. Don Ivan Morales was surveying his empire.

He had worked hard for years to build this mill: the complicated engineering, finding investors, arranging the financing, and all those goddamn hoops to jump through for the environment. But it was finally paying off; things could not be going better. He was making an obscene amount of money. And he was spending it. He might be a little overextended with the building of his villa in Viña, and the condo he bought in Bariloche, but at the rate the money was coming in, he could have it all.

His local investors, many of them from wealthy Chilean-German families, were extremely happy with the return on their money. They had even hinted that he would be invited to join the exclusive Club Aleman of Valdivia, unheard of for a swarthy-skinned *moreno* of ordinary Latin blood. He knew it was only because he was making the members money. That made him smile because he was cheating every one of them. He was required by law to treat the wastes of the mill before discharging them into the river. This required expensive chemicals, and caused inconvenient delays in production. As it was, he could barely keep up with all the orders from China. So he had decided to bypass much of the treatment and, once a week, dump untreated wastes into the river. And the environmental watchdogs? What a joke! All he had to do was provide a lavish midday meal with a lot of wine, then take them on a cursory stroll through the plant. If anyone ever checked, the books would show he was spending a small fortune on all the right chemicals. But it was a sham. That money went straight into his pocket, funding a good portion of his personal expenditures.

After pouring a glass of single malt whisky, he returned to the window where he looked out at the river. The late afternoon sun brought out the lustrous, rich red-brown of his mahogany speedboat tied to the dock. Maybe he should take a little cruise before he attacked the pile of paperwork on his desk; but then he realized how late it was when the mill's whistle blew. He watched the workers shed their hardhats and punch the time clock as they exited the mill. This was his favorite time of day because now he had the mill to himself: he never tired of looking down at his creation.

A couple of hours later, Morales drove the gleaming Mercedes out of the mill. It was a short drive to the subdivision that had once been an old farm with a large wooden house surrounded by well-tilled fields and rolling green pastures. Now, monstrous homes on half-hectare lots sprouted like weeds in all directions. The original house was still there, stark in its simplicity. The only other vestige of former days was the line of Lombardy poplars alongside the gravel entry road. Passing two cement lions, Morales entered his property. The groundskeeper, on his way home after a twelve-hour day, was walking down the driveway. When he saw the Mercedes, he stepped off to the side and took off his hat. Morales expected nothing less. He parked in the three-bay garage before entering the front door where he literally bumped into his wife. Dressed to the hilt, with eyes heavily made up, she was madly rushing around with the young maid in tow.

"Oh, hello dear," she said, and gave Morales a peck on the cheek. She turned back to the maid. "María, where's that lightweight beige jacket of mine? I swear it should be right here on this hook."

"Señora, you had me send it out to the cleaner's. It won't be ready until tomorrow at the earliest."

"Then run up and get my navy blue one out of my closet. Hurry now, I don't have all day!"

The maid rushed up the stairs. Morales watched her cute little body in the tight uniform before turning back to his wife.

"Going somewhere, dear?"

"Garden club meeting tonight, Ivan. And you're late as usual. I've already eaten, but I told the cook to stay to make you dinner."

The maid quickly came down the stairs with the jacket.

"Here you are, Señora."

The *señora* took it and turned to Morales in one motion. She gave him another quick peck on the cheek.

"Got to go!" and she quickly left the house. A little overdressed for a garden club meeting, he thought. Maybe she's having an affair. But the idea didn't bother him in the least; he had his own diversions. He turned towards the maid who was quietly leaving the room.

"María…"

"*Sí?*" she answered with downcast eyes.

Morales looked at his watch.

"Would you tell the cook I will take my dinner at nine?"

"*Sí*, Don Ivan."

She started to leave the room again.

"And María…"

"*Sí?*"

"After you tell her, make me my usual drink and bring it up to my room."

"*Sí*, Don Ivan."

Morales went up to the large master bedroom where he threw his jacket over a chair. He started to get an erection as he waited for María. It wasn't long before the light knock came on the door.

"Come in, María."

The maid entered with the drink. Eyes still downcast, she handed it to Morales before turning to leave.

"María, stay here and shut the door."

She stopped, but didn't shut the door.

"I said 'shut the door.'"

She turned to look at Morales with pleading eyes.

"But, Don Ivan, I should go down and help in the kitchen and…"

Morales walked past her and shut the door.

"You like your job, don't you, María?"

María looked down at the floor again.

"*Sí*, of course!"

"And your son likes that private school we are sending him to?"

She beamed, but still didn't look up.

"*Sí*, Don Ivan; the teachers all say that he is doing very well."

He cupped her chin with his hand and lifted her face so she had to look at him.

"And you wouldn't want to lose your job, or lose having your son go to such a good school, would you?"

"No, Don Ivan."

He walked over to put his drink down at the bedside table. He started unbuttoning his shirt.

"Take off your clothes, María."

Chapter Nine

Jorge entered his apartment, shutting out most of the mill's noise. Just like the machines he maintained, he kept the apartment fastidiously clean. A kitchenette was to his right, the living and dining to the left, and a double bed and bureau were back near the bathroom door. Next to the bureau was a small closet. Calendar pictures of scantily clad women were tacked to the walls, and a simple round clock was above the kitchen sink. He unclipped his pistol and placed it on the small dining table behind an easy chair. Flipping the eye patch down next to the gun, he rubbed his badly scarred socket hard with the heel of his hand. It itched like hell.

He had his routine. After working all night, he would return to prepare a leisurely meal of thick vegetable soup, a plate of boiled potatoes, and several thick slabs of bread. He would watch his special TV program after the meal, then sleep until he had to go to work again. He hated weekends because his program wasn't on then.

He was late middle-aged, burly with heavy shoulders, thick arms and neck. He was also flabby from lack of exercise and eating too many potatoes smothered in hot sauce. Eating the boiled potatoes reminded him of Cufeo where he had grown up on his grandparents' farm. Although Cufeo was less than an hour's drive from the mill, he never went to visit. He could never go back. He knew he had done something bad to a little girl in Cufeo, but couldn't remember what. That was when he had lost his eye. He didn't remember that either. The doctors had told him it was because he had been hurt so badly that he couldn't remember things. However, there was one thing he did know: that if he ever returned to Cufeo, the people there would kill him. He looked at his gun on the table lovingly. Maybe with his pistol, he thought, then maybe he could go back.

But he would lose his job if he did. And his pistol. No, he didn't want to lose the pistol. He picked it up and fondled it. His boss, Don Ivan, had taught him how to shoot down at the dock where they aimed at the debris floating by. Don Ivan was really good. Once, Jorge had watched him hit a seagull in the river thirty meters away. The wounded bird had thrashed around in circles while they laughed, emptying their pistols until it was still. A plastic bottle, a stick, a bird: it didn't matter, everything was a target.

While waiting for the potatoes to cook, Jorge took his pistol apart, carefully cleaning each piece with an oily rag. Don Ivan provided him with a small pickup truck that was parked outside. Once a week, he would drive to Valdivia to buy supplies. He kept the little pickup as spotless as the apartment, and as well cared for as the pistol.

He worked six nights a week as both watchman and mechanic. He could barely read a newspaper, was terrible with numbers, but give him a broken piece of equipment, and he could fix it. He loved his job and apartment; he had a hot water shower, the TV, and a fresh uniform once a week. Don Ivan even covered the expense of a woman at Nena's on his night off. He lived for those nights off!

And Don Ivan said that his was the most important job at the mill. It wasn't because he could fix machinery, Don Ivan had told him, but because he was his most trusted employee. That's why I'm the only one with a pistol, Jorge thought proudly. They had their little secret, too. Jorge could never tell, Don Ivan said, or he would lose his job. He was to tell absolutely no one that he opened a big valve every Friday night, and that he closed it exactly seven hours later. Don Ivan said the whole operation depended on him—that there were industrial spies everywhere. He depended on Jorge; said Jorge was his special secret agent.

He certainly did not want to go back to his old job of leading that stinky old horse and cart around all day, picking up trash and cleaning out gutters. Everyone treated him so badly. People never greeted him, they only looked at him like he had fallen out of a garbage can. They walked way around him on the sidewalk. The neighborhood children were the worst. They would laugh at him, and play tricks on him when he wasn't looking. The only good part of the job was that he saw a lot of pretty girls when he was downtown. He liked looking at them, especially in the summer when they wore shorts and skimpy blouses.

Sometimes, though, when someone laughed at him or called him names, he would get angry. He knew he was very strong and could hurt those people. A couple of times he had gotten in trouble for beating a heckler, and had spent time in jail. He hated jail. The *carabineros* went out of their way to treat him badly, using their nightsticks on him whenever they had a chance because they knew what he had done to that little girl. The family of the little girl hadn't wanted the public to know, so they never pressed charges. But the *carabineros* knew and beat him for it. No, he did not want to get into trouble again.

Before moving to the mill, he had lived in a shack on the outskirts of town. It was nothing more than a small room with two electric lights dangling from the ceiling and a single water spigot next to the toilet. He had a creaky old bed with a lumpy mattress stuffed with wool. The damp winter wind blew through the walls and the roof leaked. Even loading up his brazier to the top with charcoal couldn't take the chill out.

He had helped a man fix a water pump in his neighborhood. The man, who worked at the mill, had been impressed with Jorge's skill. He told his boss about Jorge, and one thing led to another. Now, this job along with the apartment was perfect. Well, almost perfect. He wanted to ask Don Ivan for one of those new-fangled things that record TV programs. Then he could watch reruns of his favorite program during the weekends; or, if he was called out to fix something, he could tape shows he missed. Wouldn't that be something! That meant if he felt like it, he could watch two or three in a day! He looked at his watch; only ten minutes until his program. He finished eating lunch and quickly did the dishes. After making sure the curtains were pulled tight, he locked the door. He stripped down to his underwear before walking up to the TV.

After an ad for some dishwashing liquid, his program came on. It was a talk show hosted by not one, but four buxom women dressed in low cut, silky blouses and short, tight skirts. The blond was Jorge's favorite. Oh, how he loved those tits! The four women continually played up to the cameras with winks and full-lipped pouts. They leaned forward often, offering wonderful glimpses of black bras and cleavage. Today, golf was one of their topics, and an Astroturf putting green was set up on stage. The blond asked their guest, the young national champion, to show her how to putt. She stood up with club in hand, and he positioned himself behind her with his arms around her, holding her hands in his. When he brought the club back, she wiggled up against him. His eyes opened wide in surprise while she posed for the camera with a look of raw rapture. She looked like she was being penetrated from behind, and the predominantly male audience loved it. It drove Jorge crazy. He ripped off his underpants and vigorously stroked himself.

The golfer stepped back to let the blond try it by herself. Jorge looked at the man to see if he had a hard-on. He couldn't tell. The blond smiled out to the audience again as she ran her hands provocatively up and down the club. The audience groaned. She wiggled her hips as she lined up the shot. When she sunk the ball on her second shot, she started jumping up and down. Oh God, Jorge thought, oh God! Those *tetas*! She sashayed up to the cup and posed for the camera. Smiling broadly and leaning way, way over, she picked up the ball. Jorge couldn't hold back anymore. He rushed up to the TV and spurted all over the screen, rubbing up against the smiling blond.

When he was done, he was exhausted. He turned off the TV, and slowly put his underpants on. By God, that had been wonderful! One of the best ever! Oh how he wished he had one of those recording machines. He must ask Don Ivan soon. He didn't care if it took a year to pay for it out of his wages. He walked over to the bed and pulled back the covers; he was totally relaxed and knew he would sleep soundly. He climbed into bed. When he got up for work later, he would clean off the screen; but, for now, he left his mark.

Chapter Ten

The Colony of Cufeo lay below Tomás, almost one solid patch of dark green instead of the earlier checkered pastures of scattered farms. More fitting to call it the 'Lost' Colony of Cufeo, he thought. He could just see Juan's house way off and the school across the road. Both were specks; but no other farms were in sight, just pine. The trees hid the road below Juan's except for the last curve down where it dead-ended at the penciled line of the Pan American Highway.

He stuck the shovel into the ground, and stretched his back. Looking up the ditch, he thought, a hell of a lot easier than in Vermont: no rocks, plus it only had to be a foot deep—no solid freezes here. He looked down to the house site, he was maybe halfway there. He walked up to the spring where he grabbed hold of one end of the thick black plastic waterline. As he fought the large coils, he thought about the Cufeo he had known.

It had been easy to convince the *campesinos* to plant trees because most everyone knew that there was no future if they didn't. The difficult part was to find ways for them to afford to do the work; they needed money, not pine seedlings, to feed their families. Reforesting meant no time to chop firewood and make charcoal which, in turn, meant no income. Fortunately, Tomás had found a source of surplus food from the States, and created a food-for-work program.

With only hand tools, the *campesinos* had to clear the steep land of all the bamboo-like *quila* and brush. They would set off early in the morning with only a heavy ax and a kerchief-wrapped meager lunch. By mid summer, absolutely monstrous piles of brush were torched. In the fall, with luck, they would have finished splitting out fence posts and stringing barbed wire around the area. Finally, during the abysmal heavy rains of winter, they would plant the seedlings. Compared to their work, his job was easy. He monitored their progress, doled out the food, and delivered the trees. Still, he had to slog through the rain and mud to notify the farmers when the trees would arrive. During the deliveries, he and the driver more often than not would get stuck somewhere. They would be soaked by the time they had jacked up the vehicle and thrown rocks and pieces of wood under the tires. It rained over a hundred inches during the planting season, was cold, and nothing ever dried out. And for what? Maybe a half dozen families had benefitted. The others weren't able to wait until the trees matured. They had sold out at rock bottom prices to the large timber companies who were cashing in big time on their efforts. And now the pine was contributing to the pollution of the rivers, killing the swans, and God knows what else. It wasn't supposed to work that way. That wasn't why he had joined the Peace Corps.

And he wasn't alone. His Peace Corps group had been actually two groups. His was forestry, the other was fisheries. Volunteers had helped to start salmon farms, with most located in the south below Puerto Montt where large pens were fenced off in the pristine narrow coastal inlets. By all accounts, it was a tremendous success, so much so that Chile had become the second largest salmon exporter in the world. Only Norway shipped more. Back in the States, he had bought Chilean salmon filets at the Food Coop across the river in New Hampshire. That, and Chilean wine.

But, like the pine, he had learned that there was more to it. Salmon farms polluted the inlets, poisoning the natural ecosystem and throwing it out of whack. Indiscriminate use of antibiotics for the farm-raised fish threatened the wildlife that inhabited the area. Millions of salmon escaped each year which transmitted diseases to native species, as well as contributing to hybridization, competition, and predation. The farm-raised salmon began to have genetic problems, like two heads and other mutations. When the waters became too polluted, the salmon farmers would gather in the cages to move south to new fjords. Slowly they were moving down the coast, leaving poisoned bays in their wake. The big salmon companies, with their connections, were awarded huge tracts of the ocean to farm which, in turn, choked out the small fishermen.

Carlos and Amanda were doing the right thing trying to expose that pulp mill. They were idealistic and angry. Good for them. It was so necessary to keep man's poor decisions and greed in check. And usually it was the younger generation, not yet tainted by the ways of the world, who tried. Someone had to keep all the old farts, with their Exxon and Chevron quarterly dividends, in line. That is, at least for awhile before they too became complacent or tired of beating their heads against a wall. So many stupid things, like in Costa Rica, a country that, percentage-wise, had more protected land than anywhere else in the world. Yet, it was there that one of man's follies really hit home. Four days he had spent wandering around the beautiful cloud forest of Monteverde with its numerous waterfalls, lush green canopy, and myriads of hummingbirds of all vibrant colors and sizes. He had even been lucky enough to see resplendent Quetzals land in trees only meters away. But when he left on a public bus, parched pastureland soon appeared on both sides of the highway with a few Brahma cattle myopically foraging on the dusty growth. He looked back towards the park. What a sight! There was a perfectly straight line bisecting the mountain, the boundary between the park and ranchland.

On one side was the forested Monteverde, dense textured shades of green with cumulus clouds directly above. Butting up to it was the cleared cattle land, brown and desertlike, totally clear sky above. It would take at least a couple of hectares to properly feed a single steer there, and in the rainy season there would be mudslides. It just didn't make any sense.

But he was over fifty now. Let the young people espouse what's right, like Carlos and Amanda. He'd help them anyway he could, but all he wanted to do was to live simply with as little impact on the environment as possible. Wind and solar for electricity, a gravity-feed system for water, a composting toilet. Peace, brother! But time to get back to work, this ditch wasn't going to dig itself. He picked up the shovel, realizing that he was just another man with his own selfish agenda.

* * *

"So what do you say, Jaime? Part time to start, then full time when we get things really rolling."

Jaime's *señora* answered for him.

"Of course he wants to, Tomás."

Jaime didn't say anything.

"You're a good driver, Jaime, and this would mean good steady money…and you would be working with your friends. And Tomás said you'd always have time for your work here. And we could take advantage of the truck to bring our supplies up when you came home after work… right, Tomás?"

Tomás nodded.

"And no more crawling around under your little pickup. This would be a good truck, and any repairs," she looked over at Tomás again, "would be done by Javier, in Valdivia."

"That's right, Señora," Tomás said.

Jaime turned to his sister.

"What do you think, Lilia?"

"I think it is a very good opportunity. You should do it."

Jaime was silent. He thought it through. Finally he stuck his hand out to Tomás.

"You've got a deal." He turned to his wife. "Now prepare some *maté* for Tomás, woman!" Beaming, Jaime's *señora* rushed over to the kitchen stove.

When Tomás had priced materials in Valdivia for his house, he discovered that most of the lumber was lousy. The boards had not been dried properly: they were cupped, crooked, and cracked. The straight, flat board was certainly the exception. He wanted good lumber, and he knew how to produce it. He decided to buy a portable sawmill. But what would he do with the mill after he finished the house? Bingo! He'd start a high-quality lumber business, and he knew just the people to run it. Juan and young Tomás agreed that, after he trained them, they would be the sawyers. He talked Guillermo into moving to Valdivia to run the retail facility which would be at a warehouse he was in the process of leasing. And now Jaime would do the trucking.

"How do you like your *maté*, Tomás?"

"With a little sugar, please, Señora."

She put a full teaspoon in the gourd, and stirred it around with the metal straw.

Tomás took a sip.

"Perfect. Thank you."

"Tomás, maybe Guillermo could sell some of Lilia's carvings at the lumber store," Jaime said.

Lilia was embarrassed.

"Jaime! Shh! Tomás is not interested in something like that."

Tomás looked up from his *maté*.

"What carvings?"

"Lilia carves birds and animals. She is very good," Jaime said proudly.

"I'd like to see your carvings, Lilia. That is," he added, "if you want to show them to me."

Lilia blushed.

"Are you sure, Tomás?"

He nodded.

"Then when you are done with your *maté*, we will have a look."

Tomás put his *maté* cup down immediately.

"All set. Lead the way."

They entered Lilia's room. Tomás thought it was like stepping from winter to spring. The sun shone through the window, accentuating the bright quilt and flowers. Lilia handed him a small wooden bird.

"A *cuchao*! Lilia, the detail; it's perfect!"

He examined it closely. It really was perfect.

"Do you remember that time when you showed me one singing in the *quila*?"

Lilia smiled brightly.

"Of course I do…But," she asked shyly, "do you really like it, Tomás?"

"Absolutely!"

Tomás looked around the room. There were carvings everywhere. He walked over to a *choroy*, a small parrot that nested in the tall hardwoods of the steep ravines. The base was a carved branch with the bird nibbling on a clump of berries. He held it up in the light from the window and turned it over in his hands. He shook his head in wonder.

"This one too. Perfect. Absolutely perfect."

Lilia's smile became even brighter. Her eyes shone. Tomás noticed the little brown desk. He admired the workmanship.

"Did you make this for Lilia, Jaime?"

"No, Tomás. She did. She is the woodworker of the house."

Tomás ran his hand over the rich wood. He could barely feel the lines from being hand-scraped. The joinery was precise.

"What tools do you have, Lilia?"

"Let's see...A square, and there is Jaime's handsaw, hand plane, and a couple chisels that were Papá's. There's also Papá's hammer, and that big old brace and bit..."

She hesitated...

"That's about it, I guess."

A natural, Tomás thought. He told her that once they had the shop set up, he was sure they could sell her carvings to tourists as well as to the people of Valdivia.

"That is, if you really want to part with them, Lilia. I know I would have a tough time doing that."

"I will sell them, Tomás. I would like to be able to help with some of the expenses here. Jaime has supported me for a long time."

Tomás picked up the *cuchao* again, and held it upright in the palm of his hand.

"Then I would like to be your first customer. Would you sell me this?"

Lilia walked over to Tomás, and closed his fingers around the little bird.

"No, Tomás, I won't. I will not sell him to you; but I will give him to you. It would make me very happy if you would accept it."

He looked into her eyes. How could he refuse?

"Alright. Thank you, Lilia. This is very special. Thank you."

He carefully put the carving in his shirt pocket and buttoned it. He looked at his watch.

"Now, I am afraid I must go. I have to go sign the lease for the warehouse in Valdivia."

"I'll walk you out to your truck, Tomás," Jaime said.

Tomás said goodbye to the women, and he and Jaime walked over to Tomás's new pickup.

"Tomás, it is so good to have you back after so many years."

"Believe me, I am happy to be here."

They stopped at the driver's door.

"And Tomás, I do not say this just because it is good to see you, and that you have offered me an excellent job. I say this also because of Lilia."

"Lilia? What do you mean?"

"These last few weeks she has been more like long ago. For very many years she was so sad and quiet, like a timid sparrow. You do not know how rare the smiles she gave you back there used to be. She smiles all the time now, especially when you are around. And she hasn't had one of her spells for awhile. All this makes me very happy."

"What spells?"

"When she remembers what Jorge did to her, she gets like…like when it first happened. You remember that. She just stares off into space and is gone from us. Sometimes it lasts for some time. Maybe not as bad as it was, but it is still very scary."

Tomás did remember. He had gone to see Lilia soon after it happened. She had been in bed, her face swollen and bruised. And it was like she was comatose. They had been close, but she didn't acknowledge his presence as he sat by her bed. The last time he had visited her before leaving Chile, she was in Osorno living with her grandparents. She had been recovering slowly, but she was scared to be left alone in the room with him. He realized it wasn't just him, it was because she was scared of all men. She's certainly had her cross to bear, he thought. It suddenly struck him that, in a way, they were alike—he had his cross, too. He climbed into the cab.

"If I help to make her happy, Jaime, then I'm glad. And I'm glad you and I will be working together. I'll be in touch later this week."

Tomás drove down the old oxcart path to the graveled road. Jaime watched the truck until it disappeared, thinking about his sister and Tomás.

Chapter Eleven

Blood-red sawdust coated their bodies. This was the fourth day they had been down in the *alerce* grotto at daybreak, cutting, sawing, and splitting with wedges the gigantic tree that had fallen over. Tomás hoped to build his entire house with the wood, but he needed Juan and his oxen to get the logs up to where they could be sawn into lumber. At first it was pretty easy going because the behemoth had fallen up hill, making the initial skids significantly shorter. The logs were also lighter because the tree had lost most of its sap and water over the twenty years it had been down. The oxen effortlessly pulled up the top logs, but as the diameters increased it became necessary to cut the logs shorter. The last one was so thick that it had to be split in half, then quartered with a chainsaw mill so the oxen could handle it. It had been extremely slow going, but at least the end was in sight: only the butt log remained. Still, it was huge, and the men and animals were exhausted. Tomás thought they'd be lucky to get it up the hill by dark.

Quartering the thick sections was done with an Alaskan chainsaw mill with a two meter bar and chain. The mill was powered by two of the largest Stihls made, each mounted on one end of the bar. Tomás disconnected one of the saws from the mill frame, then the frame itself, leaving him with a single saw with the gigantic bar. He tightened the chain, and began cutting the log off the tipped over stump. Chips spewed as the bar buried itself into the soft wood; but the bar didn't reach even halfway across the tremendous log. Tomás and Juan attacked the remaining solid core with a two man crosscut saw. Every few minutes they drove in wedges to keep the log from pinching the blade. After finally cutting through, they sat down on a thick bed of ferns to rest.

"A good thing you hung on to that old saw," Tomás said, wiping his brow. "No way could we have gotten through it otherwise."

Juan took a drink from a jug of water before passing it to Tomás.

"I was tempted a thousand times to make scrapers and blades out of it, but then I'd think of Papá. We sawed with it many times. I felt that if I ever chopped it up, it would be a violation of his memory. I hung it on the wall of the shed instead; and every time I passed by it, I thought of him."

Tomás passed the jug back to Juan. Both of Juan's parents had died in the devastating earthquake of 1960. It had also made Juan a cripple.

"How's the leg today, Juan?"

"So so, although I have to tell you I'm not looking forward to skidding this monster up the hill."

They looked at the log, then back at each other. As if on command, they stood. Climbing a simple ladder made out of lashed saplings, they snapped a line on top of the log. After sawing as deeply as he could along the line, Tomás fetched an assortment of tools: a long-handled axe, metal and hardwood wedges, long pry bars, and two sledge hammers. They tapped wedges into the saw cut, then began driving them with the sledgehammers. They were at it for hours. The breathers they took were short: wipe a brow, take off a shirt. When the log finally broke apart, they lay their sledgehammers down and clasped each other's hand.

"Bravo!" Juan exclaimed.

"You can say that again! Look at the size of these sticks! But, I'm starved; how about it, Juan? Let's see what Flor's prepared for us today."

Juan's answer was to flop down in the ferns next to their lunch which was neatly wrapped in brown paper and tied off with a string. Closing his eyes, he stretched out. "In a moment," he said wearily. "My arms are too tired to hold anything right now."

Tomás had no such trouble. His stomach began to growl as he announced the contents.

"*Sopaipilla* and some of Carlos's *ulmo* honey. Cheese, a couple of hard-boiled eggs, bread, jam, salt, and some green hot peppers. You can take a nap if you want, but I'm digging in. I might leave you something if you're lucky."

Juan groaned as he blinked his eyes open. Handing him a piece of the fried bread slathered with honey, Tomás watched Juan, eyes closed again, begin to chew contentedly. In a short while, they had eaten everything, and Tomás laid down near Juan, spreading his arms out in the soft ferns. He fought off the temptation to take a nap.

"You know what, Juan? This may sound kind of crazy, but I wonder if somehow your sister made that tree fall down to provide me with wood for the house. Do you think that's too far fetched?"

Juan sat up quickly.

"Yes, I do! What I think, Tomás, is that it's more than about time for you to let go of María Elena! It's time for you to move on. I think you're more than half crazy. She's dead, Tomás! Been dead for thirty years! Let her go!"

"Juan!" Tomás was shocked by Juan's intensity.

"Tomás, believe me, I know what you two had together. But don't forget what my sister and I had, too. You know her death destroyed me like you. God forgive me, but in the beginning I thought life wasn't worth living and I was thinking of doing myself in. But, I came to my senses: life must go on.

"Her death made me see things differently. I never considered having a family while she was alive because she took such good care of me. And she was more than a sister. We were orphans; only together could we overcome losing our parents...which is why I was so scared that you would take her away, back to your country. But after her death, I realized that I had to adjust. I needed help on the farm. I began to notice all the things Flor could do, which made me see her as more than a neighbor. I thought she'd make a good companion, housekeeper, mother. And I was right. We have had a wonderful life all these years. I am not saying having a family is easy, but it is wonderful: it is everything. That's what life is all about, Tomás: having children, continuing the cycle. Look at the birds and animals. We have the same instincts; it's just that our brains get in the way. It's time for you to let go. It's time for you to plant your seed."

"Too late, Juan. The only person I ever wanted to have children with was your sister—period, end of conversation!"

They lay in silence until Tomás asked with a smile, "Does your daughter share your views about the cycle, or does her 'brain get in the way?'"

Juan snorted.

"Don't get me wrong, I am very proud of Amanda, very proud; but sometimes I think she's a little too smart for her own good. But she's young still, Tomás. We will see with time."

"Speaking of 'time,' it's not getting any earlier. Are you ready to eat some sawdust for dessert?"

"Right! Let's get at it," Juan said, feigning enthusiasm. Tomás noticed that Juan was slow to push himself up, and limped heavily over to the oxen. Tomás didn't have a bad leg, but like Juan, every muscle in his body ached. Juan backed the oxen up to the log by tapping their noses with the *garrocha*. When he was close, he laid the long stick up against the yoke. After hooking up one end of a long chain to the team, and the other to a large hook they embedded in the half log, Juan urged the oxen slowly forward until the huge section rotated ninety degrees. Tomás quickly wedged it with triangular chunks of wood along both sides, stabilizing it so they could saw it in half with the mill.

After snapping two parallel lines, one on each side of the log, Tomás reassembled the mill. Donning safety goggles and ear protection, they started the powerful saws. The saws slowly ate through the bright red wood, creating a dense cloud of noxious fumes and fine sawdust that recoated their bodies. Tomás had forgotten to bring dust masks, forcing them to take breathers often. With the saws idling, they drove in wedges behind the cut so it wouldn't pinch the bar and chain. Continually pushing the saw and keeping it straight along the lines was exhausting isometrics. There was no celebration when they finished the cut. Juan brought the team over again while Tomás gassed up the saws: they had another half to do.

The shadows were long when they made the final skid. Juan led the oxen with Tomás following with a chainsaw body in each hand. The tired oxen and men stumbled over the roots and stones laid bare by the logs skidded up the hill. When they came to the steepest section, Juan urged his team.

"*Déle! Déle!* Come on! You can do it! *Oosh! Oosh! Oosh!*"

Tomás stopped to watch the oxen strain, gaining foot by foot. He felt himself urging them with the core of his body. Six more meters! You can do it, he thought. Only twenty more feet! Juan was no longer in front. He was along side, tapping their flanks with the pole, coaxing, screaming. Finally, they crested the hill. Juan quickly limped in front of the oxen again and placed the *garrocha* against the yoke for them to rest. The oxen's chests were like gigantic bellows. Their heads were angled forward and low, and they exhaled so sharply that it sounded like strident whistles. Tomás came up to Juan who stood proudly by his team. Without a word, he put down a saw so he could shake Juan's hand and pat him on the back. Continuing on to the truck, Tomás put the saws in the back with the other tools, then pulled a demijohn of red wine and two cups from the cab. He sat down on a yarded log, waiting to celebrate the team's arrival.

Chapter Twelve

"Why so late? And why all night?"

"Look, Carlos, either you want to come, or you don't."

Carlos pulled the aluminum rowboat out of the back of his father's truck. Amanda helped him slide it into the river.

Her tone softened.

"It's because certain days the pollution is much heavier than others. I think the wastes from the mill are being routinely dumped and I am trying to figure out when."

She smiled.

"And lucky you. My schedule calls for this one to be all night."

Amanda spied a gristly pile of feathers and bones in the headlights of the truck near the river's edge. She went down to examine it.

"Oh, Lord. Here's another one."

Carlos walked over. She looked up at him.

"This one didn't die from the poison. Something killed it. Fox or dog probably. That's great. All the crap's in its system now."

She pulled a plastic bag and rubber gloves from the box of vials and notebooks she had placed in the boat. She carefully put the remains in the bag and placed it into the rear of the truck.

"Let's go."

Carlos sat at the oars while Amanda pushed off. They slowly rowed upstream to the shallow area near some reeds. The moon was up early, dimming the stars while bathing the river and shore in silvery light. Carlos rowed smoothly. The only sounds were the plunge and dripping of the oars. After twenty minutes, Amanda asked him to stop. She threw out a little mushroom shaped anchor, and turned on a battery lantern before arranging her clipboard. She dipped a small vial into the river, capped it and labeled it. After noting the time, she looked at Carlos.

"I take readings every half hour."

She took a plastic tube-like thing, open on both ends with a little dial in the center.

"What's that?"

"A gauge to measure the current of the river. It's not precise, but it gives me a pretty good idea."

She looked closely at the gauge.

"About four kilometers an hour."

She wrote that down, too.

By her third reading, the wind had picked up, creating a light chop on the river. Amanda buttoned her jacket and pulled up her collar. Carlos, ever the photographer, looked at her. The silvery light shone on strands of her long hair wisping across her face. Graceful, muted reeds formed the backdrop. He pulled out his Nikon and took a picture.

"Hey! What's that all about?"

"Just documenting everything. Plus it was a great shot; you look very pretty, you know, with the moonlight on your hair."

Oh boy, here it comes, she thought. Right on schedule. She frowned, ready to fend him off. But all he did was put the camera away before pulling on his *manta de Castilla*. Leaning back, he looked very comfortable and, though she would never say it, handsome. They were silent for another reading. The constant rocking of the boat was making her sleepy. She needed conversation to keep her awake.

"What made you want to be a reporter?"

"I love taking pictures and always liked to write, although I've never been disciplined enough to write a book. And I guess I'm sort of the nosy type. It was a perfect fit."

"Did you go to school for it?"

"Yes, the School of Journalism at Columbia University...in New York City."

"I suppose your father paid for all that."

"That's right."

End of conversation for another two samples.

"Amanda, I realize I am very fortunate and that financially I have had it easy—alright? And I know it has been anything but easy for you. But don't let that affect what we're trying to do here. We are going to have to work together and it will be a lot more fun if we are friends."

He leaned forward with extended hand.

"Okay?"

She hesitated before extending hers.

"Sure."

It was turning much colder. Amanda hugged herself to keep from shivering.

"Have you ever written about pollution before, about what man in his infinite wisdom is doing to this planet?"

"All the time...that is, whenever my boss will let me slip one in."

"Like what?"

"I've written about the copper and nitrate mining in the Atacama with all its poisoning of the soils and streams. Six months ago I did one on the air quality in Santiago. Do you realize the smog there has doubled in the last eight years? You can hardly see the Andes anymore."

She nodded.

"I've never been there; but yes, I know. The professor in my Environmental Study Group said that in Santiago it's mostly from all the cars and buses; but there are plenty of other causes, some of which you'd never suspect. Like in Temuco. The air quality there is four times worse than the World Health Organization's recommended limit, but it's due to so many people cooking and heating with wood." Amanda looked at her watch, then back to Carlos. "What do you think the worst thing is man has done?"

"You mean, like invent the combustible engine?"

Amanda laughed.

"No, more like man-made disasters."

Carlos put his hands behind his head and was silent.

"Chernobyl in 1986? One hundred times more radiation was leaked there than the atom bombs dropped on Nagasaki and Hiroshima."

"How about the Valdez off Alaska? Over 250,000 animals died."

Carlos chuckled.

"You would be more concerned about animals than people. But we do tend to forget that wildlife is always caught up in our follies. The Valdez, though, was small; it just got a lot of press. Look at the Niger Delta. There have been over seven thousand oil spills between 1970-2000."

"And what American company is behind those? It's always an American Company."

"Right. Mostly ExxonMobil....And then there's the one in the rain forest of Ecuador. Texaco is accused of polluting eighteen billion gallons of runoff into a river there. That's," he stopped to calculate, "about thirty times the Exxon Valdez spill."

"Good God!"

She buttoned the top button of her jacket.

"Do you want my *manta*, Amanda?"

He started to pull it off, but she stopped him.

"No, I'm fine. Really."

Amanda looked at her watch, and pulled another vial from the box. Stifling a yawn, she labeled it and put it with the others.

"When's your meeting with Sr. Morales?"
"What time is it?"
"Three-thirty."
"Then, in twelve hours."
"Are you sure I can't go with you?"
"I should go alone, I think. I don't want to raise any flags. But, don't worry. I'll take a lot of pictures and we can study the whole layout."

After the four o'clock sampling, Amanda, hugging herself, drifted off to sleep. Carlos took off his *manta* and wrapped it around her. He began taking samples at four-thirty. A little after eight she woke up with a start. She looked at her watch.

"Oh, damn!"

She looked over accusingly at Carlos who was smiling at her.

"Why didn't you wake me? Now I am going to have to do this all over again next Sunday! Why are you smiling? It's not funny!"

"Amanda?"
"What!"
"Count your vials."

She looked in the box and saw that each vial was full and neatly labeled. And it was then that she noticed the *manta* wrapped around her.

Chapter Thirteen

As Jaime backed the truck up to the deck, the safety beeps startled several *choroys* in a nearby tree. They flashed emerald green as they flew away. Thanks mostly to the dry, warm spring, the house was coming along much faster than Tomás had ever hoped. Juan and young Tomás had proven to be quick studies with the sawmill, and had sawn out all the lumber. He had taught them how to use skill saws and pneumatic nailers, and they had helped him with the frame which was ready now for the milled siding and windows piled on the truck. Jaime turned off the engine, and came back to help with the nylon straps as the passenger door slammed shut. Lilia appeared, carrying a basket covered with a white cloth. She smiled at Tomás.

"Baked *empanadas de pino* and sweet cider for lunch."

"You're an angel, Lilia! And I'm starved; but let Jaime and me unload the truck first. The sooner we have the windows safely on the ground, the better I'll feel." He turned to Jaime. "Let's unload the two monsters first."

They leaned one of the picture windows against the large framed opening on the far side of the house. The other they carried upstairs. It was a struggle. Once it was safely in place, they scattered the rest of the windows around the house, and piled the siding next to the sawhorses. When the last board was off the truck, Tomás walked up to Lilia.

"Let's go upstairs to eat; the view is incredible."

Lilia brought her basket up, and they sat on cut-off chunks of beam. She passed around a plate heaped with *empanadas*. They were still warm.

"Did you bring any pepper paste, sister?"

"Of course, Jaime."

Tomás slathered his *empanadas* with the paste. Jaime laughed.

"Tomás, you are more Chilean than the Chileans."

"What can I say? I love hot sauce—addictive, I think," Tomás mumbled with mouth half full.

The waterfall and Volcán Puntiagudo looked very close.

"What a beautiful view," Lilia said as she collected their plates. "Where are the *copihue* clearing and *alerce* trees?"

"How do you know about them?"

"Tomás," Jaime said, wiping his mouth with a sleeve, "are you joking? Everybody knows about the clearing and trees. You'd have to have your head stuck in the ground not to know about them."

Tomás didn't say anything. Jaime stood up.

"Sister, do you want to come with me, or stay here and help Tomás while I go get logs?"

"Stay and help…that is," she said looking at Tomás, "if there's something I can do."

"Sure. I can always use another set of hands. You can help me start putting up the siding."

Jaime went down to the truck. As he climbed into the cab, he yelled, "I'll return in two hours. Three at the most."

The truck pulled away. Tomás stretched.

"If I sit here any longer, I'll begin thinking about a nap. C'mon, Lilia."

Tomás carried the basket down to the first floor. He walked up to a spigot Lilia hadn't noticed to rinse off the plates.

"Tomás! Running water! Where does it come from?"

Tomás grinned.

"Gravity feed, Lilia." He pointed up the hill. "I dug a ditch from a spring up there and laid a waterline. But, c'mon. Let's get to work."

With Lilia holding the wide *alerce* boards in place, Tomás fastened them with the nailer. It went quickly. They took a break after finishing the front of the first level. Tomás switched off the generator, and gave her a tour.

"Except for a bathroom and two little rooms, this will all be wide open. I'll be able to look out the big window whether cooking, eating, or just sitting."

"Bathroom? You'll have indoor plumbing?"

"That's right. And upstairs, too."

Lilia saw four stakes set in the ground. She pointed to them.

"What are those for?"

"A woodworking shop to build all the doors, cabinets, and furniture. The generator is big enough to run most of the tools for that. There's bigger equipment at the warehouse in Valdivia if I need it."

"Jaime says the business is going well."

"Too well: Guillermo can't get his orders out quickly enough. We're going to have to hire someone to answer the phone, take orders, do the billing—things like that. I also plan to buy a forklift which should really help. One thing's for sure, the other lumber businesses are starting to pay attention. A lot of their customers have switched over to us."

They climbed the stairs.

"The bathroom will be there, my bedroom here with the big window, and another two small rooms over there."

"Will those be for your children, Tomás?"

He looked incredulous.

"Not a chance! I'm way too old to start a family, Lilia."

"No, you're not," she said seriously. "You have plenty of time. You're still young enough and strong; just look how quickly you put up this house! And it will be so beautiful and comfortable. You can find yourself a young woman who loves the *campo*. She would be very lucky to share this house with you."

"Nope. No interest."

Lilia shook her head.

"What a pity."

They went back to work. Lilia was a terrific help. Another two hours passed, but there was still no sign of Jaime. As they sheathed, Lilia asked if it was because of María Elena that he had no interest in having a family. The question startled him. María Elena had lived alone with him in his mind for a very long time. He was not accustomed to sharing his thoughts of her with anyone. He said nothing. Lilia frowned.

"Forget I asked. It's none of my business."

Tomás finished nailing the board. When she brought over another, he said, "I'm sorry, Lilia. It's just that I find it very hard to talk about her. I…I've never really talked about María Elena before except maybe a few times with my father…and with Juan, of course."

They put up a few more boards before Tomás suddenly laid the nailer down.

"Let's stop. My arm's about to fall off."

They sat on the edge of the rear deck, legs dangling, looking out at the volcano. Tomás surprised himself when he started talking about María Elena.

"I still think about her everyday. I even have conversations with her in my mind after all these years. Is that crazy, Lilia?"

"No, it's not crazy. Believe me, I understand. When something so powerful, so catastrophic, happens to you like that, I think it stays with you forever. You just have to try to control it and not let it ruin your life." She uttered a short laugh. "'Try' is the key word there."

She would know, he thought. He looked at her. She looked so vulnerable sometimes. He stood up.

"Do you want to see the clearing?"

She held out her hand, and he pulled her up. She smiled her thanks, and they began to walk down the hill.

They entered the *alerce* grotto. Lilia marveled at their girth as they visited each tree. Tomás took her down the path to the *copihue* clearing, crossing the stream, and finally stepping out onto the broad shelf. The *copihue* was still not in bloom, but the view took Lilia's breath away. Tomás thought she looked very pretty, framed by the tall, noisy waterfall and the volcano. She walked up to the *ramada*. Tomás hung back. An odd feeling gripped him in the pit of his stomach. For some reason, he couldn't go in while she was there.

"This is the wedding *ramada* you built, Tomás?"

He nodded. Lilia walked around touching the branches.

"You have kept it up nicely."

He nodded again. He had paled, looked strange all of a sudden, she thought. María Elena. Something to do with María Elena. She quickly stepped out of the *ramada*.

"We should go back, Tomás. Jaime is probably already waiting for us."

He followed her out of the clearing. She walked up the trail, thinking of María Elena's effect on Tomás. He was trapped by her memory. Such a waste! He needed a young woman; he needed to start a family. He was so nice. She smiled sadly to herself. Too bad she was so old. For his part, Tomás wondered what had happened in the clearing. He had never felt like that before. Guilt, he decided. Had to be. Guilt that he was not being faithful to María Elena? Now that's crazy! Or is it? He pictured Lilia framed by the waterfall and volcano. She was striking. There was a stirring in his inner being. He had not felt a stirring like that in over thirty years.

Chapter Fourteen

White smoke shot straight up from the tall stacks, their sheer height making them look skinny as they jutted up amongst the web of buildings and vats connected by steel walkways and ladders. Loaded log trucks and trailers were waiting their turn in front of the scales. Front end loaders and cranes were in constant motion. The tremendous piles of logs dwarfed the two well-dressed men in yellow hardhats who walked beside them. The taller of the two stopped to take some pictures as they approached one of the large buildings.

"We use the Kraft process like most mills now. Although it is complicated, especially the recovery process, the beauty of it is that it is a nearly closed-cycle system with respect to the inorganic chemicals used. That means less pollution. And we generate more electricity than we need from the boilers. We sell that to the public utility company."

Ivan Morales opened the door to the building.

"In here you can see the finished product."

It was noisy inside; several lines of huge rolls of bright white paper were spinning on stainless steel axles.

"We produce only the highest quality paper. Your brown cardboard and paper bags are from other mills, not ours. Kraft-processed pulp is darker and stronger than other wood pulps, but we make it white. Production costs are higher, but so is the grade of paper."

"Higher costs especially because of the bleaching process, right?"

"Yes. Looks like you've done some homework, Carlos. But come on, it's hard to talk in here."

"First, let me shoot a few pictures, if that's okay?"

Morales nodded, and Carlos snapped shots from several angles before putting the camera back in the shoulder bag. They exited the building.

"This is the holding tank where the effluent is stored and then pumped to other tanks where it is re-treated. This creates the closed system I told you about. It greatly reduces the chance of any damaging chemical agents entering the environment."

Carlos took his camera from the bag and began taking pictures. Morales noticed right away that he shot more pictures here than anywhere else on the tour. He was also asking a lot more questions.

"So let's see if I've got it straight. After the impregnation and cooking stage, everything is washed several times and then bleached."

"Very good, Carlos."

"So, these tanks are where the effluent is stored after bleaching."

"Yes, before they go into the bio effluent treatment plant."

"And where is that?"

Morales pointed it out.

"And how does it get there?"

"Through that big pipe."

The pipe was two meters in diameter.

"And this valve opens and shuts the pipe?"

"Right again."

Carlos took a picture.

"And the other two pipes and valves? Where do they lead?"

"Why all the questions, Carlos? Wouldn't all this detail be boring for your readers?"

"Oh, it's just me, I guess. I like knowing how things work."

"That one is for filling the tank with the effluent from the bleaching process."

Carlos waited for Morales to explain the other; but instead he changed the subject.

"What do you say we go up to my office, Carlos, where we can talk in comfort?" He smiled. "And maybe have a little refreshment."

Carlos looked down to the river which was just below them. Sr. Morales eyes followed his.

"Sure. Just a couple more pictures first."

Carlos took pictures of the two pipes. He stepped back a few paces so he could include the river's edge. Morales frowned. Carlos turned toward him.

"And what did you say the other pipe was for?"

"I didn't," he said shortly. "But it's to drain the tank so we can clean or repair it if necessary."

"What does it drain into?"

Morales's eyes, Carlos thought, took on a hooded look.

"Oh, into a lined pit somewhere so that it can't leach into the soil."

They walked over to the elevator which took them up to the office.

"Here we are. Make yourself comfortable. Would you like a little libation?"

Carlos shook his head. He was thinking that Morales had knowledgeably talked about all the processes of the mill. He had explained in detail how no expense had been spared when it was built. He had boasted that only the best concrete mix was used, and that the concrete was reinforced with over twenty kilometers of rebar. He seemed to know everything about the mill…except where the pit was to drain the effluent tank.

Morales walked over to the mahogany bar where he put ice cubes in a small glass. He reached for a dark green bottle.

"I know it is sacrilege to drink single malt over ice, but that's the way I like it. Sure I can't interest you, Carlos?"

"No thank you, Sr. Morales."

"Call me Ivan," he said walking over and sitting across from him. "How is your father? You know he is one of our major investors." Morales's glass had a likeness of the mill etched into it.

"Yes, he told me. He also told me one of the reasons he invested in your plant, besides it being a good investment of course, was because it was so clean. Other mills have had a pretty poor track record. Isn't it usually the bleaching process that causes most of the problems for the environment?"

"Yes. But we've passed every water quality examination easily. I didn't show you, but there is a spigot at the bottom of the bio effluent treatment plant that can be tested any time, any day. Anybody can take samples whenever they want. This mill is clean."

"Have you heard anything about the swans downriver?"

"What? No. What swans?"

"You must be aware of the black-necked swans in the refuge near Valdivia. There have been thousands there as long as I can remember. Besides being one of the most important breeding grounds in South America, it is also a very big tourist attraction in the summer. But their numbers now are way, way down. It seems that many have died; and the ones that were able, have gone elsewhere. The businesses that make a living off the tourists are very concerned."

Morales was paying close attention.

"So, what does that have to do with anything?"

"Some are saying it's more than a coincidence that their numbers began to decline soon after you started production: that you must be doing something to the river."

"That's absurd! I've just told you we are a clean mill, and the government has the test results to prove it." He stood up and walked over to the window. "Have they checked the other businesses along the river? The tannery? The furniture plant? There are a dozen of them and," he said turning back to Carlos, "I'll bet not one of those businesses is checked as closely as we are. Tell those tourist merchants to blame someone else. It's not this mill."

"I'm sure it's not; but you can understand their concern."

Carlos laughed and shook his head as he stood up.

"But it does seem that people only pay attention to the environment, Ivan, when it hurts their pocketbook. Thanks very much for the interview."

Morales escorted him to the elevator door. They shook hands.

"Oh, do you mind if I take a sample from that spigot you mentioned?"

"Whatever for?"

"I think it would be good to have it tested, and if the results are like you say and I write about it, then it will help put to rest this swan thing."

Morales was suspicious. This young man was a little too nosy, and a little too interested in the effluent. And this swan thing. He would have to look into that. He'd bet this whole damn interview was about the swan thing.

"Where will you have it tested?"

"At the university in Valdivia. I have a friend who can do it."

Morales went over to his desk where there was a radio. He turned it on.

"Jorge, there's a gentleman here who wants a sample from the big tank. Meet him at the elevator."

He turned off the radio.

"You can't miss him. He's got an eye patch." As the elevator door opened, Morales added, "Give my best to your father…and to Esteban Espinosa."

Esteban Espinosa was the owner of Carlos's newspaper.

"You know Sr. Espinosa?"

"Quite. I've known him for a very long time. You might call him a past business associate. I made him a lot of money on one occasion."

On the way down in the elevator, Carlos wondered why Morales had mentioned Sr. Espinosa, and why had he pointed out that they had been business associates? Veiled threat? And, more importantly, why had he been evasive on where that third pipe drained? After the man with the eye patch gave him a sample of the effluent, Carlos returned to Valdivia. He decided he would find out who had built the plant; he was very curious to look at the blueprints to see where that third pipe went. Back upstairs in the office, Morales sipped his single malt in front of the large window. He went over the interview in his mind. That reporter asked too many of the wrong questions, and what was all this swan business? Maybe he should give Esteban a call to learn more about this nosy reporter. He looked at his watch; not now though, too late. Esteban was probably at home, and that's where I should be, he thought. He drained the glass and set it down on the bar. Pulling his lightweight jacket from the back of the chair, he left the office.

Chapter Fifteen

"Carlos is a very good reporter, Ivan. Maybe an even better photographer. He is thorough and careful, which is why I trust him to travel around and pick his stories. I am surprised, though, that he asked you for an interview. Usually, he looks for things with an environmental angle, human interest, or both…like his pieces on the pollution in Santiago and the miners up north."

Ivan Morales frowned into the phone. Anytime he heard the word 'environment,' it raised a red flag. Esteban Espinosa chuckled before continuing.

"Now if you were doing something like screwing up the air or water, then I'd be concerned. But I know you're not stupid. How is business?"

"Excellent! Can hardly keep up with the orders."

"Actually, I know that. I've been doing research on your company, and I'm seriously considering investing. Your Chinese contract is the envy of Chile…especially during these times. I also hear you're building a palace in Viña."

"I wouldn't call it a palace."

"What would you call it? Over five hundred square meters, pillars, pool, big windows and terraces looking out to the Pacific. I'd say you're doing very well for yourself."

"Not without a hell of a lot of hard work, I'll tell you that! Which is why I don't need your reporter creating some crazy story that we're killing all the swans down here."

Esteban's tone cooled.

"If that water's clean like you say, you've got nothing to worry about. Once Carlos gets those test results, he'll probably move on to something else. But," he continued, "I'll give you the heads-up if he submits anything."

"Thanks. I'd appreciate that."

After a few pleasantries, Ivan hung up the phone. He poured a single malt. *Just what I need: a goddamn 'green' reporter sniffing around like a bloodhound! What did Esteban say? He'd only be interested if I was 'screwing up the air or water.' My God, what mill didn't pollute?* He drained his glass and filled it again. *I should stop the dumping right away. But there's no way to keep up with the Chinese order if I do that. And the contract specifies that if I don't perform punctually, they can take their business elsewhere. And God knows the other mills are hungry and would underbid me in a second.*

And my 'palace.' Money-sink's more like it. Everything's costing twice what I figured, in a depressed economy, no less! The builder should be happy just to have the work. And that bumbling architect. His blunders alone have cost me over fifty million pesos! I should sue the son-of-a-bitch. But that's just more money for the lawyers. Thank God the company stock has been rising. I may be short on cash, but plenty of money on paper. But I don't dare borrow any more against my shares, and if the stock ever crashes, I'm screwed. He sipped the single malt while walking over to the large window. *And the remodeling of the condo in Bariloche. That, too. No, I can't slow down production. Not now. I need too much cash. Just for a couple more months. But why am I worrying? The sample Carlos took is clean. And why would anyone make too big a stink about some stupid birds? Most of them are gone anyway. So, big deal. Out of sight, out of mind. You'd* think there'd be something a little more important to write about. Like how much top quality paper this mill can produce in a day. But still, I've got to be careful; especially the nights Jorge drains the tank.

I have to make sure Jorge keeps his mouth shut. That should be easy enough. He worships me and loves his job. Fool thinks he's a special agent with that pistol I gave him. Kind of spooky the way he fondles that gun, but he's faithful and will do absolutely anything I want. And especially now that I bought the recorder for his television.

* * *

Lilia slipped the last wooden bar of the gate into place before returning to the passenger side of the truck. When she was settled, Tomás drove down the gravel road to the Pan American Highway.

"...And you'd be a great help to Pablo and Miriam, as well as Amanda. She says the river thing is taking up so much of her time now that she feels guilty that she's not around to help them more. They're getting old, you know. There's Javier's empty room upstairs which could be yours, and you'd be just a short bus ride away from the shop."

Lilia didn't say anything. Tomás turned onto the highway, heading down the long hill towards Valdivia. He was right, she thought. It did make a lot of sense to take the job. She'd make a good wage and could manage her own finances. She wouldn't be a burden to anyone for a change. Just the opposite, she would be helping Amanda with Pablo and Miriam. And God knows that Jaime's *señora* wanted her out of the house. But still, it was her home too. She had been born there. And she loved her bright little room. Her whole life was there.

She looked at Tomás. So different from thirty years ago. He was much softer then without those creases around his eyes, and his hands and forearms weren't so sinewy and hard looking. He's weathered now, just like Jaime and Juan; except he's rich, or must be, considering all the money he'd been spending. But he has no airs. And he's using his money to provide us with a future—the sawmill at Juan's, the truck, the lumberyard in Valdivia. And now he's offering me a job, too.

Lilia watched Tomás smoothly downshift to slow their descent down the steep hill. She frowned as she thought of his disappointment to learn that most of the farmers had sold out. He had worked so hard to help them, suffering through the winters and walking the muddy roads to deliver the seedlings. He organized that committee to build a new road, and came up with a scheme so the community could afford it. He and María Elena had formed a team to make it happen. But now the big companies are benefitting from all that hard work; and Amanda says that many of those same trees are contributing to the poison dumped into the rivers.

The truck approached a wide curve in the road. Tomás glanced several times down the slope towards a large boulder. She recognized it immediately because it was the only one on the slope, and Jaime had told her about it. It was where María Elena had died. Tomás's face was expressionless as they continued on towards Valdivia.

"It must be hard every time you pass this stretch of road, Tomás," she said softly.

He nodded.

"Yes, but not so bad now. Not like thirty years ago. It really has helped to return here, and Juan has been such an inspiration. His sorrow is every bit as deep as mine, maybe deeper, but he accepted her death and moved on. He will always miss her, of course, but he hasn't let it dictate his life. It's about time I did the same." A few minutes later he added, "And you've helped too, Lilia."

"Me? How?"

"Your smile, for one thing. Every time you smile, you remind me of those first days in your home, before the accident, when life was still exciting and everything so new and different. You taught me so much about the *campo*, and helped me to adjust to such a different way of life. I don't know if you realize how important that was for me...I also have a confession."

She looked at him questioningly.

"Sometimes, when you were helping me with my Spanish at the table, I'd make a goofy mistake on purpose—just to make you laugh. Your whole face would light up."

Lilia laughed. Tomás smiled as he glanced over.

"Just like that, Lilia! Your face looked just like that."

She continued laughing. Tomás loved it.

"What's so funny?" he asked.

She looked at him with mischievous eyes.

"Was the *chuchOS* one of those mistakes you made on purpose?"

"Oh God, that! Of course not! Will I never outlive that story!"

"I'll always remember the look on your face. You were mortified."

Tomás looked straight ahead, shaking his head. Lilia was still chuckling when they approached the outskirts of Valdivia.

They pulled up to the shop. Tomás waved to Guillermo who was on the forklift in front of a tall three-sided shed full of lumber. He and Lilia entered the shop. Except for a good-sized office on the left, the building was wide open. Woodworking machines were strategically placed all around. Tomás showed Lilia the large, powerful table saw for ripping, and the twelve-inch jointer for straightening and flattening lumber. After handing Lilia some earphones, he ran a rough board through the planer. Lilia ran a hand across the board.

"So smooth, so quickly! It would take me a half hour to do this."

Tomás turned off the planer while Lilia removed her earphones.

"That would be one of the benefits of the job," he said smiling at her. "I can teach you how to use all these machines, and you can use them whenever you want for whatever you want. Come on into the office."

The office door had a window facing the shop area. Tomás reached for one of the scaling sticks hanging on the wall. He showed her how to place the stick on a board to calculate the volume, then what to charge for it.

"You would answer the phone, give prices, take orders, and maybe fill some of the smaller orders for the general public. That would free up Guillermo to take care of our bigger customers like the builders, woodworking shops, and so on."

Tomás pointed over to a corner where there was a leather padded stool and workbench. He hoped this would be the coup de grâce.

"I set that up. When there's nothing going on, you can carve to your heart's content. I don't care if the wood chips are a foot thick. And, if you like, we can display any carvings you want to sell. My guess is that they'll eventually bring in a lot more money than this job would ever pay you."

Lilia looked at the carving corner, then out to all the woodworking machines. She looked back at Tomás. It didn't take her more than a few seconds to make up her mind.

"If it's okay with Pablo, Miriam, and Amanda, then it's fine by me!"

Chapter Sixteen

Lilia arched her back. *My God, this is worse than washing clothes in the* campo, *she thought. Two hundred and twenty cutterheads in this monster!* But she could understand why Tomás had her rotating them instead of Guillermo: she was better at it. She was methodical and had more patience. That's why the Ministry of Agriculture hired women to weed the pine nurseries instead of men, Tomás had told her—same sort of chore. He also had stressed how important presentation was in the lumber business. When boards came out of the planer shiny smooth, customers would return.

She picked up the portable drill armed with a star-patterned driver. She loosened one of the square cutterheads before turning it ninety degrees and retightening it. This would be the second time the cutterheads had been rotated. After the third, all four faces would be dull and they would have to be replaced. But Tomás said that their planer was much better than the old knife planers which were finicky and often tore the wood.

When she was done, she lowered the large protective hood over the spiral head. The clock on the wall said 11:05. Not bad, just over three and a half hours. And the planer was all set for Tomás who would be coming in soon to plane wide *alerce* boards for his interior paneling. She donned a leather apron and, after selecting a small gouge from the set of knives Tomás had given her, she sat at the carving bench. He's so good to me, she thought, as she reached for a chunk of *nogal*, her favorite wood. She sat motionless, picturing a *cuchao*. Moments later she slowly started to rough out the bird. Large dark chips fell into her lap.

    She was so much happier living with Amanda, Miriam, and Pablo. It was fun; quite a change from tiptoeing around her sister-in-law. Hah! I wonder how she likes doing all the laundry now! Still, she and Amanda did most of the chores, but it was Miriam who was the early morning baker. It was wonderful waking each morning to the smell of fresh bread! Pablo was always up second, going straight out to his little shed where he built saddles, braided leather lassos, and fashioned oxen yokes. She smiled when she recalled how he had eagerly accepted her offer to carve decorative motifs in the yokes. Tomás saw the carved yokes and asked if he could borrow one. He showed it to the tourist shopkeepers down by the river who immediately ordered different sized yokes for the tourists to hang on their walls. Tomás was so clever, she mused. The yokes had become the rage, and Pablo couldn't make them fast enough. Their sales had improved the household budget so much that Miriam bought a chest freezer on time, and she didn't even complain when Pablo bought himself a new *huaso* hat. It felt so good to contribute financially. And the house was comfortable too, plenty big enough for the four of them. And she had her own room. And a hot water shower! What luxury!

    The best part was that she hadn't had one of her spells in a long time. She couldn't even remember the last one. Maybe they were all done now. Maybe she was cured and could truly be at peace. Somehow, she knew, it was because of Tomás. She looked down at the little bird that had appeared in her hands. Even with all her daydreaming, her hands had breathed life into the piece of wood. I really am talented, she thought, just like Tomás says. The cranking of the chain fall of the large shop door startled her. With wood chips cascading from her lap, she quickly stood to look out the office window. Tomás's truck was there, sagging under the weight of a tall pile of *alerce*. Flinging the apron onto the bench, she straightened her blouse and ran her fingers through her long dark hair. She rushed out of the office to help him unload.

* * *

When Carlos had studied in the United States, he had taken a summer off from Columbia University to bus and hitchhike cross country, then around California and up through the Northwest. He had never thought about it before, but now, returning to Santiago, he realized that his country was the mirror image of the U.S. west coast. The fjords he had seen down south book-matched those of Alaska. The Alaskan King Crab was very similar to the *centolla* crab in Magallanes. The giant sequoia's closest cousin was the *alerce*. The lake area around Valdivia and Osorno with all its lush green and heavy winter rains paralleled coastal Washington and Oregon. Today he was driving through the fertile Central Valley with vineyards everywhere, just like central California. To the north there was the Atacama Desert; in the south of California, the Mojave. Unfortunately though, he thought as he spied the Santiago skyline off in the distance, we have the same pollution: Santiago has to be as bad as L.A., or worse.

The traffic picked up considerably as he approached the capital. Give me the south any day, he thought as he mentally prepared himself for the smog and hubbub of the sprawling city of five million. He was soon surrounded by a bevy of noisy *micros* belching their noxious fumes as they leapfrogged down the broad avenue. Santiago had one of the highest density of buses in the world which explained why it was rare these days to see the snow-capped Andes. He rolled up his windows and turned on the a.c., debating whether to check in at the newspaper building or go home first. He decided to go home, driving as quickly as he could through the downtown area. He turned on to the Pio Nono Bridge, crossed the Rio Mapocho, then entered the Barrio Bella Vista.

Bella Vista was considered the bohemia quarters of the city, and was a popular dining and party area. It was still early enough, however, so that he found a parking space close to his loft. Slinging pack and cameras over a shoulder and grabbing the laptop, he locked the car and entered his building. The loft was wide open with only furniture separating the living, sleeping, dining, and kitchen area. He put the computer down on the large coffee table in front of a light brown leather couch and easy chairs. Stifling a yawn, he flung his pack on to the bed, and began to strip. It had been a long drive, over ten hours, and he couldn't wait to get into the shower.

A half hour later with a cup of black coffee in his hand, he checked messages on the answering machine. The most recent was from his editor earlier in the day. He wanted to discuss Carlos's idea for the article about the swans, and to meet with him at nine the next morning. Most of the other messages weren't important, although there were three from a woman he was dating who wanted him to call her as soon as possible. He walked over to the couch and sat down at his computer. The couch faced a large window that framed the eight hundred meter Cerro Santa Lucia. The funicular was moving slowly up its side, no doubt loaded with tourists to visit the statue of the Virgin and to look out over the city. If they were lucky, he thought, they might even be able to see the Andes today.

Carlos re-read the two articles he had written while staying with his parents. He changed a couple of things, but for the most part they read through fine. He switched over to the Picasa program to select the photographs to go with them. There had to be at least two hundred pictures.

He selected twenty for his editor to choose from. He made an extra copy of three for his personal portfolio. The first was a close-up of the glacier San Rafael just as a section calved. The lifeboat, full of tourists in the foreground, was framed by a rainbow of spray as the blue-colored chunk of ice hit the water. The second was an action shot of a bright blue and yellow raft full of screaming passengers as it plunged into the monster hole on the Futaleufú River. Finally, there was an early morning shot of a rock climber so high up a dome in Little Yosemite that he looked like a Lilliputian. The photo made Carlos's stomach queasy.

He quickly scrolled through the rest of the file. There were several of the *asado* in Cufeo. One was of the whole group, himself included, when he had mounted the camera on a tripod and set the timer. He shook his head when he recalled the soccer game. That had been embarrassing. He decided to print a few of the group to give as presents whenever he returned to Valdivia. He came to the picture of Amanda in the silvery moonlight. A few silky wisps of hair lay across her face. She was timeless perfection—a river goddess. He printed that one too and put it off to the side.

Finally, he came to the pictures he had taken of the pulp mill. He had found out the name of the architectural firm that had designed the mill, also learning that its headquarters were in Santiago. Maybe his editor knew some way to obtain the mill's blueprints; he'd ask tomorrow. He switched off the computer and went into the kitchen to make a light dinner. Afterwards, he was ready for bed. As he walked by the coffee table he saw Amanda's picture off to the side. He looked at it for a minute or two; calling the woman on the answering machine never occurred to him.

The next morning, Carlos took the metro from Baquedano to Los Héroes where it was a short walk to the newspaper building. It was just nine o'clock when he stepped out of the elevator and knocked on his editor's door.

"Come in," he heard.

His editor and the owner of the paper were standing together looking out over the city. They turned as one when he entered.

Uh oh, Carlos thought, something's up. Why's Espinosa here? Morales! I'll bet he asked him to shut me down. Carlos handed his folder to the editor while Espinosa smiled at Carlos.

"You're looking fit and tan, Carlos. Did you see your father down south?"

"Yes, sir, and he told me to send his regards."

"Good man, your father."

Espinosa motioned for Carlos to sit in one of the two easy chairs in front of the desk. The editor was looking at the pictures in the folder when Espinosa said, "I had a call last week from an old business acquaintance..."

"Ivan Morales, I'll bet."

Here it comes, Carlos thought, but Espinosa chuckled.

"Yes. You seem to have stirred him up with the implication that his mill is responsible for killing all the swans down there."

"I think it is," Carlos said quickly. "And I also think that, given some time, I'll be able to prove it." Carlos told him about what Amanda had learned as well as his suspicions about the mysterious pipe. Espinosa leaned forward.

"Let me tell you a little about Ivan Morales. That man will do anything, absolutely anything to make money. He will step on anyone in his way, and he is a master at using people. I am not proud to say that I once was his business associate. He made me a lot of money a few years back, but when I found out how he did it, I terminated that relationship immediately. He has risen very, very quickly, which I believe was partly through connections with the criminal world here in Santiago. And I am absolutely sure that he wouldn't hesitate for a second to dump toxic wastes into the river if it would increase profits. Carlos, if you think you can come up with absolute proof, do it!

I'm here to tell you that I'm behind you one hundred percent. Joaquin and I want you to return to Valdivia as soon as possible, and, as far as the blueprints of the mill, I'll make a couple of calls. I think I know someone who'll be able to get us a copy."

Espinosa stood up, holding out his hand. Carlos quickly took it.

"Good luck."

"Thank you, sir," Carlos said and turned to leave. When he opened the door, his editor looked up from the folder.

"Carlos..."

"Yes, Joaquin?"

"These photos are exceptional! Good job. We'll run the first travel article in next Sunday's edition."

Carlos smiled and nodded. On his way down in the elevator he started making plans. He would need every camera he owned, his laptop for sure, maybe some binoculars; he'd have to wash all his soiled travel clothes before he could pack; and he'd definitely have to get his car serviced, including new filters—those dusty roads down south had been brutal. As he entered the noisy street, he also realized that he would soon be spending a lot of time with Amanda. The thought put a smile on his face.

* * *

The buildings around the downtown plaza cast long shadows as early morning shoppers jostled their way out of the number thirteen *micro* to head down to the outdoor market by the river. Amanda and Miriam, armed with empty string bags, were among them. In a few minutes they arrived at the street in front of the market where, waiting for traffic, Amanda looked over at the V-shaped, two-story restaurant, La Perla del Sur. Beautifully restored, it was one of the few buildings left standing after the massive earthquake of 1960. Painted bright blue with tall, tan-trimmed windows and doors, 1910 was emblazoned in large tan numbers at the top of the façade. Well-dressed shoppers and tourists were sipping cappuccinos at the outdoor tables.

They crossed over to the busy little market where Miriam and Amanda admired the hydrangeas and birds of paradise before strolling down the narrow corridor between the vegetable and fish vendors. Two long roofs of taut, brightly colored nylon tarps offered protection from the weather. The sunlight filtering through the nylon bathed the vegetables and fish in false tones. Miriam prodded farm-raised salmon before buying two filets, an extravagant purchase for them at fifteen hundred pesos per kilo. As they filled their shopping bags with items they couldn't or didn't grow behind the house, a young woman selling *avellano* nuts and small bundles of brown and white *chupónes* called over to Amanda.

"Hey, Amanda. What, are you such an important student these days you don't greet me anymore!"

Amanda rushed up to hug the daughter of one of the few remaining families in Cufeo.

"Aii, María, I did not see you!" Amanda looked down at the neatly separated piles. "I see you have been busy. How are the *avellanas* this year?"

María smiled, revealing bad teeth.

"Many, because there are so few pigs."

"Yes, it is different now." Amanda pictured the pigs from years ago wearing large triangles of stout branches around their necks, fashioned by the farmers so they couldn't pass through fences. Somehow, though, they always found a way out to rut their way straight to the *avellano* trees. She had competed with the pigs for the nuts, collecting burlap bags full and dragging them home where she split the black husks open with a hammer to get at the little white seed. She fondly recalled the many winter nights spent in the *fogón* with Papá telling stories while they roasted the nuts over an open fire in a big tin pan. The *chupóne*, though, was not a favorite of hers. The faintly sweet fruit lay hidden among long bayonet-like fronds that had to be pushed away with a stick. The sharply pointed leaves could spring back at any time, and many a *campo* child had injured an eye harvesting *chupóne*.

Amanda looked longingly at the little bags of *avellanas*. María knew Amanda's family's financial situation was no better than her own. She bent down to pick up one of the little bags.

"Here, Amanda."

Amanda started to protest, but María shook her head.

"This way you won't forget your *campo* roots."

Amanda laughed as she took the nuts.

"I don't think you'll ever have to worry about that."

Miriam came over to greet María. The trio was soon bemoaning the loss of the tightly knit community in Cufeo.

"But it is so much easier here in town," Miriam said. "I just have to walk to the corner for the salt or butter, or to take the *micro* to market. No more kilometers of muddy road just to catch a bus so crowded you can't breathe. But still, there are things I miss. Like the quiet. And Pablo complains that he cannot walk out the door whenever he wants to make *pichi*."

"María, if I write a letter to my parents, would you deliver it?"

"Of course."

"Come on then, *abuelita*, let's enjoy this treat from María while I write. Over there on that bench where you can rest and watch the sea lions."

The vendors, gutting and cleaning fish, tossed the entrails out into the river. The sea lions were a regular fixture, feasting on the scraps or basking on the nearby docks and moorings. Once in a great while, one would climb up over the concrete seawall to flop down on the warm macadam of the busy market street. Traffic would back up while excited tourists took pictures until the *carabineros* came to herd the complaining animal back to the river.

The perched, bewhiskered sea creatures arched up towards the sun. One had climbed up onto the wharf next to the fish vendors. The railing shrouded in page wire kept the beggar out, but with bulging eyes it stretched its long neck past a bent section to reach the scraps. Not five meters away on a dock, Amanda saw a large bull yawn, displaying four prominent yellow-brown teeth. Behind each tooth was a single row of small black teeth that, set in the cavernous pink mouth, reminded Amanda of watermelon seeds. The sea lion's button ears weren't much bigger than the little black teeth.

Miriam, falling asleep in the warmth of the sun, began to snore lightly. Good, Amanda thought while pulling pen and paper out of her satchel, she should rest. Two tourist boats slowly pulled away from the main wharf, heading downriver to the Pacific. She watched them for awhile before beginning to write.

Queridas Papá y Mamá,

Miriam and I are sitting on a bench by the river market. It is a beautiful day, the sun is out, and Miriam is taking a little nap like the sea lions down on the docks. It must be beautiful too in Cufeo. How I miss the summer days there! The 'asado' was a lot of fun, and I have discovered that Carlos is very interesting and intelligent. When he and I went out on the river to take water samples, we found another dead swan killed by a fox or a dog. I think it was one of the very last ones on the river. It is so sad, and such a crime!

The tourist boats just left for Corral and Niebla. They were full of happy vacationers going to the beaches. But I do not see any of the little boats that used to take people up to see the swans. I hope that maybe now that people are losing business, they might start paying more attention to what that awful mill is doing. I think I know now when the poison is put into the river. Carlos is investigating how. But all this has been taking a lot of time. You must know by now that Lilia moved into the house here. She helps me take care of Pablo and Miriam, and she is fun to have around.

I hope you are well, and that my brother and nieces and nephews are too. Guillermo loves his job with Tomás. Other than for the swans, life is good here in Valdivia.

Affectionately,
Your Amanda

When Miriam woke, the pair crossed the street to the indoor market to finish shopping. Soon their string bags were bulging with staples like rice, salt, vegetable oil, sugar, *maté*, a tin of Nescafé, detergent, and a large plastic bottle of the red pepper paste for Pablo. Even though Amanda carried most of the bags, Miriam was soon out of breath as they walked up to the plaza. They arrived just in time to see number thirteen pull out. Amanda swore under her breath. They walked over to sit at one of the nearby hand-wrought iron benches. It wasn't long before they heard, "Well, look who's here."

A well-dressed young woman with a stylishly logoed bag in each hand approached their bench. Amanda recognized her as a fellow student, but couldn't remember her name. The young woman glanced haughtily at Miriam, then back to Amanda.

"Aah, I see you have been shopping with your maid, Amanda." She smiled. "And she seems quite done in."

Amanda fought the urge to stand up and slap the girl. Instead, she coolly introduced Miriam.

"This 'maid' happens to be my great aunt, Sra. Miriam Carcamo Rodríguez. *Abuelita*, this is a fellow university student."

"Oh, I am so sorry," the student said.

Amanda didn't think she looked sorry. Miriam smiled up at the girl and extended her hand. Begrudgingly, the girl shifted a package so she could shake.

"It is all right, young lady," Miriam said, laughing as she looked down at her clothes. "I don't blame you for thinking that. And I am so happy to meet a university friend of Amanda's. She never brings anyone home for *onces* or a cup of tea. What did you say your name was, dear?"

"Sofía," she said, quickly letting go of Miriam's hand.

Amanda could not think of a thing to say. There was an awkward silence until the young woman said, "It was very nice to meet you, Señora, but I should be going or I'll be late for lunch at the university. I must get a taxi, there is no way I can walk across the bridge with all these things." Amanda knew it was less than a ten minute walk, and her packages didn't look heavy—probably a couple of the latest blouses. Sofia looked at the pile of groceries to the side of the bench. "But I'll wait until you get your taxi first," she added graciously.

"No, no, dear. You go right ahead. We are waiting for the bus to come, over there," Miriam said, pointing. "Oh my, there's one now, Amanda." She looked back to the young woman. "So nice to meet you," she said, bending to pick up bags.

"Well, off I go then. Enjoy your little bus ride. *Ciao*." Sofia strolled quickly over to the taxi stand as Amanda and Miriam gathered up their bags.

The bus was almost empty, allowing Amanda and Miriam to sit together for a change. As they slowly made their way to the Las Animas suburb, Amanda began thinking of Carlos. Why, she wondered, was she thinking of him all of a sudden? Sofia and her fancy bags and airs—that's why. Carlos was from a wealthy family too, yet he didn't flaunt it. He would never act the way that girl did; he was a real gentleman. Both Carlos and his father had been as natural and nice as could be at the *asado*. Obviously, Papá really liked Kurt, and had been impressed by Carlos. She realized now that she had showed off during the soccer game because of Carlos.

She could talk intelligently with him. He certainly knew his current events, was mature, multi-talented. He oozed confidence and capability. And he was so handsome: tall, a *rubio* with blond hair. He was almost too good looking. Why hadn't he made a pass at her? Most other men, young and old, came on to her at some point. But not Carlos. She had been alone with him all night in the boat, but he didn't flirt, not even once. Maybe he's gay? The thought jolted her. There were more and more of them now, especially in the large cities like Santiago. He had studied several years in the United States, in New York City which had a large gay community. Carlos must be in his late twenties and, as handsome, smart, and wealthy as he is, he's still single. Why? He hadn't said a word about dating any girls. Some of the gays in Santiago were models, really handsome men like him. Maybe he's got a boyfriend model. The more she thought about it, the more she became convinced. He was gay, she knew it. Just my luck: I finally meet someone I'm attracted to and he's gay. Wouldn't you know it!

Suddenly there was a loud thud as something heavy hit the roof of the bus. The driver quickly pulled over. Amanda saw that cars were dodging a white and black bulk weakly flopping around in the street. Oh, my God, a swan, too weak to stay aloft! It was dead by the time she reached it. Horns honked as she scooped it up and returned with it in her arms. The driver, balancing on a rear tire and holding on to the edge of a window, was inspecting the roof. He jumped down when he saw Amanda.

"What do you think you're doing! That damn bird has done enough damage without bleeding all over my bus! Put it down."

Amanda ignored him. He followed her into the bus, screaming at her. The passengers looked at the bloody, dirty bird with revulsion. Only Miriam showed any concern.

"*Abuelita*, empty some of those plastic bags and spread them out here, please," Amanda said, indicating the aisle, and blocking off the area from the driver. She gently laid the bird down.

"See, no blood on your bus, Señor. And just to the other side of the river; that's all. We get off there. Please…"

The driver hesitated when he saw the pleading in her eyes. He looked around. Everyone was looking at the swan with sympathy now. Shaking his head, he turned his back to her and returned to his seat. Moments later, he pulled out into the traffic.

"Poor thing," Miriam said softly.

Amanda turned to her.

"At least it was fairly quick; quicker, anyway, than the last one I saw die."

Miriam looked questioningly at Amanda.

"I was rowing out to take some water samples when I spotted one a ways off. I could see that it was so weak that it was having a hard time holding its head up. I rowed as fast as I could, but by the time I got there, it had drowned."

Miriam looked back at the swan.

"What are you going to do with this one?"

"If it's all right with you, wrap it up and put it into your new freezer…so I can study it later."

Without taking her eyes off the swan, Miriam nodded. The bus stopped at the other side of the bridge where the driver pointedly looked straight ahead as Amanda and Miriam struggled down with their bags and the dead swan.

Chapter Seventeen

Carlos and Amanda were bent over Miriam's kitchen table looking at a large blueprint of the pulp mill.

"How on earth did you get this, Carlos?"

"I can't really say, except that a few well-placed people in the capital don't like Sr. Morales very much."

He pointed to the schematics.

"This is the waste pipe I told you about. When Morales said he had no idea where it led, it made me suspicious. I thought he was hiding something, and I was right. It doesn't go to any pit or reservoir," he said as he followed it with his finger, "it goes under the concrete straight to the river. By periodically emptying the tank, much of the effluent bypasses the purifying stage, production is speeded up, and they can make a lot more paper. And consequently, a lot more money. No wonder the plant's doing so well."

"What a son-of-a-bitch!"

She looked up at him.

"Excuse my language, but he is! What a name. Morales! That man has no morals at all."

Carlos thought she was pretty even when angry.

"Easy, easy," he said, gesticulating with his hands.

He pulled out a handful of pictures from a manila envelope.

"This is what all the pipes and tanks look like. I'll try to lay them out so that they make sense."

Amanda noticed a little knit in his brow as he carefully placed the pictures around the blueprint.

"Would you like some water, Carlos?"

He shook his head. She walked over and filled a glass. Leaning against the sink, taking sips, she watched him. He was so tall. And those shoulders! He looked over.

"All set."

They stood matching the pictures to the diagrams. His closeness made it hard for her to concentrate. When her hand inadvertently touched his, she reacted like she had been burned. She blushed, and went back to the glass of water by the sink.

"Do you have a camera that works in the dark?"

"Sure—modified Nikon that's infrared."

"Good. Then we'll make a little visit to the mill Friday night."

His head snapped around.

"What!"

"That's when they dump, Friday nights; I'm sure of it. Judging from your photographs, it'd be possible to take pictures from the river when they open that valve for the discharge pipe. And while you're taking pictures, I'll get some samples."

She took another sip of water. He was looking at her with his mouth open. She continued.

"It's been hard to pinpoint the exact time because river conditions vary—like if there's been a heavy rain and more current, or dry with less—but my guess is sometime between nine and midnight. After dark, anyway. With the samples and your pictures, you would have the proof you need for an article. And then we could notify the environmental watchdogs. We'll crucify him!"

"And just how do you propose to get samples?"

"From the pipe in the river, of course. I can use some of the university's diving gear—wetsuit, tanks—anything I need."

"You know how to use that stuff?"

"I'm a certified diver. Most every student who has studied advanced pisciculture had to learn. That enabled us to observe the salmon at the fish farms near Puerto Montt as well as the shellfish off Chiloe. I've done a lot of diving."

The girl continually surprised him. They heard a car door shut; moments later, footsteps came around to the kitchen. Lilia entered with a smile that grew when she saw Carlos and Amanda.

"Hi there," she said, as she draped her daypack over a chair. "What do we have here?" she asked, looking down at the table.

Carlos explained, while Amanda looked at Lilia. Such a difference since moving to Valdivia. And Amanda believed that she knew the reason.

"Did Tomás give you a ride home?"

Lilia nodded as she studied the photographs.

"I thought so."

Lilia looked up curiously.

"Because you always glow after you spend time with him."

Lilia blushed.

"I don't think that's true."

"I do, and I think it's great. And you know what? I think the same goes for Tomás."

"Oh really, Amanda. You're imagining things. Tomás is just being nice. That's the way he is."

She reached for her daypack, slinging it over a shoulder.

"I'm going upstairs to put these things away. I'll be back down in a jiffy. I want to hear more about this mill thing."

She left the room. Amanda turned back to Carlos.
"She may not know it, but she's in love with him."
He smiled.
"I wouldn't be surprised."
His face turned serious.
"But let's talk about next Friday night. I don't know if your plan is such a good idea."
Upstairs, Lilia sat down next to her daypack on the bed. Could Amanda be right? Could Tomás have feelings for her? Wouldn't that be wonderful! She lay back, imagining him reaching for her hand. Smiling nervously, he leaned forward for a first kiss. She smiled back, waiting. Suddenly, Jorge's awful face filled her mind, lust oozing from every pore. He reached for her with those thick, hairy arms. "You're mine, Lilia. And you know you'll always be mine." He leered. "Because we have so much fun together!"
Lilia shuddered, but couldn't shake the picture. How could she think Tomás would ever want her? She was soiled, dirty! Tears began to slowly streak her cheeks.

After dropping Lilia off, Tomás drove out to Cufeo. He was excited that Lilia would be coming out to the house during the weekend to help him install the freshly milled paneling. Was he feeling this way, he wondered, because he would have her help, or was it because they would be alone at the house? He had been spending a lot of time with her, showing her how to run the shop equipment, how to write up orders, and how to make bank deposits. She was a quick learner. She also knew a lot about the different native hardwoods, and, with hand tools, she was at least his equal. When they discussed building custom furniture for his house, she lobbied to make certain pieces. She was something else. She was wonderful.
He turned off the Pan American Highway onto the graveled road. Thirty years ago, it would have taken all

day to make this trip: catch the crowded bus in Valdivia, then lug his pack for hours up these hills. Now, especially because of the graveled road, the whole trip took a little over an hour. And he and María Elena were the main reasons the graveled road had been built; at least the first half of it. When he stopped at Juan's farm to drop off supplies, Flor told him that Juan and young Tomás were sawing late. He could hear the whine of the sawmill down in the lower plantation, but he continued on to the house. He wanted to get the paneling safely out of the weather.

By the time he had unloaded the pickup, there was still an hour before sunset. He poured himself a glass of wine out on the rear deck. No more work on the house tonight; tomorrow's another day. He took a sip while looking out to the waterfall and to the volcano crowned by a few wisps of clouds. Spectacular! How María Elena, like Lilia, would have loved this house. He felt the guilt begin to creep up again. This is ridiculous, he thought; about time to have a little conversation with María Elena! Grabbing the bottle of wine, he trod purposefully down the narrow path. When he entered the clearing, he immediately felt her presence. He sat in a chair he had placed under the *ramada*; the sound of the waterfall was a tonic.

"Okay, *querida*, what am I going to do about all this? You know I love you...will always love you. But, I have feelings now for Lilia too. Is that wrong? Can't I finally have someone else in my life besides you?

"You make me feel so guilty, like I am being unfaithful. But you've got to understand that she's wonderful, and I think she would make a good companion. She enjoys the things I do, and we have a lot of fun together. And I think she's as lonely as I am.

"I know...I'm quite a bit older than she is, but I don't think that matters to her; that is, assuming she has the same feelings for me. The vote is out on that. But I have so much here to share. And she is pretty…And yes, damn it, I would like to sleep with her!"

He looked around helplessly.

"Yes, yes. I have you here. But this isn't real, is it? Yes, I do feel you, *mi querida*, but I want something, someone I can touch. Is that asking too much?"

He shook his head and refilled his glass. The sun was edging behind the volcano.

"But what do you think, *mi amor*? Give me a sign. Please! Let me know if it's all right to love Lilia…and maybe live with her some day."

He looked around in every direction. Everything was normal. No bird came out of the forest to land on his shoulder. No animal ventured into the clearing. There was no thunderbolt. No condor descended from the sky. He waited a long time, drinking wine. The sun dropped behind Puntiagudo, taking the green out of the hills. There was still no sign.

"Goddamn it, María Elena, you're not being fair! Let me know!"

But everything was still. Finally, he stood up, a little unsteady. He caught his balance as he looked angrily around the clearing. It was dark by the time he returned to the house.

Chapter Eighteen

It was a little after dark when they anchored the aluminum rowboat outside the mill's curtain of light. Carlos knew immediately that he didn't need his infrared camera: the plant was lit up like a shopping center. He zoomed in with his telephoto. There was no movement other than the smoke belching from the mill's tall stacks, and the air smelled like rotten eggs. Amanda put on her gear before setting out to locate the underwater pipe.

It wasn't long before he saw her trail of bubbles returning to the boat. She surfaced by the stern. Handing the underwater compass and light to Carlos, she said, "I located the pipe. It's huge, with a big screen at the mouth. Nothing is coming out of it yet…give me a hand with these tanks."

Carlos hefted the tanks into the boat before helping her out of the water. She took off her hood and shook out her hair. The wetsuit outlined every curve of her body. She was ridiculously sexy, like out of some girlie magazine. He forced himself to look her in the eye.

"No action on top either. I guess we wait."

Amanda reached for the binoculars and scanned the mill.

"How are you going to take samples without them being diluted by the river?"

"The pipe sticks out more than a meter from the concrete. I'll get behind it and fill the vials right over the opening. If I screw the tops on right there, I should be able to get close to a hundred percent effluent."

He nodded while looking out to the mill. Still no action. Putting his hands behind his head, he stretched out as best he could.

"Guess we might as well make ourselves comfortable. We should have brought some *empanadas* and a bottle of red wine."

"This isn't a picnic, Carlos."

"I know, I know. But I'm hungry, and it'd help pass the time."

They watched the mill in silence. When Amanda started fiddling with her regulator, Carlos asked, "What do you want to be when you grow up?"

"I am grown up."

"Yes, I can see that."

She gave him a quick sidelong look.

"But you know what I mean. After the university."

She put down the regulator and leaned forward, hugging her knees.

"A veterinarian. I'd like to go to the vet school here; or even the one in Santiago."

A vet. Not surprising. He thought of her dedication to the swans, and that she was studying the sciences. The other day Pablo had told him that she knew as much about farm animals as he did.

"Pablo told me that you have always loved animals—all animals. Like in that book the English veterinarian wrote. What was it called?"

She smiled.

"*All Creatures Great and Small*. I loved that book. But with me it goes maybe even deeper." She looked over at him. "This may sound like I'm strange or a misfit or something, but I have always been more comfortable around animals than people. Like here in Valdivia. When I moved in with Pablo and Miriam, it was really hard. Not because of them, of course, but everyone else. I was a bumpkin to the other kids, and they let me know it. And the university girls! We're so different. They are way out of my league: financially, their clothes, the things they talk about, you name it."

"Did you ever think that maybe it's the other way around; that it's you who's out of their league? Most of them are pretty shallow as far as I'm concerned. These nights out on the river would be pretty damn dull if all you and I had to talk about was what clothes were in fashion. But, of course, we wouldn't be out here at all if you were like that."

His comment surprised her.

"I guess that's a compliment, Carlos. Thank you."

They looked back to the mill. Amanda continued.

"Anyway, the river was my escape. I had several places where I'd go to read, and hide, I suppose. No people, and it was so peaceful. My favorite thing was to watch the swans. I loved to watch them interact. The parents were so territorial, and they'd fiercely protect their young. And they would put the babies on their back, and swim around, all the time whistling at each other." She looked at him sadly. "But now the whistling has stopped."

They were silent for a few moments before he said, "Wanting to be a vet is commendable. Lofty goal, maybe, but commendable."

"Why do you say 'lofty?'"

"It's damn tough to get into vet school. The competition is fierce."

"I'm not worried about getting in. I just worry how I can afford it." She looked at him evenly. "I'm not so lucky that Mom and Dad can pay for it."

They stared at each other in silence before Carlos said, "I thought we made a pact, Amanda, last time we were out on this river."

She couldn't hold his gaze.

"I'm sorry, you're right…really, I am sorry; it's just that it is always on my mind. I have absolutely no idea how in the world I could come up with the money."

"There are scholarships for vet schools too, you know."

"Yes, but very few. And like you say, just to get in is difficult, let alone getting a scholarship."

They looked back over at the mill.

"What about raising a family? Do you ever want children?"

"Pretty personal question, Carlos."

"Sorry. Just curious. I'll shut up if you want."

She watched him pick up the camera and check the battery. Why was she so short with him sometimes? There was nothing wrong with his question.

"I don't know, Carlos. But right now I think that there are too many people on this planet. If I mate and have kids, and those kids mate and have kids, and their kids mate and have kids, the number of humans I would be responsible for putting here would be exponentially scary. And I am just one female. Each year man takes up more and more territory; and the wildlife, which is already threatened, loses more of theirs. Nature's balance just gets more and more out of whack, which in turn causes more problems. And then you have the greed factor. Like Morales. Most humans can't help themselves. They want more and more: more money, bigger houses, prettier things, fancier cars…and they don't care what they do to the environment to get it. Look at all those man-made disasters we talked about last time we were on the river. Behind every one is human greed."

Carlos couldn't argue with that. A movement near one of the main buildings caught his eye.

"Uh oh! Here we go, Amanda! We got action."

Amanda reached for the binoculars. She saw a man walking, then stop and check a meter on the side of a tank. She turned to Carlos.

"He's a stocky guy, and has an eyepatch."

"That's Jorge. He's the one who gave me the water sample."

Jorge walked up to the discharge valve and started to turn it. Carlos began taking pictures. The camera had motor drive. Amanda continued to watch the man.

"He's got a big pistol on his hip."

Carlos looked over at her, camera still poised.

"And I'm sure it's not for show. Be careful."

She nodded, and reached for the hood and fins.

* * *

Tomás put two chairs in the center of the room so they could inspect their work. With the wide-open floor plan they could look at every wall.

"Wow! Definitely worth it. I mean, my God, look at this paneling!"

He swept his hand around the room. Lilia agreed.

"Beautiful. Such a deep red, and the width," she added smiling and turning towards him, "sure made it go fast."

Juan and young Tomás had sawn out the lumber from the *alerce*. The smaller logs had been for the beams, joists, rafters, and house siding. They also had made shakes for the roof. But from the big logs came the clear wide boards for the paneling which Tomás and Lilia had planed and joined at the shop. The boards were nothing short of spectacular.

"Lilia, how about me taking you to the rodeo next weekend in Valdivia, and dinner afterwards, as a thank you for all your help? Plus, I've talked to Amanda and Carlos; they'd love to join us."

Lilia lit up.

"That would be fun, but you don't have to do it as a 'thank you.' Putting up the paneling was an honor, really, and I enjoyed it. I feel privileged to work with wood like this."

Tomás knew that she was sincere. He felt the same way.

"Okay, then let me rephrase it. How about, 'would you like to go to the rodeo and dinner next Sunday? I want to spend a whole day with you without any work involved.'"

"Then I accept." She stood up. "But it's getting late. This will be the first weekend in over a month that I will be staying in my old room at Jaime's, and I better not be late for dinner. I'm sure Jaime's *señora* is not so keen on my little visit, and I don't want to give her any excuse to get more upset."

Tomás pulled Lilia's light jacket from a hook and held it open for her. He left his hands on her shoulders after she slipped into it.

"I want to spend the day with you" he said with his head close to hers, "because I enjoy being with you."

He turned her around to face him, hands still on her shoulders.

"I hope you feel the same way about me."

Lilia's smile vanished; her eyes panicked. He dropped his hands quickly.

"I'm sorry, Lilia. I didn't mean to upset you."

"No, no, Tomás. Believe me, you didn't...well, not really...it's just..."

She began to cry softly. He didn't know what to do. After a few moments, she took a deep breath.

"I feel the same way about you, Tomás. Really I do. And I've never felt this way before. I've never wanted to... been able to."

She turned towards the big window that looked out to the volcano.

"I have strong feelings for you, Tomás. I want you to know that. But this is new for me, and it scares me."

She turned back to him, looking him straight in the eye.

"I've never been with a man before…except…except for what Jorge did to me."

Tomás lifted her chin and very lightly kissed her on the lips. She looked at him like a startled doe, her eyes filling with tears again.

"That was in the very distant past, Lilia, and in no way was it your fault. I am so sorry for what that has caused you. I'm trying to let go too. I know it doesn't compare with what you went through—nothing like the scars you have—but let's try, both of us, to put everything behind us. Let's begin new lives right now. What do you say? Deal?"

He extended his hand. Slowly she took it.

"Only if you can be patient with me, Tomás. It may take some time."

"Usually I'm not a patient guy, but I can make an exception for you," he said, smiling. He led her out to the truck and opened the door for her. "Lilia, I want you to know that I am happier right now than I've been in a very long time."

"Me too, Tomás. Me too."

As he walked around to the driver's side, he cast a defiant glance down towards the *copihue* clearing.

Chapter Nineteen

Carlos watched Jorge climb back down the metal ladder attached to the effluent tank. Probably checked to see if the poison was draining out okay. Something moved down by the dock. What the hell! Amanda, tanks and mask no where in sight, was pulling herself up over the side of Morales's speedboat. What in God's name was she doing? He quickly swung the binoculars back to Jorge. He was walking towards a nearby building with, luckily, his back to the water. He entered the building. Carlos looked back to Amanda. She was crouched on the dock, looking up at the mill. She turned towards him, and smiled and waved. Oh my God, he thought, get back in the water! She pointed to an empty vial she had taken from her belt, and then to the effluent tank. Turning her back to him, she ran lightly up towards the mill, ducking behind a series of valves mounted on a large concrete square. She peered around the valves, then sprinted towards the effluent tank before she disappeared again behind a series of horizontal pipes. Good lord, that girl's crazy! This is no spy movie! What is she thinking! He scanned the mill in all directions, praying Jorge wouldn't come around a corner. Amanda appeared at the base of the metal ladder. She looked all around, then began to climb. She climbed as quickly as she could, but she was totally exposed. He felt sick. She reached the top where the ladder curved down into the tank. She scrambled over and disappeared. He nervously scanned the mill. No sign of Jorge. No sign of Amanda either. I should document this, he thought. He picked up his camera and waited.

Fog was beginning to roll in, but he could still see the mill clearly. After what seemed like forever, Amanda's head appeared. She carefully looked in all directions before beginning her descent. He snapped several pictures of her. As he framed her with the telephoto, her backside was to him. He couldn't help thinking she had about the cutest rear end in the world. God, what a time to be thinking that! He had better….Oh shit! There was Jorge, slowly walking toward the valve. Only a small building stood between him and Amanda who was half way down the ladder, and she had no idea Jorge was around the corner. What could he do! Jorge took out his pistol. Oh God, he must have heard her. No, the idiot's practicing quick draws, for Christ's sake. Come on, Carlos, no time to lose! Do something! Think!

He yanked up the anchor and rowed into the mill's light. He started banging on the side of the boat with an oar. Both Amanda and Jorge looked out. Jorge holstered his gun and ran down towards the dock, passing right below Amanda who was frozen on the ladder. By the time Jorge reached the dock, Carlos had rowed back into darkness. Amanda scurried down the ladder, hiding behind pipes while Jorge scanned the river. He pulled out a cell phone and punched in a number. He nodded several times before he ran back up to the mill, straight to the valve. He began to turn it off.

Amanda had made her way towards the dock while Jorge had been on the phone. Carlos could see her hiding behind the concrete square again. There was nothing between the concrete square and the dock that was at least fifty feet away. Jorge had his back to her. Amanda took off, but Jorge turned and saw her. He pulled out his pistol. Carlos furiously banged on the boat again with the oar, putting quite a dent in the side. It distracted Jorge long enough for Amanda to reach the dock, and she dove into the river just as he fired. Carlos had no idea if she had been hit.

Jorge ran down to peer into the river. The fog was thickening, which was good, Carlos thought. Jorge walked up to the speedboat, pistol still in hand. He looked curiously at the far side of the boat before climbing down in. Maybe he saw bubbles. He hoped so because that would mean she was alive. Jorge pulled out his phone again as he looked out over the river. Carlos waited in silence, hoping for the best.

He had no idea how long he waited, but one minute was like two. Jorge had left the dock and gone somewhere up into the mill. Very thick fog had rolled in; the mill was hazy, its lights faint starbursts. He shivered with the dampness. Suddenly the headlights of a car speeding along the river appeared. It screeched to a stop at the mill's front gate. He could just see a man get out, probably Morales, he thought. Jorge went running up to him. They soon were headed toward the dock.

"Carlos! Help me get into the boat!"

Carlos jumped a foot. He turned towards the stern. He hadn't heard Amanda surface.

"Amanda! Oh Amanda, are you okay! Did he hit you? You fool, what the hell were you doing!"

He rushed towards her, struggling to keep his emotions in check. He didn't know if he was more relieved or angry. But he stopped and turned back towards the dock when he heard the speedboat sputter, and start. One of the two men was throwing the lines into the boat. They had to get off this river pronto!

He roughly pulled Amanda in, tanks and all. She flopped into the boat. Carlos didn't help her. He was too busy pulling up the anchor. As Amanda gathered herself, he began rowing like a madman.

"You could have been a little more gentle, Carlos!" she said indignantly.

"What? No time! Take a look behind you. Jorge and Morales are in that boat. They're heading out to look for us, and if they find us, we're in big trouble!"

A spotlight suddenly came on in the speedboat. It looked like a bright star.

"Why did you climb that tower? That was a fool's stunt if ever there was one! I just hope we don't get shot because of it."

"To get these," she said. She began pulling plastic vials from her belt. "These will match the effluent from the river. It's just more proof against Morales, another nail for the coffin we're going to put him in."

Frowning, Carlos shook his head and muttered, "Totally unnecessary."

He rowed as hard as he could. Luckily, the speedboat was beginning its search downriver.

"I disagree," she said, reaching for a marking pen and a flashlight in her pack of supplies. She turned on the flashlight and started labeling the vials.

"Turn off that light," he hissed. "Are you crazy, girl? If they see that light, we're screwed!"

She quickly snapped it off.

"Sorry. Wasn't thinking. Just wanted to make sure these didn't get mixed up with the others."

She looked out towards the speedboat. They could hear it better than they could see it. The engine made a low, steady throb.

"If we can get around that wide bend and up to that creek we passed on the way down, we'll be all right. It's too shallow for their boat in the creek, plus I saw a tree that had fallen near the mouth. They couldn't maneuver around that for sure. If only we can make it that far!"

Carlos was sweating heavily. After a few minutes, the noise of the speedboat got louder.

"They've turned around!"

He started rowing harder. Amanda turned in her seat again. The speedboat wasn't going fast, but it was going a lot faster than they were. As it came up river, they could see the spotlight continually sweeping side to side.

"Damn!" Carlos said. "Talk about vulnerable! And I can't tell if we've gone around the bend or not. With this fog, who knows how far the creek is."

The speedboat was steadily gaining, hugging the same shore. Carlos was tiring. Amanda watched him in silence. She wished she could help.

The speedboat was getting uncomfortably close when Amanda saw the mouth of the creek.

"There it is," she whispered excitedly. "Only a little farther!"

Carlos didn't look. He didn't want to miss a stroke.

"Just tell me when to turn."

The speedboat was almost on them. The motor was very loud, and they were almost in range of the light.

"Now! Turn!"

Carlos pulled hard on the right oar while pushing on the left. The current against them was immediately stronger. The sound of the speedboat was very close. He pulled as hard as he could. He was exhausted. They could see the beam of the speedboat's light sweeping the middle of the river just as they came up to the fallen tree. They quickly pulled in behind it.

"Down, Amanda! Down in the bottom of the boat—quick!"

They flung themselves down, and lay close together. The speedboat slowed to an idle, and the light played on both banks of the creek. It slowly swept over the fallen tree. They held their breath.

Carlos's sweat chilled him. He began to shiver.

Amanda whispered, "Carlos, you're shaking. You must be scared to death."

"Damn right I am! Who wouldn't be! But that's not why I'm shaking. I'm freezing! I don't have a rubber suit on to keep me nice and warm."

He began shivering so much, the little rowboat rocked. The speedboat must be idling in neutral, he thought. The light swept over the log again. They waited. There was nothing they could do. Finally, after what seemed an eternity, the speedboat clunked into gear, and slowly continued up river.

"Whew!" Carlos said, sticking his head up and peering over the tree. "That was close. But we better stay here until they head back down river. If they go up as far as Dad's truck, I just hope that they won't see it in this fog."

Carlos continued to shiver as they lay in the bottom of the boat. Amanda, feeling guilty, unzipped her wet suit. She moved close to Carlos who immediately felt her heat: she was a furnace. As he warmed up, they lay close together, talking about the best approach to expose Morales. Carlos couldn't help but notice her softness and curves. Try as he might not to, he became aroused. He backed away from her a little, hoping she wouldn't notice. Eventually, they stopped talking, both very aware of their closeness and shared danger. Amanda reached up to touch his head.

"You're soaked."

"Sweat and fog."

Tentatively, she began to run her fingers through his hair which took him totally by surprise. Her face was turned up to his. He hesitated, then kissed her very gently. She responded. He kissed her again…and then again in earnest. It wasn't long before they were so intent on struggling with her wetsuit that they never noticed the speedboat when it returned to the mill along the far bank.

Chapter Twenty

Amanda looked around the dining room of La Bomba while they waited for their check. Tall, formal windows with deep burgundy curtains looked out on Avenida Arauco, ornate molding divided ceiling and wall, the wainscoting was finely crafted. The restaurant was three-quarters full with two waitresses scurrying back and forth.

"I can't believe I've never been here before. It's really nice; sort of an old time feeling."

Carlos smiled at her.

"I used to come here often with my father, especially on Sundays after mass. It was almost as much about visiting friends as it was about the food. And today has been a good little break for us, plus going to the rodeo tomorrow will be even better. Monday we'll get back to work, but these next two days are about having fun."

He reached for her hand.

"Did I ever tell you I think you're the most beautiful woman in the world?"

"No. Tell me."

He laughed.

"I just did."

After paying the bill and leaving a generous tip, they made their way, hand in hand, down the narrow hallway that passed the bar. They stepped outside.

"Uh oh! I don't believe it! Don't look now, but a certain Sr. Morales is walking this way. He's passing my car right now."

"You're joking."

Morales saw them. He didn't look very happy.

"Aah, young Carlos the reporter," he said with a forced smile. "And who is this lovely lady?"

Carlos shook his hand.

"Sr. Morales, may I present Amanda Montoya. She is a student at the university."

Morales extended his hand. She withheld hers. It was awkward. Carlos tried to make a quick exit.

"It's good to see you, sir; but I'm afraid we are in a bit of a hurry…"

Carlos took Amanda's arm, but Morales stepped in front of them.

"Just a minute, young man. I want to ask if you were perhaps…," he hesitated as he looked at Amanda. "Let me start again. By any chance did you two happen to pay a nighttime visit to my mill…by boat?"

Carlos tried to look incredulous.

"A visit by boat? Whatever for?"

Morales noted he did not deny it. He asked again.

Carlos looked indignant.

"And why would you ask us?"

"We had two visitors at my plant last night. One was a tall man in a rowboat, and the other was a young woman who illegally trespassed onto my property. They disappeared in the fog before I could question them."

Before you could shoot them you mean, Carlos thought.

"However, we did find a pickup truck parked along the river a couple kilometers or so above my mill. I had the license plate number traced. Funny thing, it's registered to your father. How do you explain that?"

"Ask my father."

"I'll do that, Carlos. But I bet I know his answer already."

"Let's go, Amanda, or we'll be late. Please excuse us."

But Amanda didn't budge. She smiled thinly at Morales.

"Sr. Morales, do you like seeing your name in print?"

"What do you mean, young lady?"

"I mean in the newspapers. In a week or so, you and your damn mill will make headlines from Arica to Punta Arenas. Your intentional poisoning of our rivers is nothing less than heinous, and, believe me, you're going to pay for it!"

"I don't know what you're talking about. My mill is clean. Our treated effluents have passed every environmental test."

"Oh yes. I too have tested your 'treated effluent,' and yes, it passed. However, I've also been testing your 'other' effluent for months now. There is enough proof in the university's science building to show that you are a lying, greedy monster! And, furthermore…"

Morales's face was turning red and ugly. Carlos pulled Amanda away.

"Come on, Amanda!"

Morales watched them get into Carlos's car and drive away. His appetite suddenly gone, he walked past the restaurant, continuing up to the shady central plaza where he sat on a bench. Pigeons landed at his feet. He kicked at them.

Those nosy kids were going to bring down everything he had worked for. Because of some damn birds! Screw those birds! And screw those kids! They don't know who they're messing with! They're just a couple of goddamn adolescent pimples that need to be popped. That's the right word, 'popped!' And it has to be soon, before whatever proof they have gets out. Who else knows about this? But Carlos is a reporter. Most likely he's held his cards close: he'll want all the credit.

For damn sure I can't dump anymore into the river, at least not right now. But that Chinese deadline's coming up, and I need their money! I can't afford to lower production for any length of time. That idiot contractor is leaving messages that he has to be paid or he'll take his crews off the job in Viña. And I can't fudge the books anymore than I already have. And what did that girl say? That I'd make the headlines in a week or so. I don't need this!

Maybe I can scare them off. Have a little accident. Let them know it's because of their meddling, that things could happen to them unless they stop poking their noses into my business. Carlos looked protective of that girl; he wouldn't want anything to happen to her. So, if I scared them enough...No, that won't work, that girl's manic! She'd push Carlos to write his articles regardless. They have to be silenced for good. But it'd have to look innocent, look like an accident. Get them somehow out on the river at night as his guests in the speedboat, give them some alcohol, and... But I'd never get them in the boat. They'd suspect something for sure. And I can't be connected to them in any way—too dangerous.

But they have to be eliminated. Maybe hire a pro. There are the guys in Santiago who'd do it. But that would take time and money. I don't have either right now. But I can't let this swan thing get in the papers: the value of the stock would crash and then I'd really be in trouble. That would cost me a lot more than hiring some thugs. But I couldn't trust those guys. Hiring them would give them leverage. I'd be compromised in the future for sure; have that hanging over my head. No, that's too risky. Not enough time anyway.

What about Jorge? He'll do anything I say; the idiot worships the ground I walk on. He wouldn't blink an eye to do those two. Violence is one thing that moron enjoys. And he'd never, ever say anything because he knows he'd lose his job. He loves his truck, pistol, TV, and whores too much. Maybe Jorge could fix Carlos's car for a little 'accident.' He could follow them until he had an opportunity to run them off the road or something. Yeah, that might work. Force them off the road into the river or bay somewhere. Off a mountain, or into a creek. Tamper with their brakes. Slice a tire and run them down when they changed it. Loosen up the lug nuts on their front wheels. Plenty of options.

He pulled out his cellphone, punching in Jorge's number.

"Jorge. It's me. I want you to meet me at the mill in a half an hour. I've got a job for my special secret agent. It's extremely important for the safety of the mill. I'll explain everything when I see you…Right—those two spies the other night. I've just learned they're trying to bring down our whole operation. I'm not sure, but I think they're Russian…Yeah. Oh, and Jorge, if you do a good job, I promise you a raise and I'll buy you a woman at Nena's every day for a month…Yeah, you got my word on it. Now, meet me at the gate in thirty minutes."

Chapter Twenty-One

The lead rider carried the Chilean flag into the ring. Pairs of *huasos* in matching *chamantos* followed.

"It's been over thirty years since I've been to a rodeo, Carlos. I've forgotten the name of the padded area below us," Tomás said.

"*La quincha.*"

Lilia was excited. It was her first rodeo.

"There's one over on the other side, too," she said. "What are they for?"

Carlos and Amanda smiled at Lilia. They couldn't believe she had never been to a rodeo.

"It's where they turn the steers," Carlos said. "It's all about controlling the animals, Lilia. Two *huasos* work in tandem, driving a steer through that gate from the *pinadeiro* over there into this area which is called the *media luna* for its half moon shape. One rider drives the steer while the other gallops sideways keeping it close to the walls until they force it into this *quincha*. The riders switch positions and then drive the steer to the other *quincha* where they turn him around again. Points are given or deducted depending on how well they do it. It's not easy, believe me. I know because father and I used to compete."

Amanda was surprised.

"Really? How old were you?"

"Young, really young. I competed at this level when I was eleven. They made me wear a safety helmet under my hat." Carlos laughed. "I was so embarrassed, but I had to wear it. I was at least ten or fifteen years younger than everyone else."

"You must have been very good if they allowed you to compete at that age. How long did you do it?"

"Until I was fourteen. We stopped because father refused to buy a better *corralero*. A good one costs many thousands of dollars."

"Is that what they call the horses?" Lilia asked.

Carlos nodded.

"It's a special breed trained to gallop sideways. The riders are all skilled, but the better the horse, the better you do. You'll see soon enough."

"Juan says Amanda would have been good too, if women were allowed to compete," Tomás said. "He told me that she can make a horse do what she wants by just talking to it."

"Papá has been known to exaggerate, Tomás."

"We should try it sometime, Amanda. You and I," Carlos said. "We could go out to my parents' farm. It'd be fun."

"I'd like that, Carlos," she said, blushing.

Blushing and smiling, and especially because she had her hair in that long thick braid today, Amanda looked so much like María Elena. Sometimes she's the spitting image, Tomás thought. He stood up.

"How about I get some *empanadas* and sweet cider? But not too many; we have to save room for the *asado* in Niebla after the rodeo."

Tomás went down to the concession area after they had agreed on two *empanadas* each. He watched the women roll out the dough with empty wine bottles, and shape the little tarts, filled with a mix of meat, onions, raisins, and pieces of hard-boiled eggs, before dropping them into a large pan of sizzling oil. It was slow. How many times had he seen María Elena rolling out the dough like this at soccer tournaments and horse races? When he returned to his seat, Lilia smiled radiantly at him.

"Oh, Tomás! This is so exciting. Thank you for bringing me here."

She turned back to watch as two riders slammed a steer into the *quincha* below them. The crowd, including Lilia, cheered. Tom divvied up the *empanadas* and sweet cider. They watched all afternoon, applauding good turns, groaning when the steer missed the *quincha*, and laughing when a steer lay down next to the wall refusing to move despite furious coaxing from the riders. Although late in the afternoon, the sun was still high when they left the rodeo. As they walked towards Carlos's car, Amanda suddenly grabbed his arm.

"Look! Over there! Isn't that the watchman leaning against that little blue pickup?"

"Yeah, that's him alright."

Lilia and Tomás looked over. Jorge was smoking a cigarette, looking towards Carlos's car. Lilia uttered a little cry and looked like she was about to faint. When Tomás quickly reached for her, she buried her head into his chest. She was trembling.

"Lilia, what's wrong!"

"It's Jorge…It's him!"

Tomás looked over, but didn't recognize the man with the eye patch.

"Are you sure?"

She nodded into his chest. A muffled "I'm sure" was her answer.

Carlos and Amanda looked at each other before Amanda said, "He's 'that' Jorge!" They all knew about the rape.

"C'mon, let's get out of here," Tomás said.

He walked Lilia to the car. She didn't look towards Jorge.

As they sped away, Amanda said, "Lilia, he's the watchman for Morales's pulp mill."

"Small world," she answered in a little voice.

"I can't believe you recognized him," Tomás said. "I used to play soccer with Jorge, but I didn't have a clue."

"I've seen his face in my mind most everyday of my life. I don't care how many years have passed, I'll always remember that face."

They were silent until Carlos turned onto the island of Teja. As they drove by the university, he said, "They've torn up the road to Niebla along the river, so I thought we'd take the back route. It may be slower going over the mountain, but it's beautiful looking out at the Pacific. And I don't think it will take that much longer today. With the weekend traffic all going on the other road, it will be a mess. But this way is steep and curvy, so everybody buckle up."

"Is there a trick to fastening this seatbelt?" Tomás asked.

"Oh, right; sorry. That one's jammed; been meaning to get it fixed."

The Pacific Ocean came into view.

"Look at how it sparkles," Lilia said. "It's so blue and so big."

They began to climb; it didn't take long before the ocean lay far below. There was no traffic, and they took their time, enjoying the scenery.

"Look," Amanda said, "There's a turn-out. Let's stop for a bit."

Carlos pulled over.

"Get my binoculars out of the glove box, please, Amanda."

"Carlos, you have a gun in here!"

"If you went to some of the places I do for my stories, you'd have a pistol, too. But, it's all right. I'm licensed and everything."

He went to the trunk to get his camera while the rest of them piled out. The view was terrific. There was a tanker way out, and a few fishing boats closer in. Two frigate birds were soaring up above. Carlos began snapping pictures of the birds. Tomás looked at his watch.

"We better get a move on; I've reserved a table at one of the little restaurants."

Carlos put his camera in the glove box with the binoculars, and they started off. When they crested the mountain, the little beach town of Niebla lay far below them.

"I bet we could coast all the way there," Tomás said.

"No doubt, but I'm not that brave," Carlos answered.

"Without a seatbelt, I think I'll second that motion. But I'll tell you what, this view is absolutely spectacular!"

"And it should be just as pretty on the way back," Carlos said. "The moon will be almost full tonight, so it'll be up high and bright by the time we leave."

"Just make sure you don't drink too much wine, Carlos; we don't need to take any shortcuts down the mountain. As for me, I'm not driving. I'm celebrating! It's been a long time since I've been on a date with a pretty woman."

"Oh, Tomás," Lilia said smiling and shaking her head.

They parked under a lamppost on the edge of a field crowded with cars in front of El Encuentro Costumbrista. Following a stream of people, they entered the walled compound where, inside, the area was ringed by concession stalls. At the far end was a stage, and to their immediate left, by the entry door, was a little bar serving Kuntsman draft beer.

"Best beer in Chile," Carlos said. "How about a glass before dinner?"

The two women and Tomás sat down at a little table while Carlos fetched the beer, soon returning with two large mugs in each hand. "Cheers," he said, handing them out.

As he drank the amber bock, Tomás looked around. Vendors were selling meat and fish *empanadas,* skewers of lamb, toasted *avellanas,* souvenirs, even *huaso* broad brimmed hats, colorful ponchos, and shiny spurs. On the stage the men were dressed as *huasos,* and the women wore white blouses and long skirts. He checked his watch.

"Come on everybody; as we say in the States, 'Bottoms up.'"

They entered a little restaurant with a simple dining area facing the stage. Tomás knew Irene, the owner, and she had agreed to reserve them the best table. Lilia's eyes sparkled. "Tomás, this is perfect!" she said. Carlos gave Tomás the thumbs-up sign. After ordering, they turned to watch the performers. The band had two guitars, an accordion, two tambourines, and a slatted wooden box called a *tormento* played like a bongo drum. They listened to ballads and watched couples dance the *cueca.* Irene poured them red wine to go with the lamb roasted on a spit, potatoes baked in coals, a salad of sliced tomatoes and onion, and very soft, fresh bread. After dinner they sat in plastic chairs directly in front of the open-air stage.

"Tomás," Lilia asked, "would you mind going out to the car and getting my sweater?"

"Sure thing."

Carlos tossed him the keys. It was dark now, but the car was easy to spot because of the lamppost. He stopped in his tracks. Jorge was standing next to the car wiping his hands on the back of his pants. He leaned over to pick up a little bundle on the ground before quickly walking off. Tomás hurried over to the car. Nothing looked amiss. The windows weren't broken, and the doors were still locked. He checked the glove compartment. Everything was still there. Strange. He must tell Carlos. He quickly headed back with the sweater.

As Tomás handed Lilia her sweater, she pointed up to the stage. The audience had been invited to dance a *cueca*. Carlos, twirling a white handkerchief above his head, was circling Amanda who was holding a corner of her skirt and coquettishly sashaying in front of him. Tomás immediately recalled the road benefit fiesta he and María Elena had organized so long ago in Cufeo. At the time, he was competing with Kurt for María Elena. She had danced with Kurt just like this, and he had become desperately jealous. It was then he had realized how much he loved her.

"Why are you smiling, Tomás?"

"Oh, I was remembering watching Carlos's father dance the *cueca* in Cufeo thirty-plus years ago. Carlos looks just like him."

Carlos and Amanda joined them after the dance. They listened to a few more ballads and ribald *campo* jokes before Tomás said he was too old to party all night. As they went out to the car, Tomás suddenly remembered seeing Jorge. He had forgotten to tell Carlos; but he didn't want to upset Lilia. He didn't say a thing.

Chapter Twenty-Two

Jorge watched them get into the car and head up the mountain. Good, they're going back the same way. That's that then. He drove his truck over to the parking area's exit. As he waited for a couple of cars to go by, he thought, what a waste, such a waste of sweet young flesh! That one girl's really something, and if she's the same one in that rubber suit like Don Ivan says, then, man, I'd like to get hold of her! I'd rip that rubber suit off in a second and… honking roused him from his reverie. Some idiot behind him. "Screw you!" he yelled out the window before pulling out onto the torn-up section of the Valdivia road. There wasn't much traffic, but still it was only one lane. No hurry, though, I've got plenty of time. And I don't want to go back over that mountain; I don't want to be anywhere near that mountain now.

He smiled. Pretty clever, that's what I am. Of course, that's to be expected, being a secret agent. Those idiots didn't even know I was behind them. Even when they stopped to take pictures, they didn't see me. Just like the private detectives on TV; and I fixed them good. Don Ivan will be pleased.

That other woman was pretty too, but a lot older. I know I've seen her somewhere, but I can't remember where. Maybe while cleaning the streets. He tapped his shirt pocket to make sure he still had the little drawing Don Ivan had given him when they rode over to the university. It was the first time he had ridden in the Mercedes, and he couldn't keep his hands off the wooden dash and soft leather seats. I wonder if Don Ivan would ever let me take it out? Maybe if everything goes right; he said it was so important. And he said a girl at Nena's every night for a month! Jorge laughed and pounded the steering wheel. He'd start off with that one with the big *tetas*! What was her name? Julia, that's it. Oh, was he going to have fun with her! But she bawled her head off last time, said he was too rough. Went to Nena and complained. Said she'd never do him again. Just you wait, bitch! No way Nena'd refuse to give her to me with Don Ivan paying the bill. He passed the Kuntsman Brewery, and the Puente Cruces came into sight. He drove up over the humped bridge onto the island of Teja, and headed towards the university. It was time for special mission number two.

He drove around the campus a couple of times. There was the building. No lights on, and nobody around. Looking at his watch, he saw that he had made pretty good time considering it was single lane most of the way. Like Don Ivan said to, he parked in the arboretum. He unloaded the cans from the back of the truck, and checked again for the sketch in his pocket. Finally, he picked up the cans and walked through the trees towards the building. This was so exciting: he was a secret agent on a special mission!

* * *

The moon was up high, and the rippled ocean lay below in shimmering silver. They picked up speed after cresting the mountain. When Carlos applied the brakes, they felt a little spongy. The road became steep. Carlos didn't like the way the brakes felt: they weren't right. As he tried to slow down for a sharp curve, his foot sunk slowly all the way to the floorboards.

"What the...?" he muttered, his stomach instantly queasy.

"What?" Amanda asked.

"Something's wrong with the brakes!"

Carlos pumped them again. His foot went to the floor with no resistance. He immediately yanked on the emergency brake, but no resistance there either.

"The emergency brake too!" The others stared in horror as he frantically downshifted and the engine screamed, but it didn't slow their momentum much. He turned the key so the engine died, but not so far that the steering wheel would lock up. They started barreling down the mountain.

"Oh no, that must have been what Jorge was doing!" exclaimed Tomás.

"What! What do you mean!" asked Amanda loudly as she grabbed on to the armrest, watching Carlos negotiate a sharp curve. He was leaning into it as if to coax the vehicle around.

"When I went out to get Lilia's sweater, I saw him next to the car. He was holding a bundle."

"With a cable cutter or hacksaw in it, I'll bet. Son-of-a-bitch must have cut the brake line and the emergency cable," Carlos said through clenched teeth. The car kept picking up speed. His knuckles showed white on the steering wheel.

"Morales," Amanda hissed. "He put Jorge up to it. He wants us out of the way."

"We'll see about that," Carlos said in a steely voice. He looked to the right. Stone wall cut into the mountain. To the left was sheer cliff down to the Pacific. "But first, ladies, better hang on. Looks like we're going for a ride."

With a death grip on the wheel, he willed the car around the hairpin corners. At first there was only the squeal of tires. But then he pulled too far to the right and skidded on some mountain rubble. The car fishtailed badly, and at one point they were going sideways down the road. Lilia was on the ocean side and looked down as they skirted the edge. She screamed and grabbed Tomás's leg.

"Look at me, Lilia!" Tomás demanded. "At me! Don't take your eyes off mine!" He covered her hands with his.

Beads of sweat were on Carlos's brow. He was concentrating fiercely, trying not to panic as he held the car through the curves. Amanda was rock-solid.

"You're doing great, Carlos, great! The next one looks even easier. You're my hero, *mi amor*. Good job!"

Tomás watched Lilia's lips move. He couldn't hear her, but didn't need to. Her lips were saying, "The Lord is my shepherd..."

They slammed into the side of the mountain, and were bounced back out onto the road. Lilia dug her fingers into Tomás's thigh. This was what it had been like for María Elena, he thought. He tried not to show his fear for Lilia's sake, but his stomach was in his throat. He was terrified.

The good thing was that there was no traffic to crash into, Amanda thought. But that also meant there was no one to rear-end which would have stopped them. She looked at Carlos. His eyes were narrowed and focused. She was proud of him. He was one cool *hombre*!

Somehow Carlos kept the car on the road. He hugged the inside as much as possible, and several times they scraped the mountain with strident metallic shrieks. But he didn't lose control as they continued to hurl down the mountain. They slammed into the mountain again, and the tip of a large bolder shattered Tomás's window. He was showered with glass, and felt like his face had been stung by a thousand bees. Lilia screamed again.

"You two okay back there!" Carlos yelled, not taking his eyes off the road.

Tomás knew his face was bleeding and he could not see out of one eye, but shouted back, "Fine, Carlos. You're doing great, my man!"

The road straightened out, and they were past the worst sections. They were still going downhill, but the road was nowhere near as steep. My God, Carlos thought, we might make it! A quarter mile ahead there was one last curve—a nasty one. But if they could get around that, they might even live through this.

"Just one more, guys! One more corner, then we'll be home free. But hang on, it looks like a son-of-a-bitch!"

Entering the curve, the car started to skid immediately. The side of the mountain was not as abrupt, and the shoulder was wider, angling upward to the rocky wall. They slid onto the shoulder and up against the wall with the car suddenly tipped at a bad angle. They were headed straight towards a larger boulder, directly in front of Amanda. Carlos yanked on the steering wheel hard, managing to turn the car a little, but the passenger side slammed into the huge rock. The front tire blew, and Amanda's window exploded. She shrieked in pain. The rear passenger door was torn off: Tomás could have reached out and touched the mountain as the car scraped along it. They were abruptly slowing down, but when the front passenger wheel bounced over another large rock, it was enough to violently flip the car. Tomás was flung out. His momentum skidded him across the road and he slammed into a boulder that saved him from going over the edge. In a shower of sparks, the car continued to slide down the road on its roof for another hundred and fifty feet before it finally stopped.

Chapter Twenty-Three

The first thing he did when the car skidded to a stop was to look over at Amanda. Her head was slumped, eyes closed. Was she unconscious or dead! He could see her chest expand and contract. Thank God! But her face! She was sliced open from above her right eye, diagonally all the way to the edge of her neck. Her cheek was like a filet hanging down. He could see part of her cheekbone through the blood that was gushing out. She had other cuts, but they didn't look that bad. Got to stop that bleeding! He couldn't see Lilia or Tomás, but at least Lilia was conscious. He could hear her sobbing behind him.

Out of here! Got to get everyone out of here. At least the motor's off. I don't think this thing's going to catch fire, but we got to get away from it. He looked over at Amanda again as he reached for his seat belt. I got to stop that bleeding! He started to unbuckle the belt when a sharp pain exploded in his shoulder. It hurt like hell. Zero strength. Must have torn something bad, he thought. He braced himself as best he could, but it was still a clumsy landing, and an awkward exit from the vehicle. Every muscle ached as he hurried around to Amanda's door. He saw that the rear passenger door had been ripped off. Tomás! Where was Tomás! He looked back up the road. He saw him lying at a grotesque angle up against a big rock. Oh my God! He forced himself to turn back to Amanda and wedged himself in the car so he could ease her fall from the seat. He was showered with her blood. There, he had her. Somehow, with the bad shoulder shrieking with pain, he managed to carry her away from the car. He carefully laid her down. He didn't want to leave her, but he had to go back for Lilia.

Lilia was still sobbing when he returned. He could see that she had several cuts from the shards of glass. When he crawled in to help her, she shrieked, "Tomás! Where is Tomás!"

"Easy, Lilia. It's okay. We'll help him as soon as we get you out of here. Can you move everything?"

She nodded. He helped her out of the car and took her over to Amanda. She kept looking back up the road. When she saw Tomás, she tried to break away from Carlos. But he held her firmly.

"Lilia, let me go to him first. You've got to help Amanda. We've got to stop her bleeding."

What to do? I don't know a goddamn thing about emergency medical stuff. I'm absolutely useless! I swear by all I hold sacred that I will take a course when this is all over. He took off his shirt and ripped a big square out of it. Amanda started to cough. Carlos looked down. She was choking on her blood. He quickly bent down and turned her head so the blood would fall away from her. He gently pressed the thick flap of skin that was her cheek back into place, and held it there firmly with the folded piece of shirt.

"Lilia, hold her head like this. And apply pressure to the cloth."

He wondered if Lilia could do it. She was in shock. And Amanda's face looked grotesque. But Lilia did as she was told. Tough *campesina*, he thought.

Carlos left them and ran up the road. It was easy to see their exact route by the scrape marks etched into the macadam. Tomás wasn't moving, and Carlos didn't like the angle of his body. He feared the worst. Full of dread, he kneeled by him. His face had been seriously cut by glass and was bleeding profusely. He couldn't even see one of his eyes because there was so much blood. But his body! The angle! He looked like he had been broken in half.

Carlos felt sick to his stomach, but made himself feel for a pulse. Nothing. No, wait a minute! Calm down, calm down, goddamn it! There was something. A flutter. Thank God, he's alive—barely. Now what? He didn't dare move him. He absolutely did not know what to do. He took his undershirt off, dabbed at the wounds, and gently put it under Tomás's head.

He stood up and looked out across the ocean. Only a little while ago, they had been laughing at dinner. Before that, eating *empanadas* at the rodeo. And now this? Why? I'll tell you why. Because you never fixed that damn seat belt! If he had had his seat belt on, he'd still be in the car. He began to cry.

After a few moments he wiped his eyes impatiently. Crying won't help anything. C'mon Carlos, get it together. You've got to be strong. He started back to Lilia, then stopped dead in his tracks. What! Can't you think straight? He quickly reached into his pocket and flipped open his cellphone. Four bars! He called for help and talked to the dispatcher. He told them the what and where. They said they'd be there as soon as they could.

Lilia looked up. Carlos took her place. With Amanda's head cradled in his lap, he said, "He's alive, Lilia, but barely. I don't dare move him. I don't know what's broken and what's not."

Lilia rushed up to Tomás and, kneeling at his side, saw how he was wrapped around the big rock. Her heart went out to him as she stroked his head. At least he was unconscious, hopefully not feeling any pain. It must have hurt terribly. Did he see the rock before he hit it? It must have been awful!

Why, Lord, why? Why did you do this? Tomás is such a good person. What did he do to deserve this? What did I do? And why did you put Jorge on this earth! That devil! That fiend! Twice now he has ruined my life! His face filled her mind. She closed her eyes tight, trying to shut him out. But she couldn't: she was back where she never wanted to go…

She was twelve years old when her mother had sent her to get the sheep that had crossed over to Jorge's grandparents' land. He had seen her coming and was sitting on a stump near where he had been splitting firewood. He was holding a brown paper bag on his lap.

"Hey Lilia, come on over and see what I have."

"I can't, Jorge. I have to get the sheep. I don't think your grandparents will be happy if they get into the garden."

"Five minutes won't make any difference, Lilia. And if you like, I might even give him to you."

Lilia stopped immediately.

"Give me what? What do you have in the bag?"

"Something very cute. Something I know you will like because you like birds so much."

"Well, tell me what it is."

"A baby *chucho*. He's tiny and just barely has feathers. But he's as cute as can be. Come on over and put your hand in the bag, and you can take him out and hold him. But be careful, he's very little."

Lilia walked quickly up to Jorge. She was excited. He had a big grin on his face.

"Watch it now. You don't want to hurt him or let him get away."

She very carefully reached in the bag. Jorge laughed. He grabbed hard on to one of her arms just as she realized what she was touching. There was a hole in the bottom of the bag, and Jorge's thick erection was sticking up. Lilia tried to draw her hand back and pull away, but he held her tight. She screamed at him to let her go. He slapped her hard. Lilia's head snapped sideways and he quickly put his hand over her mouth.

"Quiet, girl! You be quiet and I won't hurt you. We'll just have a little fun and only the two of us will know." He removed his hand, and Lilia tried to push him away. She started to scream again, and this time he hit her in the jaw. She stopped immediately. It felt like she had been kicked by a horse. She was woozy, and didn't make a sound.

"That's better, Lilia. Now we can enjoy ourselves." He smiled and kissed her jaw where he had hit her. "I didn't want to hurt you, but you made me." He kissed her jaw again. "Here, give me your hand." He took it and forced her fingers around his erection. "Move your hand up and down it like this…That's it. Just like that." He still held on to her other arm. He was very strong and the circulation was being cut off. With his free hand he started feeling her young breasts. He put his hand down the front of her dress and caressed her. "Now doesn't that feel good?" Tears started running down Lilia's cheeks as his hands groped her body.

He picked her up and carried her towards a large log. "Now we are going to have the most fun, my little lover." He bent her over the log and pulled her underwear down. He penetrated her from behind. He was so big and she was small. He ripped her and she screamed. He covered her mouth and started his rhythm. Lilia thought she was going to pass out from the pain. Jorge moved faster and faster, and then it was over.

He rolled over, not even bothering to cover up. He was breathing hard, totally satiated. Lilia slowly pulled up her underpants. She was bleeding, and the underpants soon stained. Jorge watched her as she walked painfully away.

"Remember, Lilia. This is our little secret. I promise I will tell no one. And you better not tell. If you do, then I might have to hurt you real bad. Now you don't want that to happen, do you?"

Lilia didn't say anything. Her whole body screamed pain. She hurt and bled. She came to the stream on her family's property. She walked into the middle and sat down. She watched the rivulet of blood as it flowed away. She sat in the stream a long time. It was there Jaime found her. She was catatonic.

Chapter Twenty-Four

Carlos sat in the chair by Amanda's bed. His body felt like he had gone twelve rounds, and his left arm was in a sling: an MRI had revealed a major tear in his rotator cuff. Amanda's head and face were swathed in bandages. She had received over a hundred stitches in the big gash, and numerous others where the shards of glass had been picked out of her head, chest, and arm. Because of her concussion, the lights were off and the shades lowered. But even in the dimness, he could see that she had two black eyes.

The ambulance driver had apologized for taking so long to get to them. He said that there was a terrible traffic jam on the bridge going over to the island of Teja due to a fire at the university. The fire was still raging when they returned to Valdivia. With the *carabineros* holding traffic for them, the ambulance sped by the university. Carlos saw the science building in flames.

Carlos dosed off and on while Amanda slept. He was the only one allowed in her room because he had told the doctors that he was her fiancé and would not leave her. The doctors came in and out, closely monitoring her because of the concussion.

Carlos opened his eyes to see Amanda looking at him.

"How do you feel?" he asked her.

"Like a mule kicked me in the head. How bad is it?"

"The doctors say it's a severe concussion, but you'll be just as ornery as ever in a couple of days."

He came over to the side of the bed. She ran a hand over her swathed face.

"What about this?"

What should he tell her? That half her face had been laid open? That she might be horrifically scarred for life?

"You were pretty badly cut when that window shattered, and the doctors may have set a record with all the stitches. But they say it will heal just fine."

"What about scars?"

He couldn't lie to her.

"I don't know, Amanda. Honestly. You'll have to ask a plastic surgeon about that."

He didn't tell her that he had called his father. He had asked him to find out who the best plastic surgeon in the country was, and to get him.

Tears welled in her eyes. He reached for her hand.

"I love you, Amanda. I want you to know that. No matter what, I love you, and that won't change."

He squeezed her hand. The tears were blocked by the bandages; he gently wiped her eyes with a tissue.

"Don't worry about it, please. You need to rest, *mi amor*."

"How are Lilia and Tomás?"

Carlos sighed as he walked over to throw the tissue in the wastebasket.

"Other than for some minor cuts, Lilia's fine. She was released hours ago, but she's stayed here to be with Tomás. He's been very seriously hurt. He is in intensive care and may not make it."

He sat down heavily.

"He's in a coma and will probably lose his left eye. And...the doctors think he is paralyzed from the waist down."

"Oh, God," she said softly. "Oh, Carlos."

"All we can do is wait and see if he even comes out of it. But you have to rest, *querida*. C'mon now, close your eyes, Amanda." She did as he said. He dabbed at her eyes again before he sat down. He was exhausted.

Tomás was hooked to several complicated looking machines. Only a small section of his face was not wrapped in bandages and gauze. Please Lord, let him live. He is too good a person to die so young, Lilia thought. Please let him heal. At least he doesn't feel anything. I wonder what it's like to be in a coma. They said I should talk to him, that he might be able to hear me—that it might give him strength to try harder to come back. What should I say? Oh, that monster, Jorge! He's the one who deserves to die. Oh, my Tomás. And poor Amanda! She was so beautiful. I've got to notify Pablo and Miriam, get word out to Juan and Flor. They'll want to come in right away. Carlos has already spoken with his father, so I don't have to do that. She stood up and gently patted Tomás's hand.

"Tomás, I'm going to leave for a little bit. There are some things I have to do. But when you wake up, I'll be here waiting for you. I love you. You are the best thing that has ever happened to me."

She lightly squeezed his hand. Was that a squeeze back? She quickly looked at his eye, but no, it was still closed. She held on to his hand for a few minutes. No response. She gently lay his hand back down on the bed and leaned forward to kiss his bandaged brow.

The nurse came in to tell Carlos that two *carabineros* wanted to talk to him. He glanced at Amanda before leaving the room and taking the elevator down to the lobby where two policemen were seated in front of a large window. It was sunny outside.

"Sr. Carlos Mueller?" one of them asked as they stood.

"Yes."

"We wonder if you can tell us about the accident? How did you lose control of your car?"

"It was no accident, officers."

"What do you mean?"

"I believe a man named Jorge, a worker at Ivan Morales's pulp mill outside of town, cut our brake lines and emergency brake cable. It was intentional. It was attempted murder."

The two *carabineros* looked at him in astonishment.

"Please sit back down, gentlemen. This may take awhile to explain."

Chapter Twenty-Five

"Right. Don't worry." He looked over to Amanda as he folded up the cellphone. She looked a lot better today. The swelling was down, and the color around her eyes was fading from black to an assortment of pastels.

"That was Lilia. She has to go to the house for awhile to get some things. I'm going down to be with Tomás. She wants someone there if he wakes up."

"Alright. Let me know right away if there's any change."

Carlos went down to the second floor, nodding to the nurse as he entered Tomás's room. Three days Tomás had been out. The doctors said he could come to at any time…or not. Poor Lilia had been by his bed round the clock. He sat down in her chair, close to Tomás's good eye. About time she took a break, he thought as he opened up a photography magazine. After awhile, he dozed. He had no idea what time it was when the nurse gently shook him awake. He immediately looked over at Tomás, but, nope, still out of it. He looked questioningly up at the nurse.

"There is a *carabinero* and a detective in the lobby who would like to speak to you."

Again? They had his story. What else did they want? He thanked her, taking the stairs down this time. The uniformed policeman was one of the two who had questioned him earlier. The other, a plainclothesman, held a clipboard. As he walked up to the men, Carlos asked, "Do you have Jorge behind bars yet?"

The plainclothesman stuck out his hand.

"I am Detective Gonzales, Sr. Mueller, with the Ministerio Público. I have been assigned to look into your accusations. Has there been any change with the North American?"

"No."

"Too bad. Then it's only your supposition without proof. We did check out what was left of your car, and the brake lines were indeed cut. We have also questioned the mill worker. He has, of course, denied everything. However, he has no alibi or witnesses to prove he was not in Niebla. Frankly, I smell a rat; but we need someone to positively put him in Niebla…" his voice trailed off. "For us to proceed any further, we need you to fill out a formal criminal complaint: I have the paperwork with me."

He passed the clipboard and a pen to Carlos who quickly completed and signed the form. He handed it back to Gonzales who said, "After presenting this to the public prosecutor, there will be a complaint hearing. Then I will be able to bring Sr. Jorge down to the station for a team of us to question him. I have a feeling that might prove very interesting: he has already contradicted himself several times. I don't think it will be too difficult to get to the truth.

"I have also learned that this man has some history with the police. Among other things, he raped a little girl but was never prosecuted because her family didn't want the crime public. I believe that girl was one of your passengers the night of the crash."

Carlos nodded. Gonzales picked his hat up off the couch.

"That is a very strange coincidence…I will be back in touch, Sr. Mueller, in a day or so."

Gonzales had gone only a few steps before he turned back to Carlos.

"I almost forgot. You must come down to the station to pick up the contents from the glove compartment of your car. We, of course, checked to see if you are licensed to have a firearm. The pistol was undamaged, but I'm afraid I can't say that about the camera and binoculars."

* * *

Morales glanced at his watch before looking out the motel room window. Nothing happening. The office light was on, but there was no one out in the parking lot. The windows of the other rooms were either dark, or had TV light dancing on the thin curtains. The stockholders' meeting and dinner had gone well. Those who had stayed over were full of wine, probably asleep by now; but still, he'd wait a little longer.

That bumbling Jorge. What a mess! Serves me right for trusting that idiot to get rid of those two meddlers. And bad luck there had been passengers. Jorge should have waited until they were alone. And that *gringo's* still in a coma. If he dies, there'll be murder charges, or at least manslaughter. And the police have already been at the mill asking Jorge questions. How the hell did they know to suspect him? And who knows when they'll return with more questions; just a matter of time. And any detective worth his salt could get the real story out of him—if they ever put him on the stand, my goose will be cooked for sure. So far no questions about the fire, though.

Morales nervously paced around, hands behind his back. He looked at his watch again before pulling out his phone.

"Jorge, Don Ivan here. *Sí*, tonight. I'll meet you at the gate in about two hours. Listen, I'm bringing a bottle of *aguardiente* for our little meeting….Yeah, I know I don't usually allow alcohol at the mill, but this is a special meeting with my special agent. And, we'll talk in your apartment…What's that?…Because I'm not sure if those spies have bugged my office, Jorge. We've got to make sure absolutely no one knows what we're going to do. So, I'll see you soon…and Jorge, have the police come back, by any chance? No? That's good, that's very good. Don't forget now—meet you at the gate at about 1:30. Right…"

Morales flipped his phone shut. He put on a dark jacket and hat, and looked out the window again. His Mercedes was parked right in front. He went into the bathroom where he opened the window and squeezed through. He shut the window, wedging a small wad of folded paper between the window and sill. He began walking quickly down the dark alley towards a small rental car agency a few blocks away.

There was a single light on in the office. As he approached, a nervous, wiry young man opened the door for him. Must have been watching for me, Morales thought. After looking up and down the street, the young man shut the door. Morales was already laying bills on the counter. The young man eagerly counted them.

"Remember now, this is a cash deal, off the record."

"*Sí*, Señor. That is not a problem. No one needs to know, especially not my boss. But, don't worry, I have done this many times before." After putting the money in his billfold, he handed Morales a set of keys.

"Sr. Gómez, it has been a pleasure, and I hope your little rendezvous with the *señorita* goes well. But don't forget, be back here no later than five a.m. My boss gets here around eight, and I want that engine cold. If I'm not up front here, just knock on the rear window." He pointed toward a small room in the back. "I'll be sleeping there." Morales nodded, and left the office.

Once he left Temuco, there was hardly any traffic; he passed maybe a half dozen cars before entering Valdivia.

There would be even less traffic on the return. He crossed the river, turned left, and took the river road out to the mill. It was 1:35 when Jorge pulled the gate open for him. Morales drove over to Jorge's apartment, stepping out of the car with a bottle in each hand.

"Where's the Mercedes, Don Ivan?" Jorge asked as he unlocked his apartment door.

"It wasn't running right. It's in the garage."

"I could have looked at it."

Morales ignored that, instead saying, "You like your *aguardiente* with cola, if I remember correctly, Jorge."

"*Sí*, Don Ivan; but let me do that, sir."

"No, Jorge, you're my special agent. The least I can do is make you a couple of good strong drinks. Just sit in your favorite chair and relax."

Jorge sat down in the easy chair in front of the TV while Morales went to the refrigerator. There were four partially frozen ice trays. Idiot didn't know enough to turn the freezer up. He filled the glass with crumbly thin ice, a very generous dollop of *aguardiente,* and topped it off with a little cola. He looked over at Jorge who had his back to him. Morales tapped in some Ambien from a vial. He handed Jorge his drink before pouring one for himself.

"Cheers, Jorge."

Jorge's black eyepatch raised up a little as he grinned.

"Cheers, Don Ivan."

Jorge took a large swig. He smacked his lips.

"That's real good, Don Ivan, real good. Nice and strong, the way I like it."

He took another swig.

"So, the police haven't come back again?"

"No, sir. And I told them nothing."

"Well, we do have a bit of a mess now."

"I'm really sorry that they made it down that mountain. That driver must have been pretty damn good, or real lucky, that's all I can say."

Morales sipped his *aguardiente*. It was harsh. Give him a single malt any day.

"You're right there. I saw the car in front of the *carabinero* station: there wasn't much left of it. But Jorge, we've got to make a new plan. That's why we're having this meeting. And could be we've got four persons to worry about now, not just two."

"Does that mean I have to wait until they're all dead before I can go to Nena's like you said?"

"No, Jorge. You can start tomorrow night. You did your job, they were just lucky, like you say… Drink up now. I'll make you another."

After his third drink, Jorge was slurring. Between the alcohol and sleeping powder, he could hardly keep his eyes open. Finally, on his fourth, his head fell forward to his chest, and he started to snore. Morales looked at his watch. Took longer than I thought, but still plenty of time. He pulled on thin black gloves and, with a kerchief, wiped his glass clean. He also wiped down the two bottles. He put Jorge's fingers around the bottles in several places before returning them to the counter. He looked around the apartment. He didn't think he had touched anything else as he made sure he put everything back in its place. He noticed the girlie calendars on the wall. Damn sex fiend, he thought as he walked back to Jorge.

He removed Jorge's pistol from his belt. It was oily and shiny. Have to admit he takes good care of it, Morales thought while making sure the gun was loaded. He wrapped Jorge's fingers around the butt of the pistol, positioning the hand so it would receive powder burns. Raising Jorge's head up by the hair, he put the barrel into Jorge's gaping mouth, and squeezed the trigger. The noise was deafening as blood, bone, and brain splattered on the far wall. The lights went out immediately. Bullet must have hit a wire in the wall and tripped the breaker, but there was enough mill light coming through the curtains to see okay. He let go of Jorge's hair, and the head flopped down. Morales retrieved his hat and coat from the little dining table, careful not to walk directly behind Jorge because, even in the dim light, he could see the floor was littered with bits and pieces of Jorge's head. Taking one last look around, he remembered that he had been the last one through the apartment door. He wiped the doorknob clean before leaving the apartment.

Chapter Twenty-Six

Everything so bright white. And silent. After that ride down the mountain, that was the best part—the silence. His face didn't sting anymore and he could see out of both eyes. He wondered where the others were. He turned, looking in all directions. Just white and bright. No, there was something way off. A speck in the distance. He wondered what it was. It got bigger. He couldn't tell if he was approaching it, or it was approaching him.

He watched with interest as the speck slowly took shape. It was a person. The person had his back to him. No, not 'his' back. It was 'her' back. And she wasn't moving. He was. He felt like he was slowly floating. She had long dark hair that cascaded below her waist, and a lovely figure. She looked familiar. A hairbrush was in her hand.

As he got closer, she slowly turned to face him. María Elena! She looked just the same—his dark-haired Venus. He was almost to her when she held up her hand, and he stopped. She smiled, shaking her index finger slowly back and forth. There was such peace in her face; she was so beautiful.

She drifted up to him, kissing his cheek. It was like being brushed with a feather. She smiled at him again. There was such love in the smile. Then she slowly turned and began to float away, becoming smaller and smaller until she disappeared.

Obviously, he was dreaming. But what was it all about? What did it mean? He had come to her, but then it was she who turned and left him? The light around him began to dim, like someone slowly turning down a rheostat. He felt something warm and moist, heard faint sobbing.

Tomás opened his eyes. Where the hell was he? A hospital room. Right…crashing into the mountain. He must be hurt. He looked at his right hand. A woman was holding it up to her cheek. Lilia. She was crying softly. Her eyes were closed. How sadness can distort features, he thought: it could make the most beautiful face ugly. He lightly caressed the cheek with his fingertips. Her eyes flew open.

"Tomás! Oh, Tomás!" she managed to say. "Oh, God, thank you, thank you!" She kissed his hand at least a dozen times before frantically reaching for the buzzer. Seconds later a nurse rushed in. Two doctors were on her heels. He looked back at Lilia. She was smiling at him through her tears.

* * *

Jorge's suicide had been a stunner, Carlos thought. But why? Why had he done it? Was it remorse for crippling Tomás? Something to do with Lilia? No, he didn't believe it. But he couldn't think about that right now; he had to get busy. Amanda had kicked him out of her room, telling him to begin writing. "It's past time to expose Morales for the monster he is!" she had said. He walked over to her notes on the large table in Pablo and Miriam's living room.

All the data was meticulously organized, more than enough proof to expose Morales. But he couldn't make it too scientific; everything needed to be written in layman's terms, which, coupled with pictures of dead swans and Jorge opening the valve at the mill, would be the one-two-three punch. Hopefully it would cause such public outrage that Morales would be crucified. He also hoped that the mill would be shut down, and Morales thrown in jail, though he knew that was a stretch. Chances were that Morales would only pay a few fines after tying everything up in the courts for months, if not years.

    He sat down at the computer. Easing his arm out of the sling, he lightly tapped some keys; didn't hurt too badly. The doctors said that surgery was on his horizon, but that could wait—he needed both hands now. He stared at the screen. So much had happened so quickly: the crash, Amanda's concussion, Jorge's suicide, Tomás waking up crippled for life. Where to start? He wanted to write a masterpiece. Who knows, maybe Amanda's right: this might be his chance for a Pulitzer. He put his fingers on the keys again, but they didn't move. He couldn't concentrate. Something was bothering him, pulling his mind elsewhere. It was Jorge's death. Suicide was just so implausible. But that's what it looked like…or was it made to look that way? Suicide was what the police were calling it; but it just didn't make sense. He didn't believe it. Why? It just didn't add up. An autopsy revealed he had taken a bunch of Ambien. Why would he take that if he were going to shoot himself? And where was the bottle of pills? The police had found nothing.

    If it wasn't suicide, then it was murder. And there was only one person he knew, other than maybe Lilia, who had a motive. Morales. Carlos would bet his life that Morales had ordered Jorge to cut the brake line, and Morales knew that Jorge wouldn't last long under questioning. And Jorge was the one who opened the valve, releasing the poison into the river. Other than Morales, maybe Jorge was the only person who knew about it; that is, if Jorge even realized what he was doing.

Once we exposed the pollution, Jorge would have been questioned about that, too. And that, for sure, would have made Morales more than nervous. As it is, Amanda and I were lucky we brought most of her notes here, and backed the others up on her flash drive. Plus, she still has that swan in the freezer. Otherwise, all the proof would have been burned in the science building. Pretty unusual, that fire: in the summertime, furnace off, no lights or electrical devices on. Damn strange. Could that have been Morales's doing, too? He knew Amanda's data was in the building; she had told him as much in front of La Bomba. She had said that she had all the evidence there to expose him. And the fire occurred the same night Jorge tampered with the brakes. Maybe Morales had Jorge do that too.

But there's no way to prove it now that Jorge is dead. Pretty damn convenient for Morales. And he has a solid alibi, too: he was at his stockholders' meeting in Temuco. Father was there, but he returned the same night, whereas Morales had stayed over. The motel watchman said his Mercedes was out front all night.

Maybe Morales had someone else kill Jorge. No, he wouldn't have done that. Too dangerous. No, Morales did it. And I'll bet he has a good alibi for the night of the fire, too. I should talk to that detective who's handling the case. He seems okay. Maybe I can work with him, or at least get involved. I know you're guilty, Morales; you must have slipped up somewhere, and if you did, by God, I'll find it!

Hands poised, he looked at the blank screen. He put his fingers on the keys, but his mind was still too full of Morales. He folded his hands in his lap. There was some movement upstairs, then creaking on the stairs, and the toilet flushed. A sleepy-looking Miriam appeared from around the corner.

"Carlos, you're still down here?"

"*Sí*, Miriam, just trying to write; but I'm having a tough time concentrating."

"Understandable considering what's been going on. But don't stay up all night now."

The stairs creaked again, and after a few minutes, silence returned. Carlos brought his hands up to the keys. This time he began to type.

THOUSANDS OF BLACK-NECKED SWANS DIE IN VALDIVIA REFUGE

A handful of black-necked swans is all that remains from a population of many thousands in the Carlos Anwandter Nature Sanctuary of Valdivia, the largest such sanctuary in South America. Once again, man has chosen to put himself above the environment. There is incontestable, photo-documented proof that Los Cruces River has been poisoned by effluents systematically and illegally dumped from a new pulp mill upriver. As a direct consequence, the swans have lost their food source as well as having their vital organs contaminated with heavy metals. Those birds strong enough have migrated, although many found the effort too much for their weakened systems, causing them to fall from the sky. Horrified schoolchildren and their parents gathered up any still alive, rushing them to swamped veterinarian clinics. Those that remained on the river suffered horribly, becoming so weak that they could not hold their beautiful necks up out of the water, causing them to drown.

Greed is evil. Often it leads to crime. Once in a great while, it leads to crimes so dastardly and hateful that they rise above the rest. It is never more poignant than when innocent creatures suffer from man's greed. Ivan Morales built and runs the pulp mill responsible for the pollution. Although he maintains that he knew nothing

about the disastrous effluent, many interesting events have recently surfaced concerning this international catastrophe.

Carlos read over the beginnings of his article. Not bad, he thought. Still, I have to be careful not to go too far: the paper doesn't need a lawsuit from that son-of-a-bitch. Exhausted, he turned off the computer and the lights in the living room, and slowly creaked his way up the stairs.

Chapter Twenty-Seven

Lilia entered Pablo and Miriam's living room through the front door. Carlos and Amanda were there. They didn't look happy. As if rehearsed, they asked in unison, "How's Tomás?"

"Not good. He's sleeping now. They gave him something strong again to knock him out." She shook her head. "I don't know which is worse, the pain or the depression. He makes a little progress with the therapy, but then he gets so discouraged. I try to keep him focused, but it's difficult. A big part of it is that he's been on his own pretty much his whole life, and he never, ever, liked to ask anyone for help. He told me once that he'd prefer spending three or four times longer doing something than ask for help. But now he has no choice, and it really brings him down."

Carlos looked at Lilia. Such a change, he thought; overnight, really—like a shroud had been cast aside with Jorge's death. She had become strong, tending to all Tomás's needs, always by his side, weighing every option and decision that had to be made. She went with him to therapy, conferred with the doctors, tried to learn as much as she could about the injury and what it would take for him to mentally and physically survive it. She was his round-the-clock nurse. When did she sleep?

How did she do it, day after day? Certainly, a very capable woman had emerged from her fragile former self, more confident in her actions, more assertive in conversations. Plain, too, that the spigot of her love for Tomás was wide open, and the well ran deep.

Unfortunately, Amanda had changed, too. So abrupt these last few days, jumping on him for the smallest thing. Maybe he had been wrong. Maybe she didn't really love him. Maybe, now that the articles had been published, he wasn't useful to her anymore. That's what she made it seem like anyway.

"Poor Tomás," Amanda said. "It's got to be so awful. I can't imagine what he's going through." She glared at Carlos. "And it could have been avoided."

Carlos looked at her evenly.

"Just what do you mean, Amanda?"

Lilia looked from one of them to the other. The tension was obvious.

"I mean the seat buckle. If you had that in good working condition...or if you hadn't rolled the car on that last corner, Tomás wouldn't be paralyzed!"

Lilia couldn't believe what Amanda was saying. If it hadn't been for Carlos's cool skill, they'd all be dead.

"Amanda! That's not fair!" she cried.

Carlos looked at Amanda coldly.

"Amanda, I did my best. As for the seatbelt, you're right. Tomás very well might not be paralyzed if he had been strapped in. Believe me, I think about it all the time. I have been beating myself up about it since the moment I first saw him flattened against that rock. You really don't have to beat me up, too; I can do that well enough on my own. Quite frankly, I don't know what your problem is, but you've been impossible lately! I'm leaving! I'm taking a break from this whole damn thing—from the swans, from Morales, and from you!"

He turned to Lilia.

"Lilia, I'll see you later at the hospital. What's a good time to come?"

"He had a pretty hard session this morning. I'd give him another four or five hours anyway to rest."

Carlos nodded. Without looking at Amanda again, he stormed out of the house. Lilia turned angrily to Amanda.

"What are you doing? I can't believe you said that! Can't you see that he's eaten up with guilt about Tomás? That was so mean! You're going to drive him away from you. Is that what you want? What's gotten into you, Amanda?"

Amanda had turned her back to Lilia. When Lilia walked around to confront her, she was surprised to see that she was crying. Lilia gently put her hand under Amanda's chin, lifting her head.

"What's wrong?"

Amanda wiped her eyes.

"Lilia, I'm a freak…or will be once they remove these bandages. And I know Carlos will stick by me no matter how hideous I look. Not because he wants to, but because he feels he should. I don't want that. I don't want him trapped and feeling like he has to do some honorable duty. And I don't want his pity either."

"So that's it. You're worried about not being pretty."

Amanda's eye blazed.

"No! That's not it!" She took a deep breath. "Well, not really. What I mean is that I don't care, for me, if I'm pretty or not. But I do care for Carlos's sake! The other day, before the rodeo, we went to La Bomba. When we were sitting at the table, he took my hand and said I was the most beautiful woman in the world. It's important to him—for us, I guess—that I be pretty. He hasn't seen what I look like underneath these bandages. I see it almost every day when I change the dressing and check for infection. It's not pretty, Lilia. I've got a big raw, red zipper running the length of my face. It's scary looking. I'm a female Frankenstein!

"And I just know what it would be like if we stay together. Everywhere we'd go, people will cringe, at least on the inside. They'll say 'he's such a good guy to stick by her after the accident. I don't know how he can do it, though, her face is so awful.'"

"Lilia, it would be better for both of us if I were just off alone. All I want is to be a vet, pure and simple. Animals won't care what I look like."

"Amanda, dear Amanda, give Carlos some credit. He's not so shallow. He loves you, all of you, not just your face. Besides, you haven't even talked to the plastic surgeon who's coming down from Santiago. He'll probably make you as good as new. And if he doesn't, it's only a physical scar. Be thankful: it's the emotional scars that are the tough ones to heal. You two have your whole lives ahead of you; don't waste them. Don't waste those years like Tomás and I did. We each lost the best part of our lives. But I'll tell you what: I don't plan on us losing any more!" She frowned. "I just have to convince Tomás of that."

Amanda reached for Lilia's hand, giving it a squeeze.

"Thanks, Lilia."

Lilia smiled.

"Give Carlos a chance. I believe, scars or no scars, that he will always love you. That's who he is, and it's rare. You've got something special. Don't throw it away." She picked up the shoulder bag that she had draped over the back of a chair. "I'm going up to my room to collect a few of my carving tools. They gave me permission to carve in Tomás's room as long as I cleaned up the mess. It will give me something to do, plus Tomás loves to watch me shape the wood. He thinks I should try sculpting."

Lilia went upstairs. She stuffed a few small blocks of wood and some chisels and gouges in her bag. She also put in the miniature *choroy* she was working on. Tomás would love it. She remembered walks they had taken when she was a little girl. He had been amazed when she had pointed out the noisy, bright green birds way up in the hardwood trees. He couldn't believe there could be small parrots in the cool, rainy climate.

She sat down on her bed. Amanda was thinking like a fool, feeling sorry for herself. But she's not a fool, and she'll come to her senses soon enough. She and Carlos will be alright. But what about Tomás and me? Now that's the tough nut; it's not just about a few scars for us. She hadn't told Amanda that the doctors made one stipulation on her carving at the hospital: make sure to take her tools home with her each night, and to keep them out of Tomás's reach at all times. They were worried, as she was, about what he might try to do. He was so depressed.

She had told Tomás how much she loved him, and that everything would be fine. He asked her how that could be. How could she think they could have any kind of healthy relationship? He kept telling her that he was half a man. No, he had added bitterly, he was not even half a man. He couldn't do what a man needs to do for a woman. Hell, he couldn't go to the bathroom by himself. No, she was crazy. He appreciated all her help, but she should move on. He said now that the specter of Jorge was gone, she should find herself a man, an entire man, and live a complete life.

She stood up abruptly. The muscles around her jaw tightened. She had already found her man, and she was going to stand by him no matter what! And she would make sure that they would have the best relationship ever. But it wasn't going to be easy. She threw her bag over a shoulder, and headed down the stairs.

* * *

When Tomás woke up, for a change Lilia wasn't in the room, smothering him with care. He lay there in bed, thinking back to when the doctor had first told them about his injuries.

"A T-12 and a number one lumbar burst fracture. We had to operate immediately. We took bone from your hip and inserted it so that it will fuse to your spine in time and hold things together. We also put in two pedicle screws to support and stabilize the area while the bone takes. Unless they begin to cause too much pain, the screws will be with you the rest of your life. But if they become too bothersome, you can elect to have them removed ...assuming, that is, everything has fused properly. But the bottom line is complete paraplegia."

Tomás had enough trouble understanding medical terms in English, let alone Spanish.

"What does that mean in layman's terms, Doctor?" he asked.

The doctor had had many patients over the years with similar injuries. What he was about to tell Tomás, though, was never easy. He didn't mince his words.

"You have a severed spinal cord, and will never walk again."

Then came the list of incidentals. He had lost his eye and, if he wanted, a glass eye could be installed. Either that or walk around with a naked eye socket, or a black fucking patch like a pirate. Then there were the busted ribs, the multiple cuts and stitches. Besides the morphine, he was on high doses of steroids to reduce inflammation. He was going to be in bed, a wheelchair, or sitting somewhere forever. He'd have to be turned constantly so he didn't get bedsores. Like a bloody lamb on a spit. He'd be given a mirror so he could inspect his backside for the bedsores. The doctor was a wealth of good news. When he finished explaining the injuries, Tomás looked over at Lilia. She smiled, trying to be supportive. He thought, what the hell is there to smile about!

God, those first days. He pumped as much morphine as the doctors would allow. He didn't want to wake up in the morning, much less go through therapy. He longed to return to that peaceful white tunnel with no pain and María Elena. But every morning they had him up doing therapy, increasing it to three to five hours a day. Therapy. Rest. Therapy. Rest. Ad nauseam. They put a body sheath on him for the ribs and back. What was it called? Oh, yeah. Cáscara de Tortuga—turtle shell—Thoraco Lumbar Sacra Orthodic, or some such shit. And then the leg braces so his legs might move a little in the right direction when he dragged himself along the parallel bars. He'd sweat and swear at the therapists. But they were relentless. Little by little he gained enough strength so he could climb in and out of his bed and wheelchair without help.

But that wasn't the worst of it, not by a long shot. There was the horrific embarrassment of incontinence. When the nurses came in to clean his butt, he wished he could shoot himself. He closed his eye when they entered, and he didn't open it until he heard the door shut behind them. Then Lilia had gotten the bright idea of taking their place. Said she was going to take care of him. She wouldn't take no for an answer, and convinced the nurses not to interfere. Tomás had finally given in. He had cried silently when she cleaned him for the first time.

He had to be potty trained—learn how to digitally induce a bowel movement. That meant sticking a finger up his ass and wiggling it around until things started rolling. God! And the 'cath' to take a piss. He had to put some gel on the catheter and stick it up his penis in order to drain his bladder. A lot of fun. And he had to do it four to six times a day.

The shrink had tried to talk him out of his depression. Said there would be lots of things he could do once he learned how to cope. Talk's cheap, Doc, Tomás thought. What did the shrink know about all the barriers he would face. God, it would be bad enough in the States where there were at least curb cuts, negotiable public bathrooms, wide doors. Here in southern Chile! A joke. And what about the million pleasures he'd no longer have? Hey Doc, you ever wiggle your toes in the sand at the beach? Feels good, doesn't it? Drop me a line whenever you do it so I won't forget! Oh yeah, speak about forgetting, don't forget to tell me what it feels like when you have an orgasm with your wife. I'll never have one of those either!

And Lilia. She was an angel, no getting around that. But she was suffocating him with kindness. She'd been by his bed constantly, supporting him in everything. She and Guillermo had found a replacement for her at the shop so she could spend all her time with him. But it was too much. And it wasn't right. He had been a physical person his whole life: athletics in school, blue collar labor afterwards, a traveler. His body was everything. Now that he didn't have one, he was nothing.

Adapt, Lilia kept saying; persevere, face it head on! Bullshit, Lilia! Your body isn't broken, your life isn't over! But that's not fair. She was trying so hard, trying for both of them. But what was fair? Was it fair for an attractive, talented middle-aged woman who finally had broken out of her shell to be shackled to a cripple? She kept saying she would take care of him forever. Crazy, absolutely crazy! She should get on with her life.

The door opened, and Lilia stuck her head in.

"Ah, Tomás, you're awake," she said smiling. She walked over to his bed with an armful of new magazines.

Chapter Twenty-Eight

What a thing to say! That was about as low a blow as possible! If he had made that last curve! His fault that Tomás was paralyzed! Had she lost all her feelings for him? Maybe he had been totally wrong about her. Where was the caring, intelligent girl he had fallen in love with? Who was this bitch!

He drove the mid-size rental car like he was in remote control. He left Las Animas, turning right to cross the Calle Calle River. At the intersection with Picarte, he turned left, heading east towards the outskirts of town.

Obviously she was tired of him; must be, to treat him like that. Wanted him out of her world. Maybe she had been using him all along. Now that the pollution had been exposed, she didn't need him. But that would make her a whore, and she wasn't a whore, damn it! And she couldn't have faked her feelings for him. And she certainly wasn't faking when they had made love: no one was that good an actress! No, something was wrong.

Maybe the concussion had done something upstairs, rattled her head so she was confused. Somehow that concussion had changed her, changed her personality. But the doctors said she was fine. She was perfectly normal. There had been no blood on her brain, no pressure, just a simple concussion. Juan had told him that she had been knocked woozy one other time playing soccer in the *campo*. She had probably been concussed then, too. So, maybe it was because she's had two of them. But the doctors were sure she was okay. She was fine with everybody else. It was just with him.

He passed the Valdivia cemetery. How did he get here? Where was he going anyway? He hadn't paid the slightest attention. He saw the *carabinero* headquarters up ahead. That was it, that's where he was headed. Morales! He might be able to take a break from Amanda and the swans, but he sure as hell wasn't going to take a break from trying to nail Morales. And the most logical place to start was with Detective Gonzales who investigated the suicide. Maybe he had found out something new.

He parked between two police vans facing the long, one-story building. The Chilean flag flew from a tall pole just to the side of the main door, and a sergeant in a brown woolen uniform sat at a large desk inside. His white leather belt and holster were so polished that they looked like plastic. The sergeant went to get the detective. Not more than a minute later, Gonzales approached.

"You wanted to talk with me, Sr. Mueller?"

"Please, Detective, call me Carlos. I was wondering how the investigation's going with Jorge's death."

"Over. Suicide, plain and simple."

"Pardon me, Detective, but, frankly, that doesn't make sense."

"You telling me I'm not doing my job, Carlos?"

"No, Detective, not at all. I just don't believe it was suicide."

Gonzales gave him an appraising look.

"You've got other ideas?"

"*Sí*. It was murder."

"How about proof?"

"None. Plenty of motive, but no proof."

"Then you're wasting my time." Gonzales started to turn away.

"Please, Detective, just hear me out."

Gonzales hesitated. He looked at his watch.

"Alright, you've got ten minutes. Follow me."

They walked down the narrow corridor to Gonzales's office. As he held the door open for Carlos, Gonzales softened his tone.

"I don't like suicide either, but I haven't found anything substantial enough to prove otherwise."

The office was small with a single window looking out to the highway. Gonzales pulled a chair from the corner up to the front of his desk.

"Have a seat."

Gonzales sat behind the desk which was covered with papers.

"But you have found something?" Carlos asked as he sat down.

Gonzales leaned back, placing his hands behind his head.

"First, tell me about who had motive, Carlos. That is, besides your friend Srta. Lilia."

"Morales."

Gonzales nodded.

"That's what I thought you'd say. You've implied as much in your articles about the swans. Well written, I might add, and shocking. But if I were you, I'd be careful. Morales won't blink an eye about suing you if you go too far with your insinuations."

"That's what my publisher's afraid of. But Morales makes sense. Jorge was just a pawn. I'm sure of it."

Gonzales nodded.

"I'm not disagreeing with you. When Sr. Young said that he would swear in court that he saw Jorge by your car in Niebla, and with what you and the young lady have uncovered about the pollution, in my mind that casts suspicion on Morales as well as Jorge. And it makes sense that Jorge, like you say, was a pawn of Morales. He was an idiot, for Christ's sake. Then there's the coincidence of the fire the same night. Off the record, there's obvious motive for Morales to have had Jorge set the fire at the university. But what really makes me suspect Morales's foul play were a couple of little things."

Carlos leaned forward.

"Such as?"

Gonzales walked over to the window, debating how much to tell the young reporter. He knew that the young man came from an influential family and represented a national newspaper. He looked out for a couple of moments before answering.

"Such as Jorge's fingerprints were all over everything in his apartment. Yet, when I dusted the door, I found only the prints of our man who went in and found Jorge. I'd be willing to bet that the knob had been wiped clean. I find that very unusual.

"As you know, we cordoned off the apartment, which really upset Morales; he wants us out of there so the apartment can be cleaned. Says he wants to hire another employee to replace Jorge, which means he has to have the apartment available right away. When I asked him if he had hired anybody, he said no. So, I said, then there was no hurry. He became angry and took another approach which I found very interesting. He said that Jorge had damaged the electrical service when he shot himself, and it had to be fixed before the complex burned down. I told him that the breaker had tripped, and there was no danger of that. Still, he said, and I quote, 'If this place catches fire, I'll sue your ass!' end quote."

"So?"

"How did Morales know about the bullet damaging the electric? I didn't tell him, and I doubt very much one of my men did. I asked him."

"What did he say?"

"Just what I thought he would...that he heard one of my men say something about it. But when I asked him, he had that, you know, little flicker in his eyes...like he had screwed up and better come up with a quick answer, which he did.

"The doorknob and the electrical short may be small things, but I pay attention to small things. Still, there's no proof. It's just conjecture on my part. There's nothing to place him at the scene, and that's what I need: concrete proof that he was in that room at the time of death, which, by the way, was twenty-eight minutes past two in the morning. We know that because the wall clock was on the circuit that tripped. In any case, he has a good alibi for both nights. He was in bed with his wife during the fire, and he was in Temuco the night Jorge died." Gonzales sat back down. "So I'm stuck with the suicide."

"Detective, I'm sure he has a bona fide, rock-solid alibi for the fire, because Jorge probably set it. Morales would have made sure he wasn't anywhere near the place and could prove it. But he couldn't take the chance of anyone else killing Jorge. He'd have to do it himself. So, somehow, he came here to do the deed, and then returned to Temuco before anyone noticed he was gone. Temuco is only a hundred kilometers away; he'd have plenty of time. With your approval, I'd like to get involved in this. I'd like to poke around Temuco to see if I can come up with something. Do you have a problem with that?"

"We didn't find anything, and we looked pretty hard. So, I doubt if you will; but, if you want to play detective, that's fine."

Carlos stood up.

"How much longer are you going to keep the apartment cordoned off?"

"I have to open it up by tomorrow. My boss says that Morales is giving him a hard time. So, I've got my orders."

"Any chance I could go over with you tomorrow before you open it back up, just to take a quick look around?"

"Meet me here at ten, and we'll go over together."

The detective pulled a card from his wallet.

"And here's my card. Call me if you find out anything in Temuco."

The two men shook hands before Carlos left the room.

* * *

Morales stood at the large window, watching the chimneys' streams of smoke quickly blend into the low cloud cover. He knew that he had been lucky to get away with Jorge and the science building, but no getting around the pollution thing now. Goddamn swans and Carlos! He was going to have some big fines to pay, and probably get shut down for awhile while the courts decided all the suits that were sprouting like weeds. And Carlos's damn newspaper articles! Because of them, the mill's stock crashed. Funny thing that all the investors around Valdivia cashed in when the stock was still high, before the articles. A little insider info, Carlos, you shithead?

He walked over to his desk. At least Carlos can't prove definitively that I knew about the pollution, and the other reporters seemed to swallow the story that Jorge was paid a bonus if a certain amount of paper was made each month. How was I to know that Jorge was dumping effluent in the river because of the extra money? Like Carlos's articles said, it was done in the middle of the night when I wasn't around. Those goddamn pictures were of Jorge, not me! He was the bad guy, not me!

And I've already agreed to pay compensation to the Bureau of Tourism for the businesses that supposedly lost business because of the dead swans. What a crock! As soon as they get their money, they'll all shut up. They don't care about the swans, just the money.

I'll probably lose the Chinese contract, and that means the house in Viña. At least the condo in Bariloche is in my wife's name. They can't get that. But still, I'll probably have to go through bankruptcy proceedings. But even without the Chinese, there's still business out there. Just have to reduce margin, work harder. God knows that I've had to do that before. But this whole mess because of some damn birds! Still, I'm lucky to get away with shooting Jorge. The only weak link there is the rental car guy. But he was cheating his boss, and wouldn't say anything. Plus, the guy knows me as Sr. Gómez, and would never connect me to the mill in Valdivia.

He picked up a pencil and began doodling on a piece of paper. He had learned his lesson alright. He should never pollute on a regular basis. It would still be possible to leak effluent when things calmed down, but he'd have to be more careful. It was just too easy a way to pad his pockets. He might have to pay a little something to get certain people to look the other way, but that was no big deal. The extra money would take care of that. As for the swans, he couldn't care less.

Chapter Twenty-Nine

Carlos noticed the sign when he slowed down for an oxcart in the highway. What! Only three kilometers to Temuco? Can't be! He shook his head. Just can't get her out of my mind. Can't stop thinking about her. About us. What's wrong? What's eating her? What did I do, other than love her, worry about her! Maybe I'm suffocating her, cramping her style. No, that's not it. I haven't acted any differently than before the crash. Well, other than I was damn concerned about the concussion.

Maybe she thinks we've gotten too serious. Maybe she's afraid that I might pop the big question so I could take care of her night and day. She's trying to push me away so that I won't ask. But I know that'd be a mistake. Sure I've thought about a possible future together, but now's not the time. She wants to be a vet, and I've got my career. Yeah, I'd like to settle down someday and have kids. But certainly not now. And she never wants kids anyway.

Could it be the damage to her face? The vote's still out on how bad it really is. We won't know until she's examined by the plastic surgeon. Maybe that's it. Maybe she's angry because Dad is having that doctor fly down from Santiago: another example of the rich having all the advantages. Maybe she's feeling guilty, lashing out because she has accepted his help? No, she seems genuinely grateful; she's thanked Dad several times. No, that isn't it.

Still, it would be totally understandable that she's worried about her face. She looked funny when the doctor spoke to us while we were leaving the hospital. He gave us instructions on changing her bandages. She was to return in a week so he could examine her one last time before removing them. She looked scared. Come to think of it, it was when I offered to help her with the bandages at Pablo and Miriam's that she first snapped at me. Said she didn't need any help, and had stormed out of the room. Obviously, she doesn't want me to see her face all messed up.

So what? So, she has a large scar. She was never concerned with how pretty she looked before. She hardly ever glanced in a mirror, never played on her looks. She wasn't wrapped up in herself like some attractive women. She's outdoorsy, athletic, curious, intelligent, and sensitive. Yeah, a little hot tempered maybe, but nobody's perfect. Still, that's who she is, and that's why I love her. Wait a minute there, Carlos! She's also beautiful. You know that. And you know it's a big part of the package. That's why you were attracted to her in the first place. And she knows that. Put yourself in her shoes. Even if she wasn't interested in how she looked, people still related to her beauty. Her whole life she's been gorgeous, and she knows that. People can't help but respond to beauty like hers. It's understandable that if all your life you've been attractive, and then suddenly you lose that beauty, it would be scary. You might think it will change how people feel about you. It shouldn't affect things, but it might. Crazy, though, because Amanda has so much more going for her than her looks. Beauty was all some women had, and they were driven to cash in on those good looks before they faded. But Amanda couldn't be worried about that, could she? Hell, he didn't know. All he knew was that he loved her, and that he would continue to love her no matter what.

He pulled up behind the oxcart. The man leading the team was a Mapuche Indian. No surprise there; the largest Mapuche community in Chile was scattered around Temuco. They had a great *artesanía* market in town. If there was time after poking around, maybe he'd go to the market and find a nice lightweight *manta* for Amanda. Maybe that would perk her up.

He drove around the cart and entered the city limits, his thoughts immediately shifting to Morales. He must have shot Jorge. It just fit. So, if he did, he must have somehow made the trip to the mill and back here again, no matter that his car was parked in front of the motel all night. Point was, no one could say that they had seen him in Temuco when Jorge was killed. Morales, of course, said 'Duh everybody! Guess what? Of course no one saw me; I was in my room, asleep.'

Even though Temuco had grown a lot in the last few years, it was still relatively small; it didn't take long to find the motel. He checked the odometer: a hundred and thirty one kilometers from the *carabinero* station. Late at night, he'd bet he could easily drive to Valdivia and back in three hours or less. He went into the motel office where he found a swarthy fat man behind the desk. Carlos introduced himself, showing his newspaper identification. He asked the man if he would look up the room Morales had stayed in. The man sighed.

"I don't have to look it up. I've already done that for the police a couple of times. It's room twelve. The maid's in there now, cleaning up. Go take a quick look around if you want; I don't know what good it'll do. Just don't disturb the maid."

Carlos entered the room. The bed had been freshly made, and the soiled sheets were rolled up into a ball in the center of the floor. The room was clean but non-descript except for a large flat screen TV facing the bed. There was also a bureau, writing desk, and a refrigerator along the walls. The door to the bathroom was ajar. Beyond it he could see the cleaning lady's rear end bobbing as she scrubbed the shower stall on her hands and knees. The window was wide open to vent the shower's steam. He started to turn away, but stopped. The window! He looked at it again. It was large for a bathroom, and there were no bars or grillwork. It was on the first floor, and he'd bet he could fit through it if he tried. And Morales was a lot smaller than he was. He quickly left the room.

He walked around behind the motel. The window was easy to spot: it was the only one open. He looked around. Narrow alley with no street lights. Morales might have had a car stashed here, but then whose car would it have been, or what would he have done with it afterward? He wouldn't have bought a car to do the deed, and then just leave it somewhere. And he didn't want an accomplice or any witness. He wouldn't steal a car. No, the best thing would be to rent one; but all the rental agencies would have been closed at that hour, plus the police said they checked them. There was no record anywhere of Morales or any rental cars that went that distance on that particular day. But still, there might have been some way, and it would have to be nearby. Morales wouldn't want to take a cab, especially late at night. He wouldn't want to be noticed by anybody.

Carlos walked back to the motel office where he requested a phonebook. He turned to the rental agencies in the yellow pages before asking the fellow behind the desk if any were close by. After putting on reading glasses, the man ran a pudgy finger down the page. The finger stopped about a third of the way down.

"This one. It's only a couple blocks away." He took off his glasses. "The best way to get there is to go to the little alley behind the motel, walk up two blocks toward the center of town, then turn left. It's about halfway down the block on your right."

It didn't take Carlos long before he was standing in front of a car rental agency which certainly wasn't Avis or National or any of the big chains. The lot was small. He counted only seven vehicles, mostly compacts at least two years old. The office was tiny. A very short, stocky man dressed in a green and yellow uniform was standing behind a wooden counter looking at a large ledger. The man made the counter look high. Carlos would bet he had a fair share of Mapuche blood. The man, taking a cheap plastic pen out of his mouth, looked up at him.

"Good morning, sir..." He glanced at a clock on the wall above Carlos's head. "Or, maybe I should say, good afternoon. What happened to your arm?" He was beaming at Carlos. He looked hungry for business.

"Auto accident," Carlos said.

The man continued to smile.

"That is too bad. I hope it was someone else's fault. I'd hate to rent a car to someone who might be a bad risk," he joked.

"Sorry, Señor, but I'm not here to rent a car." Carlos told him why he was there. The man's smile faded quickly.

"I've already been questioned by the police. I don't see any reason to go through it again. And quite frankly, young man, I'm not in a particularly good mood." He stabbed at the ledger with his pen. "I discovered two days ago that an employee who worked here for two years has been cheating me."

Trying to get on the man's good side, Carlos commiserated.

"I'm sorry to hear that. But, that must have been pretty hard to do...I mean it doesn't seem your business is that big."

He looked at Carlos angrily.

"We're open seven days a week, sir, twelve hours a day. I refuse to be here twenty-four hours a day. Sixty hours a week is enough! A man has to have some time for his family," he said righteously. "So I had this employee who took the office a couple of days a week, plus stayed here nights to answer the phone for after-hour emergencies and breakdowns. That and watch the place. And I paid him as well as I could." He pointed towards the door behind him. "I even put a bed back there so he could sleep if nothing was happening. How was I to know he had a little part time business of not recording short-term rentals. The jerk even rented my cars out by the hour sometimes!"

"By the hour? I've never heard of such a thing."

"Neither had I; but he did, to certain local businessmen who wanted to go to the whorehouses outside of town…rather than stay home with their families like they should be doing."

Carlos felt a tinge of excitement.

"How did you find out?"

"Even though our customers get unlimited free mileage, I require the mileage to be written down when any car leaves and when it is returned. It helps with maintenance. And there's one car I use often myself for around town, or to take my children out to the *campo* to see their grandparents on weekends. When it's busy, I have the car here on the lot. One day I noticed a lot of miles on it that didn't add up. I looked in the records, in this ledger here," he said, tapping it with his pen, "and the numbers looked smeared. I got suspicious and started to look way back. Several numbers of different cars just didn't make sense, and many of the numbers looked doctored. I confronted my employee who started crying and confessed. He begged me not to report him to the *carabineros*. He has a wife and several small children, so I didn't. That's the only reason; but I did fire him, and now I've got to work even more hours until I can find someone else."

Carlos shook his head in sympathy.

"That's tough, but kind of you not to prosecute."

"I'm a fool," the man muttered.

"By any chance," Carlos asked, "was your employee here the night of February fifteenth?"

"He was here every night. I don't...that is," he said forlornly, "I didn't stay here nights. I'll have to now."

Carlos tried to keep calm.

"Do you think he might have had one of those secret rentals on the night of the fifteenth? Do the books look altered for that day?"

The man turned back several pages of the ledger. He went down a column with the capped end of the pen. After a couple of seconds, he looked up at Carlos.

"Sure looks that way."

"Where can I find this ex-employee of yours?"

Carlos turned off the pavement near a bus stop at the north end of town. Slowly driving down a dirt street lined with streetlights attached to skinny wooden poles, he carefully dodged potholes as he looked at the numbers on the houses. A few mangy looking dogs were patrolling the street while others barked from behind fences. Other than the dogs, the only movement was a small boy running along next to a hoop he guided with a stick. There were no cars parked on the street, and although warm, almost every house had a smoking stovepipe sticking out of the roof. For kitchen ranges, Carlos knew, and he'd bet the only thing the houses had for heat besides those stoves would be braziers for burning charcoal. The neighborhood reminded him of the poorer sections of Valdivia where he and his father had occasionally driven through in his youth. There were no front or side lawns, and maybe a couple meters separated the homes.

He found the house, its wood weathered gray, down near the end of the street. It was small, and situated at the very edge of the sidewalk. A couple of chickens were scratching at some refuse near the front door. He was tired of answering questions about what happened to his arm, so he took off the sling. As he walked up, he could hear a radio. He knocked, but no one came out. He knocked again. The door was opened by a short young woman with her dark hair severely pulled back into a pony tail. She wore a threadbare dress mostly covered by a stained apron. A little girl, clutching the apron, appeared from behind her. She looked up at Carlos while the woman wiped her hands. The little girl's face was dirty and her dress threadbare also. The woman put a hand on the child's head.

"Yes, Señor? What do you want?"

"I'm looking for Señor Pineda. I was told he lives here."

"Why do you want to see him? And who are you?"

"I am not the police." He showed her his identification. "I'd just like to ask him about a car he rented out a couple of weeks ago."

"He doesn't work at the car agency anymore. Ask his old boss."

She started to shut the door.

"His boss gave me this address. I assume the man is your husband. If he's here, he should talk to me. If he won't, I can arrange for him to talk to the police."

Carlos looked at his watch.

"I could probably have them here knocking on your door within ten minutes, Señora."

With the door half opened, she turned to look behind her. Then she opened the door wide, silently stepping aside. A man he'd guess to be about his own age was sitting at a small table. A *maté* cup and a radio were on the table. The man reached over to turn the radio off. He looked up. Carlos towered over him. The man was slender, wore pressed black slacks, shiny pointed shoes, and a well pressed, button down white shirt. What looked like a new black leather jacket hung over the back of the chair. The woman went over to the kitchen stove to stoke the fire. A big pot was bubbling on top. She stirred the pot with a long wooden spoon while the child continued to hang on to her apron.

The man smiled ingratiatingly at Carlos. Carlos knew that the man thought he was rich because he was so tall and German looking.

"How can I help you, Señor?"

"I was told that you rented out a car on the night of Feb. 15. Can you tell me how long your customer had the car? And what he looked like?"

The man's face was instantly hooded.

"I don't know about any night rentals, Señor."

"That's not what your boss, er, your former boss, told me."

The man didn't offer Carlos a seat. The woman continued to stir the pot.

"Look, Señor, I lost my job. All right? I'm broke. And my boss said he wasn't going to…to pursue me paying him back for any rentals that were…were not on the books. So, I don't see why you have to know anything about them."

Carlos pulled up a chair, placing it directly in front of the man. He sat down, leaning forward. His face was very close to the man's.

"This has nothing to do with paying your boss back. And he has already told me all about your little side business. You were very lucky he didn't press charges; I know a lot of employers who wouldn't have been so easy on you. But, this concerns a possible murder, and I believe the man you rented the car to is involved. It's extremely important. If you don't cooperate, you would be obstructing a murder investigation."

The woman stopped stirring the pot. Carlos didn't have to look over to know she was watching them.

"You're really not with the police?"

"No, but I'm here with police approval, trying to help out. What you know could be very, very important."

The man hesitated, then took a sip of *maté*. He made a face.

"Woman, refill my cup, with more sugar this time!" As an afterthought, he asked, "Would you like some, Señor?"

Carlos shook his head. The woman came over with a steaming kettle of water. The man stirred the *maté* with the metal straw until it cooled enough to sip. Carlos was becoming impatient, but he didn't say anything. Finally, putting his *maté* down, the man turned to Carlos.

"The fifteenth of this month, you say?"

Carlos nodded. The man took another sip.

"Not hard to remember. Only had a handful of customers the whole month...and all regulars except for one."

He turned towards his wife.

"Bring me the calendar, woman."

She took a calendar hanging from a nail on the wall and brought it over. Carlos couldn't imagine ordering Amanda around like that—she'd let him have it in a second. The man studied the calendar.

"*Sí*, it was a Tuesday. Thought so. The fifteenth was when the guy I didn't know came in. I believe he said his name was Señor Gómez. He said that he had a meeting with a certain young *señorita*, and he'd need the car for most of the night. I saw that he was wearing a wedding ring, so it was pretty easy to figure what he was up to." He looked at Carlos. "That's how I got started in all this—guys had things going on they didn't want their wives to know about. But I'd never seen this guy. I remember him because he looked rich, and I upped my usual rate."

The man smiled smugly as he brushed the front of his spotless shirt. Carlos could only imagine why he was so well dressed, and his wife and child were not. He didn't like this little man.

"Yeah, I charged him double what I normally do. That especially pleased me because he acted so snobby-like. I remember he looked like he wanted to wash his hands after I handed him the keys. Anyway, it was around eleven thirty when he left, and he returned the car close to five the next morning."

"Do you have any idea how far he drove the car?"

"I do remember because he put a lot of kilometers on it, making it hard to fix on the books. Just under three hundred kilometers. I remember thinking that, driving all those miles, he couldn't have had time to screw the woman more than once. Twice at best."

The *señora* banged the pot with a spoon. Carlos looked over. She set the spoon down hard on the counter, and took the child by the hand into another room. The man followed her with his eyes before turning back to Carlos.

"I can't describe him all that much because he was wearing a dark hat pulled low and one of those black jackets made out of Castillean wool; you know, that thick black wool like those big *mantas* the *campesinos* wear during the rainy season? Funny thing, that, wearing such a heavy coat in the summertime. But then again, when husbands are sneaking around..."

Carlos nodded.

"He was a little taller than me, and definitely more heavy set. I know I'd recognize his face alright."

Carlos pulled a picture from his pocket. It was from the interview at the mill. He handed it to the man.

"*Sí*, that's him alright. Did he kill somebody, Señor?"

"That's not for me to determine. That's for the police and the courts. But you've been a big help."

The man handed the picture back.

"That's it then? That's all you need?"

"For me, yes. But, I dare say, the police will be talking with you soon. And I'm sure at some point they will want you to identify the man—Sr. Gómez, I believe you called him—in person." The man looked nervous again. He was about to say something when Carlos continued. "Don't worry. This has nothing to do with your little side business. There's no need to publicize any of that. This is about something a hell of a lot more serious."

Carlos stood. The man did not stand or walk him to the door. As Carlos left the house, he could hear the radio turned back on. Outside, he flipped open his cell phone. Plenty of bars. He leaned against the hood of the car as he dialed. He was smiling.

"Hello, Detective. Greetings from Temuco…*Sí,* poking around. And guess what, I've discovered a little something that just might interest you…"

Chapter Thirty

Detective Gonzales pulled away the yellow plastic tape and opened the door for Carlos.

"Not bad," Carlos said looking around. "Small, but comfortable enough. This was the way you found it, nice and tidy?"

The detective nodded.

"Yeah, except for all the blood and bone splattered on the wall, floor, and easy chair. There were even shards on the dining chair and table. Powerful weapon. It was quite a mess."

The detective walked over to the easy chair.

"He was sitting here, facing the TV. The bullet exited his head, entering the wall over there," he said pointing. "You can see the hole. The bullet hit an electric wire, tripping the breaker. The clock stopped at the time of the shooting."

Carlos looked over at the clock above the sink.

"Which, according to what the rental guy told me, Morales would have had plenty of time to make it here, kill Jorge, and return to Temuco."

"True," Gonzales said. "But that doesn't prove anything. We need solid evidence that he was here. You said that Morales told the rental guy he was meeting a woman somewhere. So, if he has to, he'll find one. If we confront him now, he'll just dig up some whore to vouch for him. Believe me, it's been done before."

Gonzales pointed to the floor.

"There was a glass set next to the chair here with Jorge's prints. He had a pretty good charge of alcohol in him, as well as the sleeping pills. Like I told you, though, we looked everywhere, including his truck, and couldn't come up with any bottle of pills."

"What was he drinking?" Carlos asked, as he continued to walk around the apartment.

"*Aguardiente.*"

"Straight?"

"No. He was mixing it with cola. Both bottles were covered with his prints. Same with the pistol, and he had appropriate powder burns on his hand."

"What about ice? Was there any water residue in the glass?"

"*Sí*, but all the ice trays were full and put away."

"If I were going to kill myself, I don't think I would bother to put ice trays away."

Carlos walked into the kitchen to open the freezer. Only water was in the trays. He looked to see if it was plugged in. It was: must be on the same circuit as the clock.

"Did you lift any prints off the ice trays?"

"No, we didn't bother. The frost would have covered any prints, and then washed them away when it thawed out."

Carlos snapped his head around to look at Gonzales.

"Did you turn the refrigerator off?"

Gonzales shook his head.

"Then it must have lost power the same time as the clock. If a tray or trays were used, they probably never froze again."

Gonzales slapped his forehead.

"You're right! There might be a chance for prints. Good thinking; although Jorge probably made his own drink. I don't see Morales being his servant."

"But if sleeping pills were mixed in without Jorge knowing it, then it would have to have been Morales."

"Right. Wait a minute, I'll be right back."

The detective went to his car, returning with several large ziplock bags. He carefully emptied and placed each ice tray into a separate bag.

"If we're lucky, very lucky, we might find something here. That is, if these weren't wiped clean too. C'mon, I want to send them up to the regional lab in Temuco. In fact, I might just drive them up myself. I'd like to talk to the rental car guy. That was good work, Carlos, to dig him up."

"Lucky timing. The owner of the agency had no idea about the night rentals until a few days ago."

The detective reattached the yellow tape.

"I know it will piss Morales off, but I think I'll leave this up for another…Oh, damn!"

"What?"

"It's Friday, and the lab will be closing for the weekend." The detective looked at his watch. "No way to get it up there in time for them to examine it today. I probably won't get the results until middle of next week."

When he finished with the tape, the pair climbed into Gonzales's car. The detective drove over to Morales's Mercedes where he turned off the engine.

"What are you doing?" Carlos asked. The detective was scribbling on an official looking piece of paper attached to a clipboard.

"Being sneaky."

He took the paper and left the car. Carlos watched him enter the elevator, wondering what he was up to. After carefully wiping the paper clean in the elevator, the detective knocked on the office door. Morales frowned when he opened it.

"You finally going to let me have my apartment back, Gonzales?"

"Lieutenant…Lieutenant Gonzales." Morales was such a jerk.

"Whatever, LIEUTENANT."

"Just a day or two more, Señor Morales. I thought we'd be out of there today, but something's come up. I'm sure it won't be much longer. Have you found somebody else yet?"

"Just how the hell can I do that! You've got the apartment blocked off, for God's sake! It'd scare anybody applying for the job if they looked at it now with all your yellow tape, and knowing someone shot himself in there. I want it opened up *pronto*. This has gone on long enough! Understand!"

"Yes, I understand. I apologize; soon, though, I promise. But, oh, here. Would you sign this? We're removing a few things temporarily from the apartment, and I've inventoried them here. By signing this, you acknowledge the fact. Just a formality."

"Four ice trays? What in the world do you want with those?"

Gonzales shrugged.

"Just trying to be thorough."

Morales took the paper over to the desk where he signed it.

"I don't know why you're spending so much time on this, Lieutenant. Seems pretty straightforward."

"You're probably right. Just looking for something to do, I guess. It's been kind of slow downtown."

Morales stood facing the door after the detective left the office. What in hell did he want those ice trays for? It bothered him the rest of the afternoon. Gonzales smiled at Carlos as he got back into the car.

"Hand me one of those ziplock bags in my briefcase, would you, Carlos?"

Gonzales put the paper in the bag. Still smiling, he said, "If there are any of Morales's prints on the ice trays, now we've got a fresh set to compare them to."

* * *

It had been several days since Carlos had seen Amanda. He was staying with his parents on their farm outside Valdivia, using his father's computer to work on another article. Detective Gonzales had cautioned him, telling him what was on and off the record: he did not want Carlos writing something that might compromise the investigation or potential prosecution in any way.

Carlos had been sleuthing with the detective when the plastic surgeon had arrived from Santiago to examine Amanda. His father told him that the doctor had been very encouraging, saying it would require more than one operation, but he was a hundred percent sure that Amanda would have little to no scarring. She would have to wait for her face to heal, though, before the doctor could get down to business. Carlos didn't tell his father about the friction between them. Instead, in confidence, he told him about his suspicions of Morales, backing it up with what he had learned in Temuco, and that they were waiting for a report about the ice trays. His father couldn't believe it. That man must be crazy, he said.

"No, Father," Carlos had answered. "Just incredibly greedy and cold blooded. He thinks that he can do whatever the hell he wants. I just hope we get enough goods on him so that whatever slippery lawyer he hires won't be able to get him off."

The next day Carlos went to see Amanda, rationalizing that he'd have to get his computer sooner or later. When he arrived at the front door, butterflies were fluttering around his stomach. He knocked.

"Come in."

It was Amanda's voice. He passed through the door, and there she was at the far end, wearing jeans and a hooded university sweatshirt, sitting at the dining room table with a pile of papers in front of her. The good side of her face was towards him. She pulled the hood up.

"Hi," she said. "Where have you been?"

Certainly a lighter tone to her voice than last time he was here.

"Trying to get the goods on Morales. With quite a bit of success, I might add."

She smiled. He could only see half of it.

"Really! Do tell!"

He walked around and sat at the far end of the table from her. Immediately, she turned her good side to him again.

"I'd rather talk about your seeing the surgeon. Father said it went well. What do you think?"

"He was very reassuring. He said that he had fixed faces a lot worse than mine, and that the operations would be straight forward. It's going to take two or three operations, but he about guaranteed me that I would look fine."

"Is that so important to you, Amanda—that you look fine?"

She looked down at her papers for a moment. When she raised her head, she looked straight into his eyes.

"Yes, but not for me."

"For whom, then?"

She didn't take her eyes off his.

"For you."

Her eyes filled with tears as she suddenly started speaking very quickly. Words poured out of her like water over a dam.

"I want to be pretty for you. I don't want you to be stuck with a freak. I know how I feel about you, and I decided quite awhile ago that I want to be with you for a long time."

Tears were spilling down her cheek.

"A very long time, *mi amor*. But I don't want you to be with me because you feel you have to. I couldn't stand that! And I am so very sorry," she was crying outright now, "about what I said the other day, about Tomás. I didn't mean it. I was so upset. I guess I was pushing you away:

I didn't want you tied down to a Frankenstein. But," she said, "the doctor has given me hope. It'll take time, but I won't look like this forever."

Carlos restrained himself from springing up to embrace her. He remained sitting, looking at her intently. So, it had been her face all along; she didn't have a clue as to how much he loved her.

"Will you forgive me, Carlos?"

"Are your bandages off now?"

She nodded. He stood and walked slowly to her. She looked frightened. He took hold of her hand to pull her up from the table. Very gently, he reached out with his good arm to turn her head. She closed her eyes as he pulled down the hood. It was bad. Real bad. Swollen, discolored, raw, running the length of her face. But it was her face, the face of the woman he loved. He didn't say a thing, but when she opened her eyes to look at him, tears were falling again. He very slowly began to kiss the scar. He kissed the length of it. When he finished, he turned her to face him again.

"Don't you ever, ever, think that my love is not strong enough to handle something like this, Amanda. You're everything to me, not just a pretty face. I love you. I always will. No matter what."

He took his arm out of the sling and gently drew her in. He kissed her. She kissed him back. It was a long kiss. When they surfaced, they held on to each other, rocking gently back and forth. Finally, she took his hand to lead him to the couch. When they sat down, she avoided his next kiss, instead pulling her hood up again.

"Now, *mi amor*, tell me about that snake Morales. What did you find out?"

He smiled. That's my girl, right back to business. He began to tell her everything that had happened since he had last seen her.

Chapter Thirty-One

Detective Gonzales made the call from his car in front of the police station. Two *carabineros* were parked along side in a van, waiting for his signal.

"Hello, Carlos?"

"*Sí.*"

"Gonzales here. I said I'd let you be the first to know if we arrested Morales? We're about to leave the station now. We should have him in custody in about a half hour."

"You got prints on the ice tray!" Carlos had been helping Amanda set the table for *onces*. He sat down at the table. Amanda was looking at him. He covered the phone. "It's Detective Gonzales. He's on his way to arrest Morales!"

That brought a big smile and thumbs up from Amanda. Carlos put the phone to his ear again. Gonzales continued.

"Believe me, we've got more than that on him now. But yes, there were prints on one of the trays. That plus the rental car guy's affidavit were enough to get a search warrant. The judge wasn't really happy about granting it—guess he and Morales are on the same social circuit—but he did, and we searched his office and house.

"Morales was at the office when we arrived. The warrant surprised the shit out of him, and he was on the phone right away to his lawyer. But there was nothing either of them could do. Guess what we found in his office?"

"I'm holding my breath, Detective."

"You remember that the rental car guy told you about the heavy dark coat Morales was wearing?"

"Of course."

"It was tucked away in his office closet, along with the hat. There was a vial with sleeping powder residue in a pocket."

"You're kidding! I can't believe Morales was that careless, or stupid! All he had to do was pitch it somewhere."

"Yeah, but even smart people do dumb things. Guess he figured no one would ever think Jorge's death was anything but suicide. But the bottle's not even the kicker."

"There's more?"

"This morning we got the report from Temuco about the jacket and hat. There were a few particles of Jorge's blood and bone embedded in the jacket. You wouldn't notice it at all, unless you looked real close because they were blown deep into that thick wool."

"Wow! Good work, Detective."

"A lot of this you made possible, Carlos. That's why I'm giving you and your paper the scoop. But, Carlos..."

"Yes?"

"After you write whatever you're going to write, bring it over to me before you send it to Santiago. I told the prosecutor how you helped us, and that I was giving you first crack at the story. He said he wanted to read it first, to make sure it in no way jeopardizes our case."

"You've got my word, Detective."

"And you've got my cell phone number. Call anytime. And you can figure you've got until tomorrow morning to write it. We've purposely timed the arrest so that the two daily detention hearings have already been held. The next one won't be until mid morning tomorrow. That'll be the earliest Morales's lawyer will be able to get him out." Gonzales chuckled. "So, Sr. Big Shot Morales will be spending the night in jail."

"You might see the article in tomorrow's paper. I'll have it ready in a couple of hours at most, Detective. I'm going to contact the paper now to let them know that it'll be coming."

"And, Carlos?"

"Yes, Detective?"

"If you ever get tired of being a reporter and are looking for a new job, give me a call."

Carlos smiled into the phone.

"Thanks, but I like my job."

Carlos snapped his phone shut, his mind already buzzing with the article. He gave Amanda a big hug.

"Did I tell you that you look especially beautiful today, *mi querida?*"

Gonzales started the car. He was really going to enjoy this. Sr. Big Shot, get ready! You're about to get busted but good! He pulled out of the station, followed by the police van. As they drove to the mill, Gonzales told himself to calm down. Above all, be professional. He didn't know exactly why he disliked Morales so much, but he did. Part of it was because of his snotty attitude, of course, and maybe also because he was so rich. But more than anything it was that the man thought he could do whatever he wanted, that he was totally above the law. Rules were for others, not for him. He had no conscience; he was devoid of morality. He had committed cold blooded murder and was responsible for the death of thousands of swans, paralyzed a man for life, and had a university building full of irreplaceable documents and artifacts burned down. By God, the monster should be hung up by his balls. Easy, easy! Remember, be professional—don't screw up.

They pulled into the mill. The detective parked directly behind the Mercedes, blocking it if there was any trouble. He made sure he took his keys, just in case. The police van parked next to the Mercedes. One of the *carabineros* accompanied the detective up to the office; the other walked towards the apartment.

Gonzales almost laughed when he saw the look on Morales's face when he opened the door. First there was surprise, then fear, and, finally, summoned outrage.

"What do you want now, LIEUTENANT? And why is this policeman with you?"

"I have some good news and some bad news for you, Señor Big Shot. I'll give you the good news first. The superintendent has ordered Jorge's apartment to be opened up again, and there is a policeman taking down all the tape as we speak."

Morales put his hands on his hips, although he was worried by the smug look on Gonzales's face. And what was with this 'Señor Big Shot?'

"About time! So, what's the so-called bad news?"

"The bad news is that you're under arrest for the murder of Jorge Espinosa. I'm afraid you'll have to come with us. You have the right to remain silent, but I suggest you call your lawyer because..." Gonzales reached behind his back, under his jacket, and extracted a pair of handcuffs. "It'll be easier to make the call now, before I put these on."

Morales's face paled. For a long moment he didn't say a word. He collected himself, arched his back.

"Is that so? I will make that call, LIEUTENANT, and you better believe it will be the first step to sue you and your whole damn department. You won't know what hit you, but you'll have plenty of time to figure it out when you direct traffic on some little corner for the rest of your life!"

He stomped over to the desk. As he picked up the phone, he looked murderously at Gonzales. The detective was laughing at him.

"Hurry now, Señor *Rico*, these are waiting for you," he said, waving the handcuffs slowly back and forth.

Chapter Thirty-Two

Morales struck his usual pose in front of the window, looking out with hands clasped behind him. But he saw nothing, he was too busy thinking. Rodrigo Bustamante, his lawyer, was seated at the large walnut desk.

"I think, Ivan, that it would be best for you to testify in your defense. We have to present a picture of you as the exemplary businessman, a pillar of the community whose only fault is mortal weakness for a voluptuous woman. We will also paint Jorge as utter scum."

Morales turned from the window.

"'Pillar of the community.' Is that why you had me contribute to the university's new science building?"

The lawyer nodded.

"Yes, it fits the picture we're trying to create. That, plus the university girl will testify that you knew about the test results being at the science building, which implies motive to burn it down. Even though you have a rock-solid alibi, we still will want Jorge to be the bad guy, and that anything he did, he did on his own. We will also let the court know that your generous donation was made even though your bank accounts have plummeted with your stock's crash.

"Ivan, we know from the pre-trial that things are going to be very rough. Still, we've had our share of luck, too;

especially finding out that Jorge abused Julia several times over at Nena's. She's grateful he's dead."

"She and Nena are grateful for a lot more than that! They won't have to work another day of their life with what I'm paying them!"

"Just be thankful, Ivan, or we wouldn't have a prayer. A bonus is that Julia is a perfect witness. I've created a mock court scene several times, with me being the prosecutor. I couldn't trip her up. She's a born liar. Have you gotten together with her like I requested?"

Morales nodded.

"Good. Do you have the condoms?"

Morales nodded again. He walked over to the bathroom, returning with a little plastic bag secured with a twist tie.

"I didn't know being a lawyer had so many ramifications. Is this something they taught you at law school?"

"Very funny. I was taught to win, Ivan; do whatever it takes."

The lawyer carefully placed the used condoms in his briefcase.

"I just wish your wife was as good an actress as that whore. She comes across like she doesn't give a shit about what happens to you."

"That's because she probably doesn't."

"That has to change. She has to portray the aggrieved spouse of a driven, but loving, husband. I'll just have to keep working with her on that. Now, as for public opinion, at least the small business owners were gratified in Guarantee Court, although nothing will be settled for some time. But that's all secondary. Nothing matters if we don't win the big one. I don't think I have to remind you that the public prosecutor is asking for life without parole."

"Gonzales is responsible for that, I'd bet anything."

"He's also the key, Ivan, to getting you off."

"What! Gonzales? He wants me to rot in hell!"

"Yes, and it's his enthusiasm to crucify you that gives us a chance. I don't give a shit about the prints on the ice trays. I've got two experts to say they could be weeks old. It's the brain particles in your jacket that puts you there at the time of the, er, 'suicide.' We have to raise the possibility that the evidence was not clean. I have to make the judges think it's possible and plausible that he doctored up the evidence before they ever arrived at the lab."

"What do you think our chances are, Rodrigo?"

"Right now, forty-sixty. That's why you need to testify also. We've got to work every possible angle. You've got to come across as an upright citizen victimized by a greedy, dastardly employee. So," the lawyer said standing up and pulling the chair to the middle of the room, "have a seat, Ivan. It's time to rehearse."

Morales sat down.

"Aren't you friends with one of the judges, Ivan?"

"Yes. We've had a couple of business dealings, some of them rather interesting, the details of which I'm sure he wouldn't want public."

"That's good. That's very good."

The lawyer walked around to face Morales.

"Now, Sr. Morales, tell me how could you possibly not have known that your mill was dumping thousands of gallons of toxins into the river?"

***

Tomás sat in the wheelchair in front of the floor-to-ceiling picture window trying to look out across the ocean, but it was so socked in that he couldn't even see the edge of the water. *Niebla*—fog—talk about a town aptly named! There had been maybe a handful of days out of the entire month they had been renting the house that he and Lilia could see the harbor. He looked down at the beach settlement; no splashes of bright color anywhere, everything was gray and misty. Understandably, it was like a ghost town in the winter. He could barely make out El Encuentro Costumbrista where they had dined the night of the crash. There was the lot in front with the lamppost where they had parked. God, if only he had mentioned seeing Jorge by the car, Carlos would have checked underneath and... Don't go there, Tomás! It's over and done with. You can't take it back. Your life's finished. What a fucking rat's nest!

He wheeled himself over to the refrigerator for another beer. He couldn't drink enough beer. He shook a couple oxycodone out of a little vial and washed them down. He wasn't supposed to mix alcohol and the oxycodone, but he did every chance he could, especially when Lilia wasn't around. The oxycodone enabled him to escape his body, go somewhere else, anywhere else, and the alcohol helped take him away farther and faster.

But he wouldn't have to ingest all this stuff much longer; that is, if he had the courage to follow through with his plan. Two days ago, he had completed the first step. Now, if he left this planet, Lilia, Juan and his family, Jaime, Pablo and Miriam—everybody would be set for life. The lawyer had written it up, and he had signed and initialed all the documents. He had shooed Lilia out of the house each time the lawyer came, telling her he was working on his finances, shifting some funds around. She had no idea that he had written up a new will.

He heard a truck approach down at the bottom of the hill. There was a sheer drop-off below the picture window, maybe two hundred feet, and he could see Lilia turning into the steep driveway, returning from Valdivia where she had gone grocery shopping. Carlos, who had a break between assignments, and Amanda were coming to dinner which Tomás was not looking forward to. Everyone tried to be so upbeat for his sake, and their continual sympathetic looks rankled the shit out of him. But it wasn't their fault; he was the paraplegic.

Things he never would have thought of ate at him. Like looking up at people. He was average height in the States, but in Chile he was tall. Now even children looked down at him with their pitying eyes. A small thing maybe, but not to him. He didn't talk with the shrink about that or a hundred other things. 'Use your mind now, Tomás, not your body. You just have to adjust,' Lilia kept telling him. Easy to say. He was not cerebral, never had been. He had made his way through life working physically—the woods, construction, light farming. He wasn't erudite, just a hands-on sort of guy. Damn hard to change something like that overnight, especially when you were over fifty years old.

He took another slug of beer. Now Carlos, there was someone cerebral. Amanda, too. She was María Elena's clone—smart for sure, independent, beautiful. And feisty! He chuckled. María Elena could be feisty too, but thankfully not very often. Amanda, on the other hand, could fly off the handle at any time. It was a good thing she was with Carlos who kept her in line. They were a damn fine match with their whole lives ahead of them. Not like him. His was over. There wasn't a thing to look forward to. Well, that wasn't exactly true. He had his pills and beer. If he had enough of that in him, it was A-okay. And he was beginning to feel A-okay right now.

Lilia came in with her arms full of groceries. She smiled at him before turning the corner and putting the bags down on the broad counter in the kitchen. When she went out for more, Tomás wished he could help; instead, he drained the last of his beer. When everything was put away, he asked, "How's the road?"

"Closer. Even in this weather they're working on it. Only a small section left to do just outside Valdivia. The rest is good. There's absolutely no traffic coming out here. How's your foot?"

He had an oozing bedsore on his left heel. Because the circulation in his lower extremities was terrible, the sore was taking forever to heal.

"I haven't checked it. Forgot."

Lilia frowned.

"Tomás, you have to pay more attention! It's really important. If it gets infected and into the bone, the doctor said amputation could be necessary."

"I know. I know." Another reason to check out of here, he thought. She came over to take a look.

"It's a little better."

She pulled up the other pant leg to make sure he was wearing his knee-high 'ted,' a special snug-fitting, support stocking. When she stood back up, Tomás said, "Grab me a beer, would you?"

She walked over to the refrigerator. Concern surfaced on her face.

"You've already had several, Tomás. Don't forget Amanda and Carlos are coming over."

Yeah, he thought, that's why I want another.

"What? Are you counting my beers now, Lilia?"

"No, Tomás...well, yes. You're not supposed to drink so much with your medicine."

"Just grab me a beer, or do I have to come around to get it?"

Lilia sighed as she reached for his beer. She watched him drink a third of it before wheeling over to the window. Her expression was difficult to read.

The rest of the afternoon passed slowly. Tomás began to slur his words. His eyes were glassy and his head felt heavy. He looked at his watch. Four hours since he had taken his last pills. He was supposed to take them every six. What the hell, he thought as he clumsily took the bottle out of his pocket. Lilia saw him.

"Tomás! Don't!"

She rushed over, but too late. He smiled drunkenly up at her.

"What's the matter? Can't I have a little fun? I feel better when I take this stuff. Hey! C'mon, what do you say we go kick up our heels a little! Yeah, let's go dancing down the hill. But, wait a second; silly me! Almost forgot, can't do that, can I? 'Cuz I'm a fucking cripple. Well, what do you say we jump in the sack and have a little go-around? Oh, yeah. Can't do that either." He glared at her. "What I can do, Lilia, is drink beer and take these pills. So, leave me alone!"

Lilia, on the verge of tears, returned quietly to the kitchen. Tomás turned to look out the window again. After awhile he looked at his watch. Time to 'cath.' As he wheeled towards the bathroom, he asked, "What time are they coming?"

"In a couple of hours, around seven-thirty."

"Can't wait. Can't wait to be pitied again! That's going to be a lot of fun."

"Tomás! They care about you. And they just want to make you feel wanted."

"Well, I don't want them!"

He banged the wheelchair into the door jam trying to get into the bathroom.

"Goddamn fucking door!" He slammed his fist against the wall before awkwardly shutting the door behind him. Moments later Lilia heard something clatter on the floor. She didn't know what to do. Maybe she should call Amanda and cancel: Tomás was especially bad today. She waited for him to come out. Five minutes became ten.

"Tomás?"

No answer.

"Tomás, are you alright?"

When there was still no answer, she carefully opened the door. He had passed out and, catheter still in his penis, he had drained himself all over the front of his pants. Lilia abruptly went back into the kitchen where she picked up the phone.

"Amanda? Lilia. I think we're going to have to cancel tonight's dinner...Yes, me too. It's just that Tomás is...is not feeling well. He's been so depressed lately that I just don't think he's up to it tonight ...Of course, another time when Carlos is in town. Please tell him I'm sorry I didn't get a chance to see him.... Right. Thanks, I'll tell him. *Ciao.*"

Lilia filled a small basin with soapy water and retrieved a sponge from the sink. She pulled out the catheter, washed and put it away. After wiping up the urine, she wheeled Tomás towards the bedroom. He woke up with the movement.

"What's going on?" he asked, blinking himself awake. He tried to put his hands on the wheels. Lilia stopped pushing him.

"Oh yeah, pissed myself again. Time for more fun, eh Lilia? You get to play mama and change the baby's diapers."

He pushed the wheelchair away, weaving his way to the refrigerator where he pulled out a beer. Lilia remained where she was, silently staring at the floor. Tomás wheeled back to her.

"Having fun yet, Lilia? Aren't you glad to be with me? You're crazy, you know that? Go find yourself a real man!"

"I love you, Tomás."

"Like I said, you're crazy. There's no future with me, woman! Don't you get it? You should find yourself someone that you don't have to take care of every minute. Free yourself up. Carve some more birds. Have some sex! God knows you've gone long enough without it."

"Tomás! Don't!"

Tomás felt remorse tugging at him from somewhere deep down, trying to hold him back from saying more. But he couldn't help himself.

"You stick around with me and I'll ruin what's left of your life. I'll be every bit as bad as Jorge was to you…probably worse!"

He reached for his pill bottle. It was empty. He threw it against the wall. Lilia looked at him incredulously.

"You went through that whole bottle, Tomás?"

"No, I always throw full bottles against the wall! Then I can pick up all the little pills. It's a game I play—it gives me fucking something to do! What the hell does it look like? But no worries; you got more today in town, right?"

She nodded.

"Yes, but that's the last thing you need now, Tomás. You're going to kill yourself if you keep taking so much."

"Promise?"

"Tomás, don't say things like that!"

"Where'd you put them?"

She didn't answer. Turning her back to him, she went into the kitchen to put away the things she had prepared for dinner: she knew he wouldn't eat anything tonight. Tomás wheeled angrily up to the counter. His eyes were wild.

"Where did you put the fucking pills, woman!"

She ignored him, and he went ballistic. Turning in his chair he flung the beer bottle as hard as he could at the picture window. The thick bottom end of the bottle shattered the window with a loud crash. Lilia jerked her head up. Fear covered her face, then anger. She slammed the pot of stew down on the counter. It spilled all over the floor. Her eyes flashed.

"Your pills are in the lower shelf of the bathroom. You can reach them just fine. There are two bottles. If you take them all, maybe you can kill yourself if you want!"

He started to wheel himself towards the bedroom. Lilia's outburst surprised him. She continued to scream at him.

"You, you, you! What about US, you fool! I love you. And the doctor says if you try, you can lead a good, productive life. WE can lead a good productive life. There are a lot of things you can do, if you don't give up. I never thought of you as weak, Tomás. Anything but! I was wrong! You're a self-pitying weakling who won't even try!"

He continued to wheel himself towards the bedroom.

"Wait, I have one last thing to say…"

She quickly walked around in front of him, forcing him to stop. She put her arms on the wheelchair rests and lowered her head until they were eye to eye.

"I'm not going to watch you kill yourself, Tomás. If you go for those pills, I will leave you, I swear. Take your choice."

Their eyes locked. She stood back up. Even in his drunken and drugged state, his mind said, cool it you fool, but his hands and arms began to push the wheels. When he passed the twin beds on the way to the bathroom, she turned on her heels and grabbed a jacket hanging by the front door. The whole house shook when the door slammed behind her.

Chapter Thirty-Three

Lilia angrily drove towards Valdivia, her mind spinning. If he doesn't want me around, why should I stay? Maybe he's right: get on with my life! If I left him, could I go back to working at the lumber outlet? I made enough money there, plus had time to carve. But then his shadow would always be there because it's his business. Sooner or later he would begin to pay attention to it, then he'd be around. That would be really tough.

But maybe he'll never be interested in the business again. Like his house. It's just sitting there, three-quarters finished. Maybe he will totally give up and kill himself. God, I couldn't handle that! I just no way could handle that. The best thing would be to move somewhere else, start over. Osorno, or Puerto Montt. Lots of tourist shops in Puerto Montt, and Tomás has said a thousand times that the tourist stores would die to sell my carvings. Plenty of others too in Temuco and Puerto Varas.

There's one problem though, one very big problem: I love him. I want to care for him, help him. If only he would snap out of it and try. We could be a team. We could have a future, a good life together; but it won't happen if he won't try.

She drove up over the Puente Cruces. Turning right, in front of the university, she crossed the bridge to downtown Valdivia. She followed Avenida Picarte, heading east, and then re-crossed the river to enter Las Animas. When she arrived at Pablo and Miriam's, Carlos's shiny new car was parked in front. She parked behind it. Carlos and Amanda were sitting like lovebirds on the couch when she entered. They looked up guiltily.

"Sorry to interrupt," Lilia said.

Amanda jumped up to give her a hug.

"You've been crying. Are you alright?"

Amanda's concern brought Lilia to the brink of tears again, but she fought them back.

"I'm fine. It's just Tomás. He's bad, he's so low. He's taking too many pills, and drinks more and more. It makes him worse. He's running away. He's a mess tonight: that's why I cancelled dinner. I don't know what to do."

Carlos stood up to put a hand on her shoulder. He knew that Tomás depended on the painkillers now. Addiction came with trimmings: the last thing Lilia needed was another monster in her life.

"It's up to him, Lilia. You can't do more than you've already done. He's in Niebla, at the house?"

"Yes. We had a fight, and the way he is now, I can't talk to him…no one can. I'll go back in the morning. Is it okay, Amanda, to sleep in my old room tonight?"

"Of course. You don't have to ask. Maybe Tomás will realize what you do for him if he spends the night alone. You have been a saint to that man for months!"

Lilia smiled sadly.

"Maybe. Who knows? But I'm really exhausted. I'd like to sleep for a million years. Good night."

Carlos and Amanda sadly watched her trudge up the stairs to her room.

Tomás entered the bathroom for the pills. He held the bottle for a few long moments before he slowly placed it back on the shelf. Lilia's gone because of those devils. Well, fuck her! Good riddance! And I'll do it tonight! With her angry, it'd be a good time. Come here, my little friends. He reached out, but stopped inches short. Congratulations, Tomás, you've made it! You do yourself in, and then Lilia can clean up the mess. You're a total asshole now, you know that? Lilia has done so much for you. No one, not even María Elena, would have put up with you for so long. And this is how you thank her? Scream at her. Get violent. Drive her away. Then do yourself in so she'll have to clean that up too.

He looked down at himself. That's right, take a good look! Peed all over yourself. Well, your turn; at least Lilia won't have to clean up this one. Don't you have any pride, *hombre?* She's not your personal slave. You've always tried to be a decent human being. But that was before you became so self-absorbed. What are you now? A total jerk!

But things have changed! I'm barely half a man, now! Okay, so that's true—obviously. But do you have to change? Do you have to become a bad person because of it? Do you have to become an addict, to lash out all the time? You know why you do that, don't you? Disgusted with yourself. You realize what you've become. You have no self-esteem left. Yeah? How can I have self-esteem with this woman who has wiped my butt so many goddamn times? She'd be better off without me! Free her up so she can have a life. That's why I've got to do it. That is, if I have the fucking courage. He reached for the pills again.

So, you're just like she said, Tomás, a weakling! Go ahead, take those pills and drink the beers. Kill yourself. That's the plan. Why don't you at least try once! Leave the pills and try to make it through a night, just one night without them. You can do it if you try. Like the alcoholics, one day at a time. Wouldn't you feel better if you could look at yourself in the mirror, and have a clear eye stare back at you for a change? Come on, give it a try. Tonight! The pills will still be here if you can't make it. He lowered his hand and looked in the mirror. It wasn't pretty. He was a mess for sure. Okay, no more pills tonight; at least not right now.

He brought the wheelchair up to his bureau. After struggling out of his soiled trousers and maneuvering into sweatpants, he went to examine what was left of the window. Tendrils of fog were curling into the room as he looked at the gaping black hole. He realized he could end it so easily right now—it could be over so quickly! All he had to do was to get a rolling start, then launch himself out the window. Could he really do it? His stomach fluttered with the possibility.

He wheeled over to the pantry area for a broom. Carefully putting the wheelchair brake on, he swept the broken glass out the window. He couldn't hear the pieces hit the ground. He knew he would only have the courage to try once, and the last thing he needed was a blowout to throw him off course. His stomach felt as heavy as lead. Throwing the broom off into a corner, he wheeled himself the full length of the room, across from the window. He slowly put his hands on the wheels. Wha'da ya say, Tomás? Can you do it! Ready, set, go? His hands were sweaty on the wheels. He wiped them on his sweatpants. Here we go now, c'mon: one for the money, two for the show… C'mon, what are you waiting for! A very long minute passed. Nope, can't do it. Why not, chicken shit? You've got nothing to live for!

He began to roll the wheelchair back and forth across the room. Seven pushes one way, turn, seven pushes the other. He pushed hard and long. Sour sweat began to pour out of him. If I can't do myself in, what the hell can I do? Start using my mind for one thing. I'm not stupid; I can still learn new things. And plenty of other people have been in this situation—had similar injuries. Look at all those athletes that compete in wheelchairs. Maybe writing. Always wanted to try, but could never find the time—too many projects. Well, I've got plenty of time now! And plenty of material with all the travels. Memoirs about all the things I've seen around the world. Or maybe write a love story. Or maybe what it's like to face life as a cripple after being active your whole life.

And I have a lot of money. Except for a new spinal cord, I can buy all the stuff a paraplegic needs to make life easier. There's going to be a settlement, too, with Carlos's insurance company. No, no problem with money. The first thing would be to retrofit a new car. Something with four wheel drive, but still lower than the truck, easier to get in and out of. And, thank God, I'm not a 'quad!' I've got use of the upper torso—my hands and arms are strong. I could have a special shop set up out at the house. I could still make furniture. Lilia and I could work together. Now that would be good! I really am much better off than some. That's right, Tomás! See there! You can think positively. The glass can be half full. There's a lot you can do!

Lilia said that it would be possible for us to have sex if I had an operation where a pump's inserted in my ball sack. When squeezed, it would inflate an erection. She's talked to patients who have had the operation, and to their mates. They said they have wonderful sex all the time. Maybe it was a different kind of sex, but no less wonderful. It was all about watching the process—watching the love act without inhibitions, touching, seeing your mate have an orgasm.

So maybe we could have sex too. Maybe we really could be okay. But I'd have to get in shape. Stop the beer and pills. Watch my diet closely so only one bowel movement a day. Hey, don't forget about the pain! How will you get through that? Bullshit! The pain isn't so bad now. You know that! You can handle most of it without any of the drugs. You've been lying to the doctors for weeks to keep getting plenty of pills. Good grief. That's right, you've become a liar now too!

He stopped wheeling. What the hell, give it a shot! And first things first! He wheeled over to the refrigerator, opening the door wide. He took out every beer and placed them by the sink. One by one, he opened them and dumped the beer down the drain. He started laughing when he recalled a scene from "The African Queen." There was Bogart, hung over as hell, waking up to see Katherine Hepburn holding a parasol while dumping his bottles of gin overboard. The camera panned over a long line of bottles floating out of sight. Pity though, Kuntsman beer is the best in Chile. Well, maybe one last one. He took a sip. Maybe I should dump the pills down the toilet. Whoa there, partner! Let's don't get hasty; this is a trial run, remember? You might not make it, and you still have some pretty intense pain on occasion. Let's keep the pills in reserve, okay?

He took the beer over to the window, carefully putting the brake on. Just being that close to the gaping hole made his stomach flutter again. But he was feeling cheery, excited by the decision he had made. Wonder where Lilia is? With Amanda, probably. Wonder if I should call her? Tell her that I'm going to try, and that I dumped out all the beer—well, almost all the beer—down the drain. He looked at his watch. God, how did it get to be so late? Much too late to call. He looked out the window. He could just see a dim light or two through the persistent fog. He took another sip of beer. He was going to miss his beer.

He was emotionally and physically exhausted. There were barbiturates and alcohol in his system, and the mist felt so good on his face. He closed his eyes. Soon he was snoring, the half-drunk bottle of beer lying at an angle in his lap. He began to dream. At first he wasn't sure where he was, but both María Elena and Lilia were there, standing side by side, smiling. They were preparing his *maté*. Then he realized they were in his little kitchen in Vermont while he was on the porch in his usual place, rocking. Lilia took María Elena into the living room to show her the paneling. But it wasn't the knotty wide pine he had put up; instead it was the *alerce* that they had installed in the new house. As Lilia ran a hand lovingly over the paneling, Tomás noticed María Elena's smile begin to tighten. Lilia walked over to the box in the corner where he kept all his athletic stuff: softball mit and bat, soccer shoes and soccer ball, bicycle helmet and gloves. After rummaging through the box for a few seconds, she found what she was looking for. It was a little bicycle pump, but it was phallic-shaped. Lilia caressed the pump as she explained how to use it. María Elena's smile disappeared. She looked furious. She said something angrily to Lilia, then strode out the front door. She passed right by him. He stuck out his arm, trying to stop her, but she was just out of reach. She stomped down the porch stairs to the small clearing around the house. There was a *ramada* in the clearing, which didn't make sense because he didn't have one on his land in Vermont. Beyond were the woods, but they weren't maples and birches; they were *alerce*. María Elena headed straight for the trees. Somehow he knew that he would never see her again if she made it to the trees. He tried to stand up to bring her back, but couldn't. Why the hell not! He grabbed the arms of the rocking chair. He heard Lilia scream, "No!" at the top of her lungs just as he launched himself up with all his strength. It was then he woke up, instantly realizing where he was. And his mistake. But it was too late. He slammed into the edge of the window frame before disappearing into the dark abyss below.

Chapter Thirty-Four

Light rain dripped from Juan's hat, falling onto the black *manta de Castilla*. The thick wool absorbed it like a sponge. The big collar was pulled up and, other than his face, only his hands were visible holding the reins and a carved wooden box. He rode slowly up towards Tomás's house. Gray, wet, dismal. A fitting day, he thought, to scatter the ashes. He looked down to the box. They were taking one last ride together.

"How many times have we been on this road, eh? I cannot remember. There is the old trail over there down to the *gerente's* house, and we are passing now the little girl's grave. But the cross is gone. Everything's gone now, my friend," he said sadly. "Remember the soccer games, and how we would tease each other on the rides home? Athough," he chuckled as he patted the box, "you and I are too old for that now. No more soccer fields, no more schools either, only your pine. But you know that already."

He rode on with his memories. The house wasn't far away when he heard vehicles approach from below. That is good, he thought, they won't have to wait long. He pulled off to the side, holding the reins firmly and talking in a low voice to his horse. He didn't need it to shy, and drop the box: for sure Tomás would not like to be spilled here.

Carlos, Amanda, Pablo, Miriam, and Guillermo passed first in Carlos's car. Somber faces, brief waves. Lilia was next, driving Tomás's truck with Jaime and his *señora*. Kurt and Carlos's mother were in Kurt's pickup. Young Tomás brought up the rear driving the company truck with Flor next to him in the cab. Holding on to the side and headboards was the rest of the family, bundled in *mantas* and hats pulled low. No one smiled. Once they passed, Juan spurred his horse into a fast walk that was not quite a trot.

"We will never have to worry about money now, my friend, thanks to you. And Amanda will be able to go to veterinarian school. I never knew you had so much money! And to live like you did, like we do! You must have been a little crazy. But what about your new house, eh? What am I supposed to do with that? Should Flor and I move there? I don't think so. We are too accustomed to the farm. We are too old. Your house needs young people. It should be finished like you talked of, with all your new systems. Maybe young Tomás, or Amanda if she ever settles down. I asked Lilia if she would like to live there, but she said no. She said it would make her too sad."

When he arrived at the house, everyone filed out of the front door. He rode past them to the trailhead. They silently followed, down past the *alerce* grotto to the edge of the *copihue* clearing where Juan carefully handed the box to Jaime before dismounting. After hitching the reins to a sapling, he loosened the cinch and covered the saddle with his *manta*. Taking back the box, he led them to the *ramada* where he placed it on a small table. Lilia had crafted the box. On the front she had carved a *chucao* in relief. Juan oriented the bird so it faced out towards the waterfall and volcano. He cleared his throat.

"How do I begin to tell you what Tomás meant to me? To all of us. It is impossible! When he first came here, he couldn't speak our language, didn't know our customs, couldn't even ride a horse. He was very young, and very alone. But he adjusted. He came to love us as we came to love him. He was to marry my sister. He was my brother… and," he smiled softly, "he could play soccer. We played many times against each other, and then together one year on the Camán team…"

Juan fought to control his emotions.

"All of you know what the grotto and this clearing meant to him…and to my sister, and over the years to most of us here. This was where he was to be married, and this was where he believed my sister's spirit lives. It is only fitting his ashes be scattered here.

"Tomás could not stay with us after my sister's accident, although I know he wanted to with all of his heart. He could not because, as he often told me, too much here reminded him of her. He felt that he had to leave or he would never heal. I said goodbye to him at this very spot, and I feared that I would never see him again. But he came back to us after all the years. And he was happy again."

He looked over to Lilia.

"And you, Lilia, were the biggest part of that happiness. It was you more than anyone who was curing Tomás."

Lilia did not respond or look at Juan.

"I know Tomás loved you, Lilia, and if not for some very bad people, I think he would have healed completely and you would have been very happy together. But it was not to be. For whatever reason, God has taken Tomás away from us."

He frowned at the box.

"I am told that you took your life, Tomás. That is bad and makes me very angry. That is against the rules of God. You have disappointed me. Maybe all the drugs clouded your thinking, but I want you to know that you have made me angry as well as sad.

"But even so, Tomás reached out, during his confusion, to help us. He has shown once again how much he cared. Jaime's and my family will never go hungry, all of us have a future thanks to him. For that we are indebted."

He took the lid off the box.

"Flor and I have bundled Tomás up into many little packages. I ask that each of you take some of Tomás to spread, and maybe say a few kind things to him in your mind."

Juan held the box in front of him as everyone lined up. The only two to leave the clearing were he and Lilia. They returned to the trail. Juan walked as far as the *alerce* grotto; Lilia continued up to the house. Juan undid the red curled ribbon that bound the package, and sprinkled some of Tomás at the base of each tree. He stood for a long time, head bowed and silent, at the stump of the fallen *alerce* where he and Tomás had worked so hard. The piles of sawdust were still there, dark red from the rain.

Lilia walked around the outside of the house, leaving ashes at each corner. She spread some around the outdoor spigot, and, finally, around the little shed that was to be his shop. She entered the house. The paneling brought tears to her eyes. Why had she left him alone? If only she had been there! She saw his body sprawled on the rocks. The picture fanned her fury. Morales! I hope he spends the rest of his life in prison with all the other murderers. I hope he get's buggered every day until he bleeds. No! I want him dead! I want him hanged. There should still be the death penalty for people like him! Like the Bible says, 'an eye for an eye.'

She lovingly stroked the paneling, unknowingly striking the same pose as in Tomás's dream. She walked around the room, looking out the windows as she waited for the others to come up the path. Finally, they appeared at the trailhead. Juan and his horse were not with them. She went outside.

"Where's Juan?" she asked Flor.

"He wants to be alone. He told me to start serving the food down at the house without him," Flor said, shaking her head. "If I know my husband, he won't return home for hours. And he'll be soaking wet."

While the mourners were getting into their vehicles, Juan was pulling two glasses and a bottle of red wine from his saddlebags. He filled both glasses, and placed one on top of the box. He lightly tapped it with his.

"Cheers, Tomás. Are you happy now? You've got me talking to you, just like you did with my sister. I guess that makes me as crazy as you."

He took a sip as he looked around the clearing.

"Listen, María Elena, if you're really here, come on over! Tomás and I are having a little send-off."

Juan filled his glass again. The immense volcano was obscured by rain falling harder now, and the waterfall, thick and white, was much louder than usual. Maybe it was the wine, but he began to feel their presence. Now he knew how Tomás felt when he came here. Juan could almost feel the cascade course through his body as he sat and drank. He had no idea how much time passed before he noticed the bottle was almost empty, enough for one more glass. He looked over to the path. His horse was soaked, head down, miserable. The *manta*, he knew, would weigh many kilos. He tapped Tomás's glass one final time before standing up.

"Tomás, I'm afraid this one is *para el estribo*, or as you would say, 'one for the road.'" He drained the glass. "I will return sometime soon and we shall have another little visit, you and me. You have my word. And you, sister," he said to the clearing, "you must be happy! You finally got your man back."

With the soaked *manta* weighing on his shoulders, he tightened the cinch, and pulled out another bottle of wine from the saddlebags. Opening it, he looked back to Lilia's box, and raised the bottle in a final toast. Bottle still in hand, he mounted, took a long swig, and turned his horse around. Slowly, he headed up the trail.

Chapter Thirty-Five

Carlos looked around the courtroom. It could have been a scene out of one of those dubbed-in Perry Mason reruns, except there was no jury and there were three judges instead of one. The judges, each with a gavel, sat at an enormous elevated desk. A door directly behind them led to their private chamber. Next to the judges was the witness stand. Everything was made out of heavy ornate dark wood, including the bench that he, Amanda, and Lilia sat on behind the prosecutor's desk. Morales sat with his lawyer across the aisle from the prosecutor. The room, other than for the few witnesses, was packed with the press and public: the trial was big news with the whole country paying attention.

"No further questions, Detective." Carlos watched the prosecutor return to his seat. The evidence was indisputable and overwhelming. Morales didn't have a chance; but he was still curious to see what approach Morales's lawyer would take.

Rodrigo Bustamante stood up. He was tall, good looking, graying a little around the temples. He buttoned the front of his charcoal gray suit as he approached the witness stand.

"I have learned, Detective Gonzales, that you had a somewhat humble background…that your parents were

quite poor, and that you grew up in a rough neighborhood of Concepción."
Gonzales looked surprised.
"Yes, that is true."
"You have come a long way in life. And now, do you make a lot of money being a detective?"
Gonzales smiled.
"Certainly not; but I never expected to make a lot of money being a policeman."
"Do you resent people who have a lot of money...who are rich?"
Gonzales hesitated before he answered.
"No, of course not."
"Then how do you explain your hostility towards my client? How do you explain the length of time you had the worker's apartment in the mill cordoned off, so he couldn't replace the employee who committed suicide? It was more than twice the time that is customary in such an investigation. Your co-workers, including lab technicians as well as members of our respected *carabineros*, whom I shall call upon later, described to me your insolence to my client, and they have told me that on several occasions you said, and I quote, that you were going to 'crucify that son-of-a-whore.' I was even told that when you arrived to arrest my client in his office, you dangled handcuffs in front of him, laughed at him, and called him '*Señor Rico.*' How do you explain this if you do not resent his being wealthy?"
"I don't see what bearing this has..."
"What bearing! I'll tell you what bearing this has!"
The lawyer turned to face the judges.
"Your Honors, the physical evidence against my client, which Detective Gonzales so graphically described, was transported solely by the detective to the lab in Temuco. This is very unusual and unorthodox. It violates protocol; yet, that's what was done. If the detective, for whatever reason, had a personal grudge or disliked my client, he

had the opportunity to tamper with that evidence...and I believe that is exactly what happened."

Gonzales turned crimson, the prosecutor sprang from his chair, and the courtroom erupted. All three judges banged their gavels. The judge in the center ordered the room to quiet. He turned to the defense lawyer.

"That is a very serious theory, Councilor."

The prosecutor added, "Your Honors, Detective Gonzales has been with the justice department for over fifteen years. His record is spotless. This," he said looking at Bustamante, "is nothing more than a very tasteless and desperate ruse."

"I think, Your Honors," Bustamante said, "that if you let me proceed, I can and will show that there should be considerable doubt about the evidence that has been presented." The judge looked at his compatriots. They nodded, and he turned back to the lawyer.

"Proceed."

"Detective, I assume you have presented all the evidence you have discovered concerning this case?"

Gonzales gave him an icy stare.

"Of course!"

The lawyer began to walk back and forth in front of Gonzales.

"You said that Morales drove the rental car from Temuco to his mill the night of the suicide."

"The night of the murder. Yes."

"My client does not deny going to Valdivia late that night in the rental car after his stockholders' meeting. In fact, as he told the car agent in Temuco, and as he admitted to you, he had a, shall we say, rendezvous with a woman, and that they parked in their customary spot for a certain period of time."

"Yes, that's what Sr. Morales maintains."

"Now let me ask you something, Detective. If you were married and had a rendezvous in the town you lived in, with a woman who was not your *señora*, might you want to use a car other than your own for that meeting?"

"Yes, that's possible, but..."

"And did you, Detective, investigate that spot where my client said he parked?"

Gonzales began to fidget.

"Yes."

"Did you find anything that may have indicated that my client had been there?"

Gonzales glanced towards the third row where the sergeant who had accompanied him to the area was sitting. The sergeant looked away.

"Yes, we found something."

"Would you tell the court what you found?"

"Some used condoms."

"'Some used condoms.' Detective, that means more than one, correct?"

Gonzales nodded.

"I didn't hear you, Detective."

"Yes."

"So, if those condoms were used by the same person, it would seem to me to indicate that that person had been there more than once. Did you have the condoms examined at the lab in Temuco?"

Gonzales looked towards the sergeant again before answering.

"Yes."

The lawyer stopped pacing in front of Gonzales. He leaned over and looked directly at him.

"And what did you find out?"

"The DNA indicated that they had been used by Sr. Morales."

"Indicated? Did they MATCH the DNA of my client?"

"Yes."

"Is that the only thing you learned?"

"Traces of the woman's DNA were a match also."

The lawyer turned to face the judges, then turned back to Gonzales. In a booming voice he exclaimed, "Then why, in God's name, was this evidence not presented along with everything else!"

Gonzales growled, "Because they were planted. I don't believe Morales or that woman ever met there—not even once!"

The defense lawyer stared at Gonzales. Gonzales glared back. The lawyer turned to look at the judges again. He was shaking his head. Almost to himself he said, "You... YOU don't believe..." Without looking at Gonzales, he asked, "Do you have any proof, any whatsoever, that substantiates that allegation?"

Gonzales looked down.

"No."

The courtroom began to buzz loudly until the judges banged the room into silence. With biting sarcasm, the lawyer concluded, "Your Honors, I have no further questions for this...this upholder of justice."

Judging from the strained look on the prosecutor's face, Carlos would bet anything that he hadn't known about the condoms. Gonzales was in hot water for sure. He might even face charges. The prosecutor stood up and did the only thing he could. He said that the defense was desperate. That they were trying to impugn the reputation of a highly respected law officer with over fifteen years of experience. He pointed out several commendations the detective had received. But, when the prosecutor sat down again, everyone in the courtroom realized that real damage had been done.

When the prosecution finished with its witnesses, the defense called Julia Mendoza to the stand. A woman stood in the rear of the room. All eyes were on her as she slowly made her way forward. Carlos wondered if it had been intentional that she was seated so far back. Although dressed in a conservative skirt and sweater, both were tight, and she was sexually stunning. She reminded Carlos of a Rubens with her hourglass figure. Her full breasts, pointed and swaying slightly as she sashayed up, looked impossibly soft in the sweater. This was the woman Morales said he had met. True or not, a liaison with her was totally imaginable—she oozed sexiness. For the first time, doubt flickered in Carlos's mind. Could Morales really have been with her? Was it really a suicide? And if he was beginning to doubt, what were the judges thinking?

Bustamante asked her where and what she did for work.

"I am an employee in Señora Nena's house on Avenida Anibal Pinto." There was a titter in the courtroom, and Julia smiled into the crowd. Every male over sixteen in Valdivia knew about Nena's.

"And do you know that man sitting over there?" the lawyer asked, pointing at Morales. Julia giggled.

"Of course I know Ivan!"

Morales, looking very much like a husband in the doghouse, glanced embarrassedly at his wife who was the epitome of hurt and forgiveness. Julia turned to smile innocently at her. The courtroom tittered again, and a judge banged his gavel, calling for silence.

"And did you meet with this man very late on the night of February fifteenth of this year?"

"Oh, yes." She smiled again at Ivan, who was looking down at his feet.

Julia cheerfully answered all of the lawyer's questions, completely unabashed and seemingly enjoying herself. Certainly those in the courtroom were enjoying her. Even the judges smiled at some of her candid answers. Carlos thought that there'd be a waiting line outside Nena's tonight.

When the defense was done, the prosecutor approached the stand.

"Young lady, I believe you said that you are an employee in the Señora Nena's house." Julia smiled up at him.

"That's right."

"And just what do you do there?"

Her smile didn't falter.

"Oh, this and that."

More laughter in the courtroom. The judges were smiling again.

"I see, 'this and that.' Isn't Nena's house where men come to buy, shall we say, pleasure from women?"

"Oh, we sometimes dance and all with men who come to Nena's. But, men don't pay me anything. Only Señora Nena pays me…for being her employee. I do lots of things besides dancing, you know—dishes, clean the house, make beds."

The prosecutor ignored her answer.

"You, young lady, are paid, pure and simple, to be a prostitute which in my book means you will do anything for money. I believe you are being paid now to lie which, I might add, is a very serious offense. I don't believe you ever met with Señor Morales that night. Are you sure you don't want to tell the court the truth before you get into some real trouble?"

Bustamante jumped up.

"Objection, Your Honors! The consul is threatening the witness!"

Julia looked totally indignant. Her response was cool.

"Frankly, Señor, I don't care what you think. I know who I am and what I am, and that does not include being a liar!"

The prosecutor continued to question her, trying to trip her up, but couldn't; she was rock solid. He ended somewhat lamely, saying, "Your Honors, this woman is a whore, a woman who will do anything for money. Who could possibly believe her testimony?"

The judges waited for Julia to return to her seat before they adjourned the trial until the next morning. Reporters scurried out, cellphones in hand.

The next day Lilia was called to the witness stand. Bustamante softly asked her to describe when she was raped as a child by the deceased. The prosecuting attorney objected, saying the question was irrelevant, painful to the witness, and totally unnecessary. The judges allowed the defense to proceed. In a small voice, Lilia told how she had crossed onto her neighbor's land to look for the sheep. The courtroom was absolutely still when she described the rape. Bustamante asked, "And how old were you?"

"Twelve."

The courtroom gasped, and Bustamante, shaking his head from side to side, turned to the judges.

"No further questions, your Honors."

The prosecuting attorney remained seated. He looked up to the judges and shook his head. Lilia, head bowed and eyes averted, slowly made her way to her seat where Amanda took her hand. Carlos had to admire the defense. It had produced experts who said the prints on the ice tray could have been weeks old, produced the whore who couldn't be rattled, challenged Gonzales's credibility with the testimony of the sergeant and others. And that condom thing! That was huge; suppressing evidence, for God's sake! But he was trying to reason why Lilia had been called. He didn't have to wait long before he figured it out. In a surprise move, the defense called Morales to the stand.

The courtroom stirred, and the judges ordered everyone still. Morales, dressed conservatively in a fine tweed suit and with head upright, walked to the witness stand. His bearing was both avuncular and aristocratic. The lawyer waited until he was settled.

"Sr. Morales, please tell the court what you do."

"I own and operate the pulp mill twenty-five kilometers out of town."

"And you are the largest employer in the province?"
"Yes, I suppose that is true."
"And Jorge Espinosa was one of those employees?"
"Yes."
"Did you know that he was releasing toxins from your mill into the river?"
"Absolutely not! I had no idea…but then, I have learned many things, many heinous things about this man in the last several months." He looked directly out at Lilia. "I am so sorry, young lady, for what that…that monster did to you." He turned back to his lawyer. "I tried only to help the man out. He was a street cleaner before I hired him. But he was also an excellent mechanic. I wanted to give him a chance. I enjoy giving an opportunity to people who are less fortunate—like the son of the maid in our household. My wife and I wanted to help him, too. We send him to a very good private school here in Valdivia where he is excelling, especially in computer studies. His mother is ecstatic, and the boy will have a real future."

The prosecutor stood up.

"Objection, Your Honors. This is irrelevant."

The judges looked at Bustamante.

"I disagree, Your Honors. We feel that you should know just what type of man the prosecution has put on trial."

The judges conferred briefly. "Please continue, Sr. Morales."

Morales's expression changed to one of mortification.

"But Jorge was the biggest mistake of my life. I have learned there is conjecture that he may have been responsible for the fire at the university. I feel so badly for the university, and the town. That man has affected us all, although," he looked over at Lilia again, sadly shaking his head, "some more than others."

Bustamante put his hand on the rail of the witness stand.

"That 'conjecture'…is that why you made such a generous donation to the university?"

Morales's head swung quickly around.

"Sir, that donation was not to be made public!"

"You didn't want anyone to know?"

"No, sir. That's the last thing I wanted. I felt that if I had never hired Jorge, none of this would have happened. All I wanted was to run my business, be a good employer, and meet my production deadlines." He looked down to his folded hands. "But even though I knew nothing about it, Jorge was my employee and I felt responsible, as his employer, for what he might have done. I wanted to help make it right, but," he said while glaring at his attorney, "privately! But, besides that, I have met several times with the businessmen who were affected by the discharge. We are working out compensation. I want to make it right with them too." He looked over to his wife. "There are many things I want to make right again."

His wife put on her best smile of forgiveness. Amanda rolled her eyes: oh please, spare me! Carlos thought, almost convincing, but not quite. Still, he had to admit, they were good. All of it was good stuff—well rehearsed and choreographed.

"Can you explain Detective Gonzales's attitude throughout the investigation?"

Morales sighed, slowly shaking his head.

"Frankly, no. From the beginning, I tried to cooperate fully with him, but for some reason he seemed not to like me. He continually made things difficult. I didn't understand it...until maybe yesterday when you said it was because I was wealthy."

He looked out towards Gonzales.

"I would just like to say to the detective that I earned my money. I have worked very hard, extremely long hours, and taken big chances. It did not come easy. And all this nonsense about me murdering Jorge has put the mill at risk; I stand to lose a big contract, and if I do, then there will be many, many jobs lost. It would be heartbreaking for me to have to lay off my employees; but it may come to that. If you, Detective, wanted to make me and possibly others suffer, then rest assured you have succeeded."

When the prosecutor questioned Morales, he held firm, continually denying all accusations. He was a wall, equal parts humility and indignation, and could not be shaken. After Morales returned to his seat, the judges adjourned the court until after lunch when both sides would present the closing arguments.

The prosecutor stood up to face the judges. He was much shorter than Bustamante, and much heavier and dark-complexioned—a *moreno*.

"Your Honors, I think we have produced both motive and solid proof that Ivan Morales is guilty of murder. The man, through greed and desperation, calculated and planned the murder of his employee, Jorge Espinosa. But who was Jorge Espinosa? Yes, he was an evil man with a police record, and who committed an unforgiveable sin over thirty years ago. But what the defense counsel has neglected to tell us is that the victim was also 'simple.' This was caused by brain damage from the many blows he suffered soon after the rape from the little girl's brother all those years ago. The deceased may have been very good at fixing machinery, something inherent, but beyond that, he was easily confused. However, much like a dog, he could follow instructions and he was faithful.

"We maintain that Sr. Morales had multiple motives for silencing Jorge Espinosa permanently," the lawyer said, raising three pudgy fingers and pointing to them, one by one. "The deceased was instructed by Sr. Morales to open the gates of toxic discharge once a week. Two, when the pollution was discovered, Sr. Morales ordered the deceased to cut the brake line of the auto of those who discovered the pollution, resulting in a horrific accident where a man was paralyzed and later died. Three, he ordered the deceased to set fire to the science building to destroy all records and evidence of the pollution. We have presented a written deposition from the man paralyzed in the automobile crash that he saw the deceased next to the car right before they were to return to Valdivia. And there is no question that the brake lines were cut. When asked by the police, the deceased denied being there. Sr. Morales knew that the deceased would never stand up to intensive questioning, so he had to remove him. He shot him dead and made it look like suicide."

The lawyer starting listing points again with his fingers.

"We have a witness who rented him a car that night in Temuco. The defendant admits he drove to Valdivia and was there during the time of the murder. We have prints on an ice tray that our technicians indicate places him in the apartment the night of the murder. Finally, we have found bits and pieces of the deceased's brain and skull embedded in the defendant's jacket.

"The defense, in desperation, has tried to impugn the character of Detective Gonzales. The prosecution will concede that Detective Gonzales acted in an unprofessional manner at times during the investigation. It also recognizes that the detective made a serious error in judgment about those condoms. However, as has been pointed out by our lab technicians when they were recalled to the stand, lending credence to the detective's supposition, the condoms were in unusually good shape for supposedly having been in the outdoors for several months. It would be very easy to conclude that they had been planted. Still, it was a mistake not to submit them for evidence. But, that said, it is absolutely absurd to suggest that the detective altered the defendant's jacket in anyway. I repeat, Your Honors, absolutely absurd!

"And, like the condoms, Sr. Morales has conveniently found a so-called witness to vouch for him. Your Honors, no matter how charming the Srta. Julia has been in court, I believe she is lying. Unfortunately, it is not that difficult to hire false witness in this country. I ask you, especially considering her profession, to ignore her testimony. She is not a reputable witness."

The prosecutor sighed, looked to the floor, then back up to the judges.

"This case, I believe, is a simple one. Motives, witnesses, tangible evidence have all been provided. Sr. Morales is being tried for only one crime, but I believe he has committed several, all with dire consequences. And this was not done because of anger or passion. It was thought out—calculated and planned. And, it was done because of greed. I ask Your Honors to find this man guilty as charged, and to sentence him to the maximum punishment of life in prison without parole…Thank you."

Bustamente unrolled his sleeves and pulled the suit jacket from the back of his chair. He slowly approached the bench.

"Your Honors, there is one thing I am in total agreement with the prosecution—that this is indeed a simple case. It is the simple case of a well-respected member of our community being wrongfully tried for a crime that was never committed. Jorge Espinosa was not murdered. He committed suicide. As to exactly why, we will never know. As the prosecutor pointed out, his brain had been addled from blows to the head. Maybe that had something to do with it. Or maybe it was guilt for the man who was paralyzed. Or maybe, it had something to do with the young girl who he had raped was one of the passengers of the car that crashed. He had never been charged for raping her. Possibly he thought he would be now. Or maybe it was because his illegal dumping was out in the open, and he would be fired from the best job and living situation he had ever known. We will never know for sure.

"But here is my client. He is the largest employer in the province and, I might add, a good and fair one. At considerable expense, he built the most up-to-date, environmentally friendly mill in this country. I ask you, why would he do that if he intended to pollute? No, the pollution was a result of his generosity. It was because he offered production incentives to his employees. One employee violated that generosity: Jorge Espinosa. It was he who was greedy, not my client.

"It is so sad that a simple incentive to produce more paper caused so much harm to the environment, the community, and to this community's businesses. The swans are a national catastrophe, and my client was absolutely devastated when he learned that his mill was responsible. That is why he has already met with the local businessmen, and is working out equitable settlements.

"And the fire. I don't think that there is conclusive proof that it was arson. However, the possibility does exist that the deceased was responsible for that too. Because of that possibility, my client felt some responsibility. Consequently, he made a significant anonymous contribution to the university to help them rebuild."

Bustamante looked apologetically towards Morales.

"I publically apologize to my client for divulging this fact. He wanted no credit, only to help make it right."

The lawyer turned back to the judges.

"Everything the prosecution has offered as proof, we have rebuffed. We have a witness who," he said looking at the prosecutor, "regardless of profession, has testified under oath that Sr. Morales was with her at the time of the suicide. That said, my client is guilty of one crime—that of indiscretion. Being the largest business owner and employer in this province, he is constantly under tremendous pressure. To fulfill his contracts both domestically and abroad is an enormous task, let alone managing the day-to-day goings on with a mega-business.

It is understandable that a man like this needs a release, a release that I would bet many here in this courtroom have taken at one time or another…some maybe even at the Señora Nena's."

A judge rapped his gavel at a few snickers in the courtroom.

"This is no laughing matter," the lawyer said seriously. "The Señorita Julia was that release, and now that my client's clandestine meetings with the Srta. are public, it has understandably affected his personal life. Fortunately, the situation is being worked out. Sr. Morales is humbly trying to repair the damage."

On cue, Morales looked at his wife, she beamed back. Amanda almost gagged. Bustamante looked to where Gonzales was sitting.

"I believe we could have this trial thrown out of court on the ridiculous actions of Detective Gonzales. However, we have continued with our defense because we want the public to know my client is innocent. The detective was not only completely unprofessional, but he has also committed serious infractions. After this trial, we will consider filing charges. We believe the jacket was impregnated by him. The prosecution said that because of blows to the brain, the deceased was 'simple.' Certainly, Your Honors, my client is anything but. To think that this intelligent, successful captain of industry would murder a man, splattering pieces of skull all over the jacket he was wearing, and then hang that jacket up in his closet to be discovered by the police is nothing short of ludicrous."

Carlos looked over at Morales. His face was a mask.

"And for a detective to consciously withhold evidence, very important evidence, is a travesty and insult to all the investigators and police of this country. He has sullied our system!"

Bustamante walked up close to the judges. He held his hands up as if pleading.

"Your Honors, I can't help myself from saying that I believe this world is a better place without Jorge Espinosa in it. But, I believe that taking a life, any life, including one's own, is a sin and should be punished. I think that Jorge Espinosa is being punished now, somewhere, somehow. He threw away his life on his own volition. But Sr. Morales is a fine man. I ask you, I beg you, please don't throw away the life of my client; above all, don't throw away the life of an innocent man."

Bustamante returned slowly to his chair, shoulders slumped as if totally spent. The judge in the center tore his eyes away from him to confer briefly with his colleagues. He rapped his gavel sharply.

"Court will reconvene at nine o'clock tomorrow morning. We believe we will have a verdict at that time."

Chapter Thirty-Six

Amanda jumped to her feet, screaming, "Ridiculous! Scandalous!" In the furor of the courtroom, she wasn't heard by the judges who gathered up their papers, and quickly left for their chamber. Members of the media were yelling into their cellphones. Carlos pulled Amanda, still screaming at the judges, towards the door. Lilia remained seated—stunned. She watched as the smiling Morales clapped his lawyer on the back and shook his hand. His wife, strutting up in high heels, gave him a perfunctory hug. The hug for the lawyer seemed more genuine.

Lilia couldn't believe it. This was justice served? This was payback for Tomás? She was transfixed, totally focused on Morales. She didn't notice Carlos come back for her. He gently pulled her to her feet. Lilia could not take her eyes off Morales. Morales, his wife, and the lawyer passed close by as Carlos and Lilia exited their row. Lilia heard him invite the lawyer to celebrate at the mill with a forty year old single malt. The lawyer accepted as the trio walked jubilantly towards the waiting press.

Carlos, arm around Lilia, escorted her by the circle of reporters. Morales's voice boomed from a microphone.

"I am so proud to be a Chilean where we have a judicial system like no other in South America. Justice has been served. An innocent man has been freed…."

Carlos and Lilia could still hear him as they reached Carlos's car. Amanda was in the front, hands over her ears, staring stonily forward. Carlos quickly started the car, and drove off. No one said a word from the courthouse to Las Animas. They filed into the kitchen where Pablo and Miriam were having a late breakfast.

Miriam looked up.

"Well? Did he get life without parole?"

Amanda snorted as she began to pace angrily around the kitchen. Carlos sat down next to Pablo where he made himself a cup of Nescafé. Lilia sat on a stool, close to the kitchen stove.

"Hardly!" Amanda spat. "The judges declared him innocent. It's a travesty. A violation. A..."

Pablo looked up from his *maté*.

"You really expected something else, Amanda?"

He looked at Carlos.

"No offense, Carlos, but this is no surprise; not to me anyway. The system has always favored the rich. And it always will. It's just the way it is."

Amanda sat down in a huff. She reached for a cup and saucer, and angrily tore a hunk of bread from the loaf in the center of the table.

"Maybe, but it was the suppressing of evidence by Gonzales that did it," Carlos muttered. "That was the key. And his lawyer. I still believe Morales murdered Jorge, but you have to admit that the defense did a really good job."

Pablo wouldn't let it go.

"Clearly. But still, rich man's justice. I ask you how many people can afford a lawyer like that one, eh? Very few, Carlos, very few."

"I can't argue that." Carlos looked around the table. "And it doesn't bode well for the civil suits against Morales and the mill. There's a good chance now that public sentiment will be behind Morales: that he didn't know of the dumping, and that Jorge acted alone on burning down the science building."

"That is nonsense, and you know it," Amanda said.

"Yes, I don't believe any of it. But I can't prove otherwise; and with Jorge's death, no one else can either."

"And Morales will get off with a slap on the hand and maybe a few fines!" Amanda's eyes were wild. "Even if Jorge acted alone, what sort of precedent does this establish? It has been proven that the mill intentionally polluted; that it destroyed a very unique and ecologically important part of this country…of this continent! Yet, for the sake of some jobs, it is deemed a minor violation. The message is clear: it is excusable to poison our waters, kill our flora and fauna, so man can amass more and more; so men like Morales can build their castles. Once again, it is man first at the expense of everything else. Screw the planet, who cares as long as we humans get what we want! That's the message. God, it makes me physically ill!"

Lilia spoke for the first time.

"Morales killed Tomás. He deserves to die."

They all turned to look at her. She was staring straight ahead at the wall. That was all she said. They lapsed into a moody silence. Although next to the stove, Lilia paid no attention to the fire. Miriam had to reach past her several times to stoke it. Lilia only stared straight ahead. Everyone but Lilia ate something. Pablo offered to make her a cup of tea, but she did not bother to respond. She didn't say another word to anyone for a long time. When she finally spoke, she startled them.

"Carlos, I left my purse in your car. Can I have your keys?"

"Of course, but I'll get it for you…"

He started to get up, but Lilia was already on her feet.

"Thank you, but sit… I need to walk around a little."

Lilia went out to the car. Her purse wasn't there, but she knew that. It was under the little stool where she had kicked it out of sight. She sat in the driver's seat and leaned over to open the glove box. She reached in for Carlos's pistol. Good, she thought: a revolver like the one Jaime has in Cufeo. She checked to see if it was loaded. It was. She put it in her large skirt pocket, and closed the glove box. She started the car and drove slowly off towards the mill.

Epilogue

Beaming and bearded, Carlos reached for Amanda's hand, drawing her into the clearing. She was followed by both their families. Next came a priest from Valdivia, and finally, bringing up the rear, was Juan, his full head of hair completely salt-and-pepper. Once everyone was in the clearing, Juan took charge, limping quickly around, arranging the families in a semi-circle behind Amanda and Carlos who faced out from the freshly thatched *ramada*. The priest was in front with his back to the waterfall and volcano. It was a breezy, beautiful day, and the *copihue* were in their full, vibrant red bloom.

Juan, stationing himself at one end of the semi-circle, looked proudly over to his daughter. About time, he thought. Amanda, seven months pregnant, was radiant; he had never seen her so serene. Much to the relief of all in attendance, she finally had agreed to take time off from the large animal practice to get married. Juan nodded to the priest who cleared his throat.

Before he could say anything, Amanda suddenly reached for Carlos's arm.

"Look, Carlos, swans!" she exclaimed pointing.

High above the volcano, silhouetted by the afternoon sun, was a long line of black-necked swans. They were so high up that it was difficult for the naked eye to distinguish how fast their wings were beating. But even at that altitude, their long straight necks were visible. A storm had blown them to the west, off course from their normal migratory route, and now they were fighting a strong headwind.

They soon spied the curved course of a river which joined two others at a large town, continuing as one out to the broad blue of the Pacific Ocean. Up river from the town, the swans began to circle a large bend where tall reeds and surface aquatic growth was abundant. It must have looked like a good spot because they came in for a landing. They weren't particularly graceful, angling out their broad wings to slow themselves down. As they skimmed the water, their webbed feet dropped down, and they began to run clumsily over the surface until they dug their heels into the water as the final brake. They sank slowly into the water much like water skiers who let go of the rope.

The swans wiggled their tails, settled their wings, and immediately began to feed. Several paddled straight to the vegetation on the surface. It was a floating green island of delicacies, chest high so that they only had to slightly incline their necks. They created narrow little channels as they ate their way into the growth. Others inspected the shallow river bottom where they found a thick carpet of *luchecillo*. Mated pairs dabbled while using their broad webbed feet to stabilize themselves as they tipped upside down with tail feathers pointing skyward. Occasionally a duo held the pose like synchronized swimmers. It was a smorgasbord bonanza, and the swans soon ate their fill.

They began to preen and clean themselves. Because of the long necks, there was no place on their bodies they couldn't reach. They dipped their heads, necks straight, into the water and scooped enough so that, as they curled their necks backwards, rivulets coursed down to their backs. They rubbed different spots, using the sides of their head as scrubbers.

Before resting, they explored the tall reeds. Somehow they knew this would be a perfect nesting area. There were no buildings or roads nearby. The hills rising up from the river were covered with only the green of pastures and trees. There was food and cover. It was idyllic, perfect for raising their young. They would remain here. Unconsciously the swans started staking out territory before they settled in for the night. As the sun dropped, one by one they turned their long necks and tucked their head into the soft feathers between their wings.

About The Story

The Carlos Anwandter Nature Sanctuary is located on the Cruces River near the town center of Valdivia in southern Chile. It is commonly believed that the refuge was the home of the largest population of black-necked swans in South America. On January 31st, 2004, the Celco (Celulosa Arauco y Constitucíon) pulp mill owned by businessman Anacleto Angelini began operation up river. By August, 2005, only four birds out of an estimated five thousand were observed. The birds strong enough to fly had left the sanctuary, the others had died. Autopsies attributed the deaths to the presence of high levels of iron and other metals polluting the river.

Since the catastrophe, the pulp mill has been periodically shut down and fined. Many irregularities in operation were exposed, and there was a scandal about the mill's lawyers "altering the scientific report on which the Chilean Supreme Court of Justice based its initial ruling acquitting Celco of the massive die off and reversing the factory shutdown ordered by a lower court." The pulp mill is presently in operation.

A long awaited report compiled by the Universidad Austral of Valdivia said, "Celco was responsible for major environmental damage in Carlos Anwandter…" On the summer day of Monday, December 3rd, 2007, the Emilio Pugin building of the Faculty of Sciences at the Universidad burned down. It was a loss of over ten million dollars for the University, as well as a rare collection of Charles Darwin memorabilia and artifacts. The fire was officially determined to have been caused by an electrical malfunction, although when my wife and I traveled to Valdivia in January, 2008, there was some public conjecture that the fire was of suspicious origin. Some also believed that the mill was behind it. I have never read anything that substantiates that theory. However, while in Valdivia, I did read in the local paper, "El Correo," that Celco was consistently in the top ten Chilean businesses fined for environmental infractions. For juicy reading about the mill and heart rending details about the swans, I suggest googling "black-necked swans of Valdivia, Chile." Listed below are some of the articles I read which gave me the idea for the story and the above information. With the exception of the brief reference to Douglas Tompkins, whose love of this planet I have the deepest respect for, all characters, names, and storyline in the novel are fictional.

* * *

1. From Wikipedia: Anderson, S. (June 19, 2007) "Celco Trashes River Yet Again, Shuts Down Plant"... article from "Patagonia Times"
2. "Revisiting the Valdivia CELCO Industrial Spill of 2005"...posted by "Patagonia Under Siege"— Mon., Jan. 7, 2008/patagonia—under—siege.blogspot.com
3. Environmental News Service (ENS), Nov. 21, 2005: "Chilean Pulp Mill Poisons Swans in Their Sanctuary"
4. The Free Library by Farlex: report from July 29, 2005.

About The Author

David Mather's Peace Corps experience from 1968-70, and subsequent trips to southern Chile, provided the background for both *When the Whistling Stopped* and its precursor, *One For The Road*. He and his wife now divide their time between their homes in the woods of New Hampshire and in a small fishing village on Florida's gulf coast.

Glossary

Abrazo - hug
Abuelito(a) - little grandfather, grandmother
Aguardiente - harsh, strong liquor
Alerce - sequoia/redwood type tree
Artesanía - craftsmanship, craftsmen
Asado - barbecue, roast
Avellanas - nuts from the avellano tree
Avellano - Chilean hardwood tree

Bolas – balls

Cacharro - rattletrap
Campesino(a) - poor farmer
Campo - countryside
Carabineros - Chilean police
Chamantos - small colorful ponchos
Choroy - small green parrot-like bird
Chucha - bitch, (Ch. Slang) cunt
Chucho - burrowing owl
Chupóne - fruit from "campo" bush
Ciao - bye

Copihue – national flower of Chile
Corralero – Horse that gallops sideways
Cuchao - small bird with loud, clear song
Cueca - national Chilean folklore dance

Déle - give it to it!
Don - respectful prefix to name, like sir

Empanadas - tarts
Empanada de pino - meat & veggie tart

Faja - sash
Fogón - outdoor cooking shed

Garrocha - skinny pole used to lead oxen
Gerente - manager
Gringo – foreigner, North American

Hombre - man
Huaso - Chilean cowboy

Lingue – Chilean hardwood tree
Luchecillo – water weed

Manta - poncho
Manta de Castillo - thick wool poncho
Maté - strong South American tea
Media luna - half moon, rodeo area
Mi amor - my love
Micro – small bus
Mi querida - my dear, my love
Moreno - swarthy complexioned

Niache - blood pudding
Niebla - fog
Nogal - walnut

Onces - afternoon tea or snack

'Para el estribo'-'for the stirrup'
Pichi - piss
Pinadeiro - Chilean rodeo practice area
Pronto - soon, quickly
Purgatorio - purgatory

Querida - dear
Quila – bamboo-like plant

Quincha – rodeo wall padded section

Radal - Chilean hardwood tree
Ramada – branch & sapling structure
Rauli - Chilean hardwood tree
Roble - oak family tree
Rubio - fair haired/skinned person

Señor(a) - Mr., male person (Mrs., woman)
Sopaipilla - fried dough

Tejo - game similar to horseshoes
Terminador - terminator
Tetas - breasts, 'tits'
Tineo - Chilean hardwood tree
Tormento - slatted wooden box drum

Ulmo – Chilean hardwood tree

Made in the USA
Charleston, SC
16 June 2014